To Norma,

Secrets at Abbott House

HOPE YOU ENJOY
this book ...
So what's next
for you ?!

Also by Crystal Sharpe:
The Mystery of the Ming Connection
Masquerade on the Net

Other books by Virginia Cornue, PhD:
The Dragon's Daughters Return
Draw on Culture: China
So Much Blood: The Civil War Letters of
  CSA Private William Wallace Beard, 1861-1865

.

Secrets at Abbott House

A SANDRA TROUX MYSTERY

Crystal Sharpe

Sandra Troux Mysteries LLC
41 Watchung Plaza, Suite 88
Montclair, New Jersey 07042
Visit our web site at www.sandratrouxmysteries.com

Authors: Virginia Cornue, Ph.D. and Linda Lombri, M.S.
Front cover designed by Ryan Durka and Judith Rew
Back cover and spine designed by Judith Rew
Front cover photo by Andrew Cohen
Back cover photo by Linda Long
Logo designed by Corinne West

Sandra Troux Mystery books may be purchased for educational, business or sales promotion use. For information, please write: Sandra Troux Mysteries, 41 Watchung Plaza, Suite 88, Montclair, New Jersey 07042

Library of Congress Control Number: 2015908980
CreateSpace Independent Publishing Platform, North Charleston, SC

Printed in Charleston, South Carolina
ISBN-13: 9781511687454
ISBN-10: 15116878452

Virginia Cornue:

To Mei Ming, a freedom fighter in her own way
And for all those who made it possible, rode the Underground Railroad
to freedom, or hoped they might.

Linda Lombri:

To Anita who continues to inspire and tickle my heart
To Liliana, may she grow up to love reading
And for the resilient people of Haiti

CONTENTS

Secrets at Abbott House

1 Escape through Applegate Farm

SANDRA TROUX FLINCHED. A leg iron snapped around her ankle. The other loop fastened with a loud click. Locked tight. An iron bar slid through the rings. She couldn't walk. A collar clamped around her neck. Four iron spikes stuck straight out from the collar and then bent upward. The ring choked her. She could barely breathe. Had she been inside a building, she wouldn't have been able to rest, lean against a wall or sit back in a chair. The spikes were too long. Only two minutes and she was overwhelmed. "OK, OK. Enough. Let me out."

"And those were only a few of the physical restraints used on some plantations – even on farms right here in New Jersey. Owners didn't need to lock a slave up if she tried to run away. It was cheaper to make her *wear* her own prison. Clamp on these leg irons and you couldn't run away. You couldn't even walk." The docent at *Applegate Farm Ice Cream Shop and Museum* called out, "Anybody else want to try while you wait for the next tour to begin?"

Sandy rubbed her neck and ankles, relieved to be free again. "Lizbet, only two minutes. I almost screamed. How could anyone stand these?" They were on line outside the

1

ice cream shop and museum's barn red 19th century farmhouse. She shook her head and shivered in relief and disgust. The cruelty…

Lizbet Sheridan clutched Sandy's arm, "One of my ancestors on my Dad's side might have suffered from something like that. But maybe not, maybe they were free." She shook her head angrily and sighed deeply. When the instruments were offered to her, she backed away, shocked. "No, I'll pass."

"That was too real, Lizbet." Unnerved, Sandy shivered still from the collar and irons. Strange images flashed through her mind:

A tall angry man wearing a punishment collar, barefooted in ragged trousers, stumbling on a dusty road, roped behind a carriage. The carriage slowed as its horses picked their way over a rocky patch. The rope slackened and the man stopped. He wiped sweat from his eyes and off his high brown forehead. The carriage picked up speed. The rope tightened. It jerked the man forward. He staggered but refused to fall. He grabbed the taut rope to steady himself and regained his balance. He began trotting again as a horseman cantered by, cracking his whip overhead. A pale face framed by chestnut ringlets and a peach frilled bonnet peered out of the carriage…

The pictures faded as Sandy forced her mind back to the present, her friends and their history vacation.

Half with Lizbet and half in the bizarre world she had conjured up in her imagination, Sandy seemed a bit dazed. Lizbet was herself unsettled, wondering again about her Black heritage – as she had so often during this tour. The two friends steadied each other, oblivious to the crowd on line with them. "Lizbet, what would I do without you?"

"The same as me, Sandy. We couldn't do without each other." She threw her arms around her friend in a bear hug of love and gratitude for their lifelong friendship. "Look, we knew this would be a challenging trip. I mean, it's not the most fun topic, right? But nobody should feel bad on this beautiful day. Especially not us." A balmy breeze ruffled Lizbet's salt and pepper curls. It lifted Sandy's silver bangs and dried the sweat that had popped out on her forehead from being locked up and from the mysterious pictures that had run like a silent movie in her mind. The air was soft and redolent with flower fragrance. Pink, yellow and white tulips bloomed, nodding their heads all over Montclair. Slender limbs of yellow forsythia arched at the corners of the ice cream shop. Red tulips bordered the antebellum farmhouse where they waited for their tour tickets and Bobbi.

"You OK, Sandy? You sure? You still look a little pale."

Sandy nodded, "Yep. You?" She took a deep breath. "Yeah, I'm good, Lizbet." She grinned, "Yeah, I'm really good. Here we are at the famous Montclair Applegate Farm. Our last stop on our New Jersey Underground Railroad tour! More time together when we go south if we decide to do that leg of our trip. And not a sign of mystery or danger or a criminal on the horizon! No kidnappers or plane crashes in swamps, or sword fights in secret tunnels. No neo-Nazis or Russian thugs. Our past is past. Our future is bright!"

Catching Sandy's more cheerful mood, Lizbet countered with a mischievous glint in her eye. "Well, you never know about *our* future. Bobbi just might show up with a new villain stalking her!"

Startled at that prospect for a few seconds, the two burst into laughter. "Nahhh," they said in unison. The crowd surged forward, carrying them to the farmhouse door and the ticket table.

"See Bobbi anywhere? I still haven't spotted her." Sandy unzipped her red fleece jacket as they stepped through the front door. Squinting against the backlight, she craned around an especially tall man whose Civil War Union cavalry slouch hat blocked her view. A woman with long dark hair, dressed in a closely tailored black business suit and almost black purple suede wedge-soled stilettos stood restlessly behind the man. The woman checked her silver wrist watch every few minutes and shifted impatiently, mirroring Sandy's movements, further cutting off her line of sight.

"You know Bobbi'll figure out any company problems and get herself here. She would never miss Real American History? Never!"

Bobbi Power was the third in their triumvirate of lifelong friendship. Sandy, Bobbi and Lizbet had been best friends since fifth grade when as nine-year-olds they played detective. Now the two old pals steadied each other against a bus load crush of parents, teachers and school children pushing to get to the head of the line for the 2:00 p.m. tour.

"Janet Emily Schaefer, you come right back here and apologize immediately!" a distracted mother ordered. A little girl – in jeans and a t-shirt reading *GIRRRRRRL POWER!!!!* – had shoved between Sandy and Lizbet.

"That's OK." Lizbet smiled warmly. "I remember when my boys were this age. A constant stampede! I'll bet she's the class leader. Enjoy her enthusiasm."

Sandy winked at the little girl and seconded Lizbet's encouragement. "It's never too young to support girls' strength. You've got a natural leader there. A modern Nancy Drew!"

Janet Emily mumbled, "Sorry." Then she winked back at Sandy, hooted and dashed off.

"Remember when we were nine? Nancy Drew groupies all the way! Oh, you'll never guess. I've been waiting for the right moment when we're all together to tell you something amazing. I wanted to surprise you both. Anyway, can't wait any longer. Lizbet, you'll never believe it! Nancy Drew was *born* in Newark. Our inspiration is a Jersey Girl. In fact, she's the Original Jersey Girl.

Lizbet's eyes popped. "Really?"

"More later, I promise. When we're all three together." Sandy checked her phone to see if she had a text from their errant friend. "Where is Bobbi? I'm getting concerned. Her project's so super secret...hope nothing's gone wrong." Sandy lowered her voice. "She hinted to me it was about some new ID and anti-theft technology." Sandy guessed Bobbi was initiating an innovative clothing labeling system. "Has she told you anything?"

"Just that it was really top secret." Bobbi's project had periodically taken her away from their New Jersey UGRR tour to a special lab in Newark's burgeoning economic zone, just four miles east of Montclair where she was directing her hush-hush project. "Now, Sandy, no mother hen-ing. She'll tell us all about…Ummph!" Holding their places against the crush of kids, they reached the registration table fairly intact. Lizbet pulled out their reservation documents for the lecture and tour of Applegate Farm's little known UGRR "station," which encompassed the main house, a tunnel, the barn, and a small compartment in its hayloft. Freedom seekers had worked their way northward from station to station after crossing from Maryland, Delaware and southern Pennsylvania into New Jersey on their way to safety in New England and Canada.

"Oh no, you don't," Lizbet put out her hand, when she saw Sandy zip open the big pocket of her waist pack and reach for her money. "You got dinner last night at that great diner, "The Charbroil," she hummed, happily remembering the deep-flavored Mediterranean vegetable soup and the crisp Greek salad she had devoured. Sandy and Bobbi had ordered zesty lemon chicken soup and mixed salad with grilled salmon "These tickets are on me!"

Lizbet was a retired restaurateur – having sold her two wildly successful Boston fusion restaurants to her sons after her wife Joan died of breast cancer. Sandy had also retired from teaching anthropology at a large midwestern university when her beloved husband Joaquin died in a freak accident falling from Peru's Machu Picchu. She was grateful she had her daughter June, son-in-law Tim and granddaughters Kat and Charlie. Bobbi, executive vice president of global marketing and new business development at an international fashion company, still aiming for the Corporate Marketing Officer (CMO) big corner office, was mother to a college-age daughter.

Sandy stuffed her money and credit cards back in place, but several bills fluttered to the floor. "I've been meaning to show you and Bobbi this incredible Norwegian money, the Kroner (NOK)." She held up a kr100 note and turned it from side to side, catching the light. "See this stripe down the middle?" It sparkled. "Each Kroner has this astonishing anti-counterfeiting technology embedded in it. See how it shines? My friend Soren sent me some from Oslo," she said in answer to Lizbet's unspoken question. "I've been wondering if this relates to the new technology Bobbi's company is working on."

Before Sandy could get enough elbow room to retrieve her money, the dark haired woman scooped them up. "Allow me," she said pleasantly handing the NOK notes back to Sandy. "I couldn't help overhearing you speak about your friend, Bobbi. Her name wouldn't by any chance be Bobbi Power?"

Both Sandy and Lizbet nodded startled. "Yes, we're waiting for her," Lizbet chimed. "She's in Newark working on some secr...ummmph," she grunted when

Sandy jerked the tail of her jacket. "Uhhh, she's just a little late getting here."

The woman seemed not to notice Lizbet's sudden shift and introduced herself. "I'm Lena Morris. If your Bobbi Power is the same as my Bobbi Power, my colleague at Auguste Fashion Marketing International, then you must be Sandra Troux and Lizbet Sheridan. Bobbi has often spoken of you. Indeed, I've sometimes felt a little envious of her – having two lifelong friends through thick and thin…"

"Lena, what are you doing here?" Bobbi interrupted, surprised to see someone from her company. "I thought you were attending the Board of Trustees' meeting. Aren't you scheduled for a South Carolina location scouting project?"

"I thought so too, and I was supposed to leave in a couple of days," Lena replied ruefully. "The meeting was postponed until the Board gets recommendations for new community members. My trip is scuttled for the time being. I'm on the search committee for community members. So, in answer to why I'm here in Montclair and not back in Manhattan at HQ…I was helping with last-minute details for a luncheon tomorrow at the New Jersey Historical Society in Newark. I volunteer there when I have time. Remember, I'm a Jersey Girl!

Sandy and Lizbet looked at each other and laughed. "Oh, not at you," Sandy said. "We were just talking about Nancy Drew and New Jers…"

Lena rolled right on, "You've been telling me about you and your friends' trip and that Montclair to be your last 'stop.' Why not, I asked myself, do the unexpected? So here I am! Ta! Da!'"

A bit surprised at this explanation of spontaneity by normally stick-to-the-plan Lena, Bobbi smiled and introduced her to Sandy and Lizbet.

"Come this way, please," the docent said. "Everyone, take your seats. After a short talk and documentary, we'll enter the tunnel. It stretches from here in the main house to the barn. Freedom Seekers sheltered there. Children, quiet down. The tunnel was dug to make it possible to bring food out to the barn without arousing suspicion."

The trio hurried to find three seats together and scanned their programs and a small booklet titled *Steal Away, Steal Away, The Underground Railroad in New Jersey* by Giles R. Wright and Edward Lama Wonkeryor. "Lena," Bobbi whispered, "there's a seat right behind us," inviting her colleague to join them. Sandy and Lizbet turned around waving and pointed to the chair. Lena sat down between the tall man in the Union soldier hat and a sixth grader who squirmed in his seat and chattered to his friends across the aisle. She leaned forward to hear better, bracing herself on the back of Sandy's chair to join their conversation.

"I'm so glad we decided to take this trip," Sandy said as they settled themselves. The friends had been ready to stay home after solving two very dangerous international cases hop scotching around the world besting vicious criminal.

"So special," Bobbi murmured.

"Yes," Sandy whispered, leaning left and right,

bumping companionable shoulders with her friends.

"Me, three," echoed Lizbet.

Lena sat back disappointment washing over her face.

The docent gave a brief history of slavery in the North and South; how many slaves resisted, challenged and escaped from bondage; and the role the Underground Railroad played in that resistance.

While deciding where to go on vacation, Sandy had told her friends about an amazing collection of antebellum and Civil War letters her father Dallas had inherited from his Aunt Babette, affectionately known as Babby. They'd been found in the attic of her New Orleans townhouse in the French Quarter. Her estate was still being finalized while cousins packed up various bequeaths for shipping. Cousin Sue had sent Dallas one of the letters and he'd made Sandy a copy. Dallas had been told some of the letters hinted at murder and other family secrets in South Carolina and that one even mentioned the Underground Railroad and New Jersey. "I really want us to tour New Jersey UGRR sites.

"Maybe we can even go south to the Carolinas. Dig around for your family, Lizbet and track down your birth dad's people, your southern people. So, what do you say? What about an historical trip for a change?" she'd asked her friends. "No mysteries. No thugs. No kidnappings. No thefts."

"Uh oh, Lizbet, secrets and mayhem in those letters. No matter her promise of nothing bad or dangerous, Sandy'll be on the trail soon," Bobbi laughed, "especially with that letter fragment in hand. A *clue*! Sandy can never resist a clue, Lena. I'll bet it's burning a hole in your pack, Sandy!" Lena had shifted forward again, hearing something about old letters. She laughed along with them, but when she sat back to listen to the presentation, a sharp crease marked her forehead.

After the presentation, the friends were soon through the tunnel and into the barn. The roof rafters soared overhead. Dust moats floated in shafts of sunlight. Bobbi and Lizbet scrambled easily up the ladder to the hayloft where runaways hid in a virtually airless box-like compartment buried under a huge pile of hay. Lena was right behind them, teetering on her high heels as she followed the docent. Freedom Seekers would be spirited to Jersey City and across the Hudson River to Brooklyn and then to the Bronx or Long Island, and then on northward. Manhattan was too dangerous. Even though there were UGRR stations there, some of the worst slave catchers and auction houses were located on Manhattan island. "Go ahead, I'll catch up with you in a minute," Sandy waved them. "Dad's calling."

Dallas Troux, a retired journalist, asked how their *Ride on the NJ Underground Railroad Tour* was going. "We're having a wonderful time, Dad. We're in Montclair now at Applegate Farm. Umm, it's one of the lesser stations, but it's fascinating. It was a working dairy farm far back into the early 1800s. It's ice cream place now. What? Great Aunt Babby's letters arrived? The whole collection? You've been digging into them – going to make a family genealogy? Who? Amaelie Anne Fleurie Abbott? Spelled A-m-a-e-l-i-e? Ummm, yeah, an unusual spelling. What?

That family secret Cousin Sue mentioned. Hmmm…tell me more later, Dad. Bobbi and Lizbet are coming down from the hayloft. Yes, I'll tell them. Yes, love you, too, Dad. Kiss Anna for me. Ha! I know that'll be an easy one."

Sandy rejoined the tour in the barn just as the docent outlining the history of Newark and Montclair. "In the 1600s Montclair was originally part of Newark and then when Azariah Crane, his wife Mary Treat Crane, and their son Nathaniel, built a home in 1694 near the present intersection of Orange Road and Myrtle Avenue the southern part of town was known as Cranetown. The northern part where we are today was known as Speertown. They eventually joined and became Montclair. in 1868. Cranetown and Speertown were rural, but businesses as well as farms like Applegate developed. Israel Crane, a descendent of Azariah and Mary, founded a wool mill on Toney's Brook. And New Jerseyans were on both sides of the slavery issue. Textile producers supported slavery, because they bought southern slave-grown cotton and then sold the cloth back to plantation owners for their slaves." Sandy's thoughts drifted to Great Aunt Babby's letters and to the Southern branch of the Troux family tree. Were they brave abolitionists who argued for human rights? Or were they slave holders? The latter prospect made her shiver involuntarily. If only she could go back in time to see for herself…

"Cherie, come away, vien ici, cherie, immediatement!" Dragging her

gaze away from the handsome, upturned face in the carriage below, the warm brown eyes, the raised hand in greeting, the strong shoulders clad in sage, and the brilliant, brilliant inviting smile, she replied softly, "Non, Maman, I am going down to the street. I have seen the man I must marry. And now I will go to meet him." Ten weeks later, Amaelie Anne Fleurie of New Orleans wed Henry Fleetwood Abbott of Anderson County, South Carolina. A trousseau-loaded wagon followed their carriage along the road north, trailed by a coffle of five chained-and-shackled slaves.

❧

Sandy broke from her reverie a little shaken, hoping her "vision" was just a wisp of fancy.

"Come this way, everyone," the docent instructed. "We'll look at some of the side rooms. The stalls have clothing the escaping slaves wore. Over there, you'll see shackles. Just wander along for about 15 minutes. Then, we'll all get some ice cream."

"Yay!" the children on the tour cheered and raced by in a whirlwind.

As the larger group moved along the sides of the barn, looking into the former stalls, Bobbi said, "Sandy, you wouldn't believe the little compartment they slept in – a packing box really, covered with piles of hay."

"And they had to be really quiet during the day," Lizbet broke in, "not everyone who worked on the farm was an abolitionist. And anyone who turned in a runaway made a lot of money. They must have suffocated under all that hay and in that box. Makes me want to know even more about my ancestors. I know my Korean family and my African American adoptive family, but nothing about my birth dad's side, the Greelys. I hope they were Freedom Seekers...that is if they were slaves. I hope they were free."

"Even more reason for us to go south, don't you think, Lizbet?" Sandy asked.

"Exactly," she answered. "Let's do. Bobbi? What about the Carolinas? We could do a genealogy trip as well as travel backwards on the southern legs of the UGRR. See some of the places where fortunes were made off the slave trade.

Lena pushed between Bobbi and Lizbet. "Lots of people here in the northeast made fortunes off slavery as well. We think it was only in the south, but that's not true. Why, even New York City..." She was cut off as another group, including the tall man, jostled them to get close to the stalls.

"While we're on this genealogy trail, Bobbi, let's visit some of your family's old places in NYC. Harlem, Brooklyn and Queens, right? I'd love to see your family's old home in Astoria. We could..."

Getting free of the crowd, Bobbi poked her head in a stall. "Hey, Sandy, here're some Civil War letters."

"Wouldn't it be weird if we recognized some of the names?" Lizbet remarked.

"Stranger things have happened," Bobbi joked.

"Well, get ready for weird." Sandy leaned over the dusty glass case that displayed several fragments of a yellowed letter. She pointed to a line in the letter. "Dad just told me that some of his letters were written by

Amaelie Anne Fleurie Abbott to her sister in New Orleans. This letter mentions an Amaelie Anne Abbott! Oh, this is too strange. Do you think it might be the same woman?" Sandy asked, a little shaken. "If she is the same woman, the woman in this letter is a possible relative! So we have to go south. Agreed? We have to go south for Lizbet and for me and Dad. We'll find your people, Lizbet, and we'll find where the Abbotts lived. But how in the world did this letter come to be here at Applegate Farm?"

Before either Bobbi or Lizbet could answer, Lena said, "I think I know why it's here. Look at the card describing the letter. It's from the collection of the New Jersey Historical Society. That's where I was this morning – in their Newark offices. How it came to be in their collection, that I couldn't say. You'd have to talk to the director of NJHS. Hey, I have a great idea. Why don't all three of you come to our quarterly luncheon tomorrow as my guests? I know there are still some seats available. Three places came free this morning – a death in the family.

Sandy began shaking her head, "No, we couldn't really impose…

Lena stopped her. "The program is about their Civil War collection. I haven't seen the whole collection yet, but I understand that there are letters and diaries."

"Well, I'd love to go," Lizbet piped up. "So put me down."

"You're sure?" Bobbi asked Lena, a bit uncomfortable to be mixing her work and her private life.

"Yes, completely sure," Lena said. "Besides, it will give me a chance to get to know your friends and hear about all your adventures."

Still puzzling over the possible name coincidence in the letter, Sandy unzipped her pack, intending to take out the letter fragment copy her dad had sent. A bit distracted, she followed along to the ice cream parlor. Lena had hung back with her and asked, "May I see…" A virtual gang of kids swooped by, bumping the adults.

"OK, this is getting to be too much. Let's get ice creams and then get outside where these children can run around, and we can hear ourselves think." Bobbi and Lizbet were waiting for them at one of the counters.

"I'll have double vanilla peanut butter fudge in a waffle cone," Lizbet ordered.

"Double chocolate for me," Bobbi said.

"I'll have butter pecan in a cup," Sandy told the young girl behind the counter who held her scoop at the ready.

"And strawberry for me," Lena said.

Sandy zipped open her waist pack to get out her money. "My wallet's gone!"

Bobbi checked her tote bag, "Mine's gone too!"

Lizbet searched her shoulder bag, but found her change purse in the bottom. And then Lena said darkly, "My wallet's missing, too."

"Quick, where's that tall man? He was hanging around us much too closely. I didn't like it. Bobbi, see if you can find the manager and call the police." Sandy ran outside. The man was nowhere to be seen. The Applegate

Farm manager called the Montclair police. Sandy, Bobbi and Lizbet wasted no time. They searched the grounds, looking behind trees, under cars, and asked everyone if they had seen anything suspicious. Lena searched along the sidewalk bordering the property. Sandy noticed her digging in garbage cans set along the street. "Find anything?"

"Nothing," Lena called back. Finally, a police car drove up and two detectives got out: one older man and a younger woman. Sandy too, looked in the street side cans after searching the ice cream shop cans. She dug deep into one after the other, nearly falling in head long. And her diligence was rewarded: she held up the three wallets. "Found them!"

"Thanks so much, I can't imagine how I missed them." Lena rifled through her wallet. "How strange, only a few dollars were taken. Not my credit cards or ID."

"Bad news here," Sandy said after searching hers. "The Kroner bill is gone and so is my precious letter!"

"Oh, my God!" Bobbi cried. "My new company security pass card is missing. It's loaded with new proprietary technology! This is a disaster."

2 Robbery Redux

"ROBBED! AGAIN." Sandy frowned, frustrated: no progress recovering their belongings – especially Bobbi's security pass prototype. "I said to you: no thugs, no kidnappings, no thefts. We're just going to have a wonderful trip together, enjoy each other's company and have fun learning something new. But here we are again." Disgusted, she slapped the steering wheel. "Why haven't the police found that Union soldier guy? We gave great descriptions. They don't seem to have any leads at all." It was unusual for Sandy to be so irritated, but the loss of Bobbi's security card was serious. She could replace the kroner and she would see the original of her letter scrap soon enough. But the theft of Bobbi's pass card was really, really bad: something that could affect her job. And Sandy did not like anything that threatened her friends or family.

They'd peeled off to the left from Newark's Broad Street onto Park. She turned their rented Prius onto Park Street looking for a down ramp the GPS indicated was coming up. The ramp led to Military Park's underground parking garage across from Newark's gleaming Performing Arts Center. The PAC was only a few years old and headliners played there – singers, dancers, musicians, actors, and comedians. A world class venue.

Lizbet scanned the billboards. "Bob Dylan and His Band. Hope we have time to go to a performance. Patti LaBelle! I love, Patti Labelle! She's just fabulous. Maybe we can get tickets for tonight. She's performing at 8!"

The Prius dashboard GPS showed the New Jersey Historical Society building up ahead. "It's right over there at 54 Park Place. Walk over to the PAC afterwards and see what's available? What do you think?"

"Sounds good. I do need to get my mind off the thefts." But her mind reverted to them immediately. "Lizbet, I can understand stealing Bobbi's security pass card. Awful as that is for her. Industrial espionage and all that kind of skullduggery. And maybe even my Kroner notes with its embedded new technology. But then, why steal them from me? It would be easy enough to get currency from any Norwegian DNB Bank. There must be one in New York. Just walk in and buy some. But, it makes no sense why anyone would want the scrap of a letter. Not even the real letter – a copy of a letter scrap. Makes no sense whatsoever. Something feels off." Sandy was renowned among her friends and family for her flashes of perception. This innate skill had served her well as an anthropologist picking apart knotty research questions. Often she'd have a pile of facts that seemed to have no relevance. And then she'd get this little gut feeling bubbling up, and the connections would be clear. Or, her skin would prickle as a threat warning. She was getting those prickles now.

"And can you believe that police officer? 'Now little ladies, don't get hysterical. Are you sure you didn't forget those items you described? Maybe you left them in your hotel?' Well, he didn't exactly say that, but certainly gave me the feeling that was what he was thinking. Detective Jonas was really uncomfortable. I'll bet she gave him what for when they drove away."

Lizbet was laughing at Sandy; her normally cool friend didn't often blow her top, but rub her up against stereotypes and watch her spout. "As you say, Sandy, some old dogs just can't learn new tricks."

"I felt like popping him in the chops. Little ladies, indeed! He almost said, 'Little *old* ladies.' Prejudice against older people runs deep, doesn't it? And stereotypes are worse about older women. Fries me! I guess he doesn't know the new 'What's Next? Generation' women, does he, Lizbet?" she grinned at her friend, feeling better for having vented. "Help me look for the parking garage entrance, OK?" Her cell rang and the Bluetooth screen on the dashboard showed Bobbi's number. "Bobbi, what's…?"

"Watch out, Sandy!!" Lizbet shouted and slammed her foot to the floor as if she were driving.

Sandy automatically jammed on the brakes and sat on the car horn. A woman darted across the street in front of them heading for the park. And out of the corner of her eye, Sandy also saw, sensed really, a looming shape about to sideswipe them – a black sedan with dark tinted windows. Caught between the sedan and the woman, Sandy veered slightly to the right avoiding a collision with the car and barely missed mowing the woman down.

Lizbet opened her window and stuck her head out. "Hey, hey," she yelled. "Hey, watch out!" Focused on her conversation with her cell plastered to her ear, the woman didn't see their silver Prius or the black car. "Hey, be careful." Lizbet waved her arms and slapped the side of their car while shouting. Startled by the commotion, the woman jumped onto the curb, paused for a moment, turned back, and crooked her eyebrow in apology. She raised her hand giving Sandy and Lizbet a friendly little wave. The black sedan raced away down Park Street, swerved right, fishtailing onto Mulberry and at last caught the woman's eye. Her face fell. Dismay washed over it, erasing her rueful smile. She jerked back, banging into the iron railing that bordered the park. Abject fear marked her features. Placing her hands on the top rail, she half straddled and half vaulted into the park – and disappeared.

"Sandy, Sandy, answer me. What's going on?" Bobbi's urgent voice sounded over the car speakers.

"I almost hit a woman on her cell who was totally oblivious to us."

"She ran right in front of us." Lizbet took some very deep breaths. It was a very close call."

"And some nut case almost side swiped us." Sandy turned onto the garage down ramp and pulled into a parking space.

"Sure you two are OK? What, Juliana? Hey, can you two hang on for a minute? I've got to talk to my associate. Listen, I said get John down here right away. I don't care what he's doing. I need him now. Call Cecelia to come over from the lab and Ursula from tech. Yes, it's serious. Now!"

"What's happening there? You sound furious. Is everything all right? When do you think you'll get here?"

Bobbi was calling from her office on University Avenue at the Auguste Fashion Marketing (AFM) Research Center in Newark's Innovation Zone. "Not good here. There are system reports that someone used my card to get into the building."

"Bobbi!" Sandy said, aghast.

"Oh no," Lizbet said. "That's bad."

Bobbi was very angry. "And worse, someone or several some ones have been in my office. I've ordered a full scale investigation to see if anything's been tampered with or stolen. It'll be a while before I can get over to the luncheon, if I can get there. Hold my place. What?" she called. "OK, John, I'm coming."

"Bobbi, Bobbi, wait a second," Sandy said urgently, "I have a bad, bad feeling about this break-in. Something that's bigger than our wallets being stolen. And...don't ask me how, but I think it's connected to the technology in the Kroner currency. And the letter copy. Now go, go. Come when you can. And, if you can't, just text me. We'll work everything out."

✄

"Our place cards," Lizbet pointed to the round table near the speaker's podium set up in the large conference room of the New Jersey Historical Society. "Lena must have called ahead. Wonder where she is. Bobbi told me she's a stickler for punctuality. It wouldn't be like her to be late." The spacious first floor room was hung with 18th and 19th century New Jersey seascapes and landscapes as well as portraits of leading people in New Jersey history: Author Stephen Crane; singer and activist, Paul Robeson, feminist Alice Paul, folk sheroe Molly Pitcher, and scores of others.

Each table was named for a Civil War Union general. They were seated at the General William Tecumseh Sherman table. The General George B. McClellan table was nearby. General Ulysses S. Grant's table flanked it. "You know, Lizbet, I think there's some connection between Sherman and the Troux family. I have some faint memory of it. Dad will know." Each place setting was laid with the general's biography. Sandy picked up the little pamphlet. Columbia, South Carolina. That's it, Lizbet, there's something about South Carolina. Sherman's army didn't just burn Atlanta and then lead the famous and devastating March to the Sea at Savannah, Georgia. His army turned north to Columbia and razed it. Then, they went northeast to Goldsboro, fought at Bentonville, North Carolina and finally accepted the surrender of Confederate troops in Raleigh. Says here, 'all along the way from Savannah to Goldsboro, about 62,000 Union soldiers cut a 50 to 75 mile wide swath – burning, stealing, killing, rampaging, terrorizing, and eating their way to victory. What Sherman called 'hard war.' Well, it was really successful. Helped break the Confederacy and end the Civil War."

"And a very good thing!"

"Yes," Sandy echoed. "A very, very good thing. But what about the Trouxs and South Carolina? Did you see where that letter was from? The Applegate Farm letter? Was there anything that connected to South Carolina? I have the impression there was…"

"Come on, Sandy. Let's wait for Bobbi out here." She led the way back to the lobby. Sandy draped her grey embroidered Kashmir shawl over the back of her chair. In the lobby, she scrutinized a large display. "Newark once included what is now Montclair. And Montclair used to be called Cranetown. Exactly what the docent said. Here're some land deeds and survey maps. Hey, those Azariah Crane deeds. Here's one signed by Eleanor Woodruff Pennington. Hummm, wonder who she was; interesting that she owned land. 'The three branches of the Crane Family documented in these papers are descended from Jasper Crane (ca. 1605-1681), one of the original settlers of New Haven, Connecticut, and his wife Alice.'"

Sandy read aloud while Lizbet, half listening, looked around at the people gathered in the lobby. She noticed a vivacious, curly red-haired woman talking to several people. Lizbet caught a few words of their conversation. "Haiti. Concert. Montclair. Saturday."

Threading her way to the group, Lizbet said, "excuse me, I couldn't help overhearing something about a Haitian Concert."

"Yes, indeed. A wonderful concert with great performers. In fact…oh let me introduce myself, I'm

Cynthia Stagoff. These are my friends…"

"We're sorry, Cynthia, but we've got to leave immediately…a crisis at home with one of the kids. Something about the microwave, peanut butter, chocolate, and something fizzy. Sorry we didn't get a chance to meet. Sam, can you get our coats? I'm calling Janie. She said something about the fire department. Sam rolled his eyes. "Yep, fire department, again" and walked off towards the coat check.

Unfazed, Cynthia carried on describing the event. "I'm waiting for our headliner. I want her to meet some people here who can connect her to the PAC. Our Montclair event is wonderful, but small in comparison to a performance at the PAC. Ours is a charity concert to benefit education and healthcare organizations in Haiti. Amazing singers, musicians and dancers. We started helping out just after the earthquake in 2010. You are?"

"Oh, I'm Lizbet Sheridan and that's my friend Sandra Troux," pointing to Sandy who was still engrossed in the display about the Crane family. We're in New Jersey on a self-guided Underground Railroad tour. We – meaning Sandy and I, and our friend Bobbi – were at Applegate Farm recently and met one of Bobbi's colleagues who volunteers here. She invited us to this luncheon. And I love Haitian music. I've always felt a connection, no, an affinity for all things Haitian." Lizbet waved to Sandy. "Come over here.'

"Sandy, a Haitian music concert in Montclair. We've got to go. It sounds wonderful."

"Lizbet, wonder if the New Jersey Crane family is

related to the Berkshires, Massachusetts Crane family. They make paper...they make all the paper for our currency. Lizbet, are you listening?"

"Sandy, are you listening?"

The two friends started giggling like they had done as girls back in Prairieview when they'd carried on simultaneous monologues. "OK, you two, cut it out and act your age," Bobbi chuckled slinging her arms around her friends.

"Never, never," Sandy said still grinning at her memory. Then she took a closer look at her friend. "Hey, Bobbi, you're stressed, ruffled, and definitely unsettled, right? Bad? Huh?"

"Bad." Bobbi scraped her fingers through her normally sleek black hair to make it lie down, but succeeded in making it more tangled. Lizbet dug into her bag to get Bobbi a comb.

"Tell us later," Sandy said softly to Bobbi.

"Cynthia Stagoff, Dr Sandra Troux and Ms. Bobbi Power."

"So pleased to meet you, and I hope you all can come to the concert. Here," she handed Lizbet a flyer. "Pardon, I see some people."

"Bad? You can't imagine. I worried I'll be called into the head office in New York. That's not all." She took the comb and stood twisting it in her hands. Sandy narrowed her eyes and shook her head slightly. She had never seen her friend so disturbed, not even when her husband had decamped shortly after they'd adopted Sophie Rose. His abandonment had just made Bobbi fierce, determined that she would make a great life for herself and Sophie. And she had done so. But now, Bobbi was furious and distraught. Sandy guided her to their table. Lizbet pulled out her chair.

"Burglars used my stolen security card to get in." In answer to Sandy's unspoken question, "We know it was mine, because all the prototypes are coded. They knocked out the guards. I mean cold cocked. Or, jabbed them with something. They were found flat out on the floor. Then the snakes downloaded encrypted files from my computer. Again, I have no idea how. They broke into a safe that had other prototypes – antitheft devices, new micro lens plans…"

Bobbi shut up abruptly as a striking woman with her hair in circular patterned cornrows hurried to their table and leaned over Cynthia. She picked up a napkin and fanned herself. She spoke to Cynthia in a low voice. "I don't know…I called and called. She was supposed to meet me in front of the PAC. I looked and waited for her. She said she had something vital to tell me."

Before Sandy could sit, Lena Morris pulled a chair out and plopped down between Sandy and Bobbi. She, too, looked harried. "I'm so sorry I'm late. I just couldn't get free. Then, I couldn't get a parking space. Then, I broke my heel and had to go back to my car for my extra shoes."

"Bobbi, we're at Sherman's table. Maybe you can get some of his soldiers to chase those burglars like they chased the Confederates," Lizbet quipped, leaning over Sandy and Lena in an effort to cheer her friend. Sandy gave her a "zip up" look, gesturing at Lena.

The woman with the spectacular corn rows pulled out the chair between Cynthia and Lizbet. Cynthia leaned forward, "This is my friend Phara Damour, the fabulous singer who is the lead performer at our upcoming fundraising event."

"I'm Lizbet Sheridan. I love Haitian music. Cynthia's told us all about the concert." Pointing to Sandy and Bobbi, "These are my friends. And this is Lena...Lena; I don't know your last name."

Bobbi supplied – "Morris," in a strained voice.

"We're on a New Jersey Underground Railroad tour. And, I love your hair style: the way your corn rows circle your head and attach to your long braids. How do you do that?" Phara's cornrows finished in a dazzling style: long braids that touched her waist, some of which were twisted into a bun tilting over her left eye. "Just beautiful! I've always imagined I was part Haitian. Silly, I know, I'm part Korean, so why not Haitian!! They're the most gorgeous people on the planet."

As chatty as Lizbet was, Bobbi was the opposite. Her usual polite self, but quiet now, almost icy. Sandy was tense, on point, something was up, and she was determined to find out what was going on. Lena tapped her foot, checked her cell constantly, swiveled in her seat, picked at her food, and was generally what Sandy thought of as 'twitchy.' "Lena, something on your mind?"

"Well, now that you've asked, yes, there is. I was supposed to meet a friend and she didn't show. That's really why I was late. I have to admit, I'm a little worried.

Not like her."

Before Sandy could probe more deeply, Oliver Tichenor the Historical Society Director, tapped his glass for order and asked for quiet. He talked about the history of the NJHS and some of its holdings. Then, concluding his remarks, he said, "We are so honored today to have Sarah Pennington make a presentation on *The Civil War and the New Jersey Cranes*. Ms. Pennington is a descendent of the Crane family and has taken an interest in searching her history in New Jersey. She is a long time supporter of the Society. And today, she tells me that she has something really exciting for us. Sarah?" Tichenor stepped back from the podium and a slight woman, with a fluff of white floss crowning her head like a corona, took his place.

Her talk was fascinating. She gave a brief overview of the importance of the Cranes to New Jersey and particularly Essex County, Newark and Montclair. They were community founders, industrialists, soldiers, and chroniclers. Perhaps abolitionists, perhaps slave owners. She talked about Stephen Crane, a New Jersey native and distant relative who had written about the Civil War in *The Red Badge of Courage*. "And now I have a special surprise for Oliver. A surprise that connects us to the Civil War. You know how I haunt the paper conventions, yard sales, barn sales…anywhere I can look for old diaries, letters and so forth. Right, Oliver?" He smiled at her. She explained how she was digging through a box at a barn sale and found some treasures. "Soooo," she dragged out the word to heighten the drama, "I am thrilled to donate something really special to the New Jersey Historical Society. Drum roll, please: parts of a Crane diary from the Civil War. And some pages, or parts of pages, from another prominent New Jersey family, the Van Vlecks. Plus a very special letter."

Lena started, almost jumping in her chair, and then quickly collected herself. Sandy took her arm to steady her. "Are you all right, Lena?"

"Yes, yes, I just had a twinge in my ankle. I think I must have turned it when I broke my heel."

Sandy laid her arm around the back of Lena's chair and nudged Bobbi as if to say, believe that? I don't think so…"Well, if you need one, I have some aspirin in my bag."

"No, really I'm fine.

Oliver joined Sarah Pennington at the podium to gaze reverently at the documents she held up for view. Tattered, burned, torn, and blotched – few pages were intact and those that had some integrity were so damaged by water that few words were readable. Oliver carefully set the first diary on the overhead projector. The name 'Pvt. Na..hal Naty Cran, 41st …is ords', showed on the screen. "I think this means 'Private Nathaniel Natty Crane 41st New Jersey Regiment, His Words.' He carefully turned to another page. The words 'kiled' and 'runned' and 'gol' were projected.

The lunch guests gasped. "Oh my God," one woman blurted, "do you think there was a murder and a theft of gold!"

"Now, don't jump to conclusions. We don't know

this. We don't know anything yet. So we have to carefully study these documents." Oliver looked at the other pages. "This one is from Clyde Van Vleck, a 'sergeant' also in the 41st. These are amazing, Sarah. They are treasures. Really, they are treasures." He gently set them aside on a table behind the podium. Then, even more carefully, he unfolded a scrap of a letter and placed it on the overhead.

Lena shivered. "Isn't this so exciting?" she said to everyone at the table.

Sandy was riveted, whether by the documents or by Lena, was hard to tell.

"'M dearst Osn.r,' I think this means, My Dearest Osn…?" Oliver read slowly.

Now Phara Damour jumped. "Osner," She blurted out loud. "That has to be Osner. That's a Haitian man's name! It means king in Creole.

Oliver thanked her and continued. "My Dearest Osner, We hav ch…' This page is so blotched that forensic investigation will be needed to decipher the rest. Wait a minute; I can make out the signature. 'I remain your devoted…with true affection, Amaelie A. Abbo.' I think it must be Abbott – there's a partial 't' at the end. And the heading might say Abbott House Farm, Storeville, South Carolina"

It was Sandy's turn to gasp. *That was the name in the Applegate Farm letter and the name Dallas had mentioned.* Bobbi and Lizbet stared at her.

"Thank you all for coming this afternoon. It has indeed been an afternoon of surprises and delights. And thank you to Sarah Pennington for handing such treasures over to us." Oliver Tichenor shook Sarah's hand while a photographer arranged them for some publicity shots. Lena slipped out of her seat, whispering she needed to go to the Ladies Room. Sandy quickly threaded her way towards Oliver and Sarah. "I want to see that letter," she mouthed to her friends. Bobbi nodded in assent. Lizbet was in deep conversation with Phara and Cynthia.

"I'd love to see the diary fragments, Mr. Tichenor," after she'd examined the letter. It was indeed from Amaelie Anne Abbott. But who was Osner? And was that incomplete word 'child'? Now there was a real mystery to solve.

Tichenor reached for the diary fragments he had put back in the case they arrived in. He had set the case under the rear table to get them out of the way of traffic. But there was nothing there. The case had vanished!

∽

"I can't believe they were stolen right from under Oliver Tichenor's nose. Well, under all our noses. How was that possible?" Lizbet asked.

Bobbi shook her head in disbelief.

"There was a lot of movement by that table — everyone going back and forth to the Ladies Room. And then that crush of women asking questions and clustered around Ms. Pennington and Mr. Trichenor. You couldn't really see what was going on back there." Sandy stared off as if she were seeing the movement and the crush in her mind's eye. She tried to picture the small brown leather case that held the documents. "You were there, Lena. Did you see anything?"

"No, I wish I had," she said. Then, gathering her tote bag, brief case, handbag, and black trench coat, Lena touched Bobbi's arm. "I'd love stay with all of you, but Frank sent me a text, and I have to run into Manhattan. Something's amiss in Finance. But what can anyone say to such an outrageous act? I mean stealing historical documents. I wish I could stay, but I have to fly. Let me know if anything turns up." Lena shrugged on her trench. Put her tote over her shoulder and strode out of the building.

Sandy was silent, but her friends knew her brand of silence. She was deep in thought. She wrapped her shawl around herself as if to concentrate better.

In the pause, Lizbet announced, "We've been invited to the Sixth Annual Concert for Haiti. It's in Montclair this weekend. And Phara Damour is headlining. Imagine. We've been in the presence of one of Haiti's most famous singers. And we've got to go, right now. We're going to meet Phara's friend.

"Yes, I just got a text, apologizing for not meeting me. She's across the street waiting for us in the Park. *She* is the very important person, not me. All I do is sing. She saves people."

Coats were collected; bags found; goodbyes said; rest stops made before the trio of friends crossed Park Place and walked into Military Park with Phara and Cynthia. "There she is," Phara sang out. "Mon amie Cassandra." President Kennedy's sculpture, a bust set on a marble column supported by a plinth welcomed visitors. Gutzon Borghum historic "War of America" sculpture memorialized the Revolutionary War. The park's central greensward was bordered by a pathway set with small round café tables and slat-back folding chairs. Tulips, pansies and daffodils bloomed in abundance. Greening trees danced in the breeze. New street lights in the style of the original ones, the first electric lights in a public space in America, bordered the walks. Children raced along the paths followed by their caretakers. A poetry reading was underway near a small kiosk selling coffee, juices and pastries. Military Park was alive with weighty history and present light hearted energy.

Wearing a short dark red jacket, Cassandra Innocent sat quietly gazing at some papers on the table. "She's working with Sweat Free Communities. Maybe she's concentrating so hard she doesn't hear me." Phara walked to her friend. She reached out and gently laid her hand on her friend's shoulder. The woman who had run in front of their silver Prius was still. She didn't respond. Slowly, she moved. She slid to her right and slipped off her chair onto the grass. "Blood," Phara said. Her voice trembled. She held up her hand. "Blood."

Sandy knelt down, facing the women. "Yes, blood," she whispered to the strained faces peering down at her. She lightly pressed her left index and middle fingers to the woman's carotid artery. "Yes," she repeated, "and dead."

3 Murder Most Foul

SHOCK MADE HORRIFIED MASKS of Phara, Cynthia, Bobbi, and Lizbet's faces. They gazed down on Sandy as she scanned the murder scene: *must be a knife in the back – and that can only be murder.* Sandy looked with pity at this woman lying crumpled on the grass – just a short while ago so spirited, so energetic, so alive. The moment she had looked into Sandy and Lizbet's eyes, with her liquid brown ones – a bit ruefully, a bit playfully from the curb outside Military Park, they had made a human connection, however brief and fleeting. Now life was gone from her lovely eyes; still partially open, pain registered in them, surprise, and a fierce anger. *Yes, I see anger. I would be angry, too.*

Sandy felt a surge in her chest, a surge of responsibility along with the tears knotting her throat. *We knew each other for just a moment, but your very last expression was fear. Of what? Of whom? Those who killed you?* A promise rose in her. *I will do my best to find your murderers.* She cradled Cassandra's hand in hers. *Still warm.* She caught Bobbi's troubled eye and mouthed "Still warm." Bobbi mouthed back, "So – very, very recently." Sandy nodded slightly. In fact the dead woman's muscles were completely relaxed, limp. Cassandra was still in that condition of primary flaccidity, a body's condition the moment of death. Sandy recalled the autopsies she had attended researching tin miners' deaths in Bolivia.

The Medical Examiner explained that after primary flaccidity, all the body's muscles began to stiffen, either from coagulation of muscle proteins or a shift in the muscle's energy "containers" (ATP-ADP), into the condition of rigor mortis. Starting between two to six hours following death, rigor mortis began with the eyelids, neck, and jaw. It then spread to all other muscles over the next four to six hours, including the internal organs. Dr. Menendez had shown her on the corpses of mine collapse victims how the onset of and degree of rigor mortis could be determined by checking both the finger joints and the larger joints and ranking their degree of stiffness on a one- to three- or four-point scale. He explained rigor mortis was affected by the individual's age, sex, physical condition, and muscular build, ambient temperatures and other mitigating factors.

Sandy touched Cassandra's hand gently and her fingers moved easily *still flexible. No rigor mortis yet.* Cassandra Innocent had been murdered within the last hour – perhaps within the last half hour. *While we were saying goodbye and getting our things together, Cassandra Innocent met her murderer.*

Anger rose up in Sandy burning away her sadness. A movement caught her attention and brought her to alertness. The form moved; Sandy sensed more than saw the dark silhouette against the cream and grey dappled bark of a plane tree. A slender silver shape glinted in the silhouette's hand. She leapt to her feet and sprinted down the path. "Bobbi, call police!" She darted through a double-dutch game, never breaking stride. The Beyoncé look-a-like turners and next jumper never broke rhythm nodding approval in time to feet and rope slapping the pavement. The silhouette now resolved into a large dark figure, *a man?* Head turned glancing over his shoulder, face featureless. Sandy side stepped a mime group: dark suits, dark stocking masks, black gloves. *Ah. The man the same.* He cut across the park's inner greensward, bounded over the perimeter railing and slipped into the open rear door of an idling black sedan. Sandy raised her hand and shot – a photo of the car as it careened into northbound traffic.

Bobbi hurried toward her. "Anything?"

"Photo of the car and license plate." Sandy's chest heaved as she caught her breath. She bent over and rested her hands on her knees. She noticed something stuck to the sole of her shoe -- a shiny scrap, cloth, paper, she couldn't tell. She peeled it off and absent mindedly crammed it in her pocket rather than toss it on the ground. "Maybe the plate number will match the dashboard cam video of that side swiping car. Maybe we do have something to report."

"Come on, two officers have arrived. They want to questions us." Bobbi slipped her arm through Sandy's. They walked quickly back, this time skirting the double-dutch game. The turners and jumper tipped their heads inviting Sandy to jump with them.

"Another time, but thanks anyway."

From behind a mimed tree, one artist sneaked a quick look and drew back, acting the hiding man. Another mimicked Sandy darting through the jump rope game; two others were surprised bystanders. "The Chase" was underway again.

"Bobbi, maybe these mimes saw what happened to Phara's friend. What if they were part of what happened? The man I followed had no face just like those mimes!"

Startled, Bobbi said, "No face!"

"Look: their faces are hidden with dark stocking-like masks. He must have been wearing a mask as well." They turned to look, but the mimes had trotted rapidly away from them. Darting into a glass and steel enclosure, they disappeared down the stairway leading to the underground garage. Sandy started after them. Bobbi pulled her back.

"No, the officers want to talk with us. They're waiting."

"Detective Breshelle Allison." The tall broad-shouldered police officer held up her badge, introducing herself to Sandy. She straightened the lapels of her black pants suit as she tucked her badge away and tugged her red blouse down. A mass of braids clasped at the nape of her neck swayed as she settled herself and squared her scuffed biker boots. Everything about her radiated power and confidence. "My partner, Sergeant Iris Pedilla," gesturing towards the slight woman taking notes. That movement revealed a bulge under her left arm.

Lizbet noticed the bulge under Officer Allison's

jacket. "Looks like a Glock G43." She held the still weeping Phara in a fierce hug, "It's a very slim pistol and easy to conceal. Also accurate and great for all hand sizes. Got a six-round magazine." Phara drew back in astonishment at this comfy-looking and mild-mannered woman.

Sergeant Pedilla's head snapped around at Lizbet's comment. "What do you know about handguns," she asked training hard eyes on Lizbet.

"I'll bet you carry a Glock 42. Probably fits your hand better. I know about getting clothes and a gun to fit a smaller frame. Well, I'm not so small any more, but I was at one time." Lizbet chatted as if she were making a customer feel at home in one of the Boston restaurants she'd owned. She had advised her sons, Liam and Robert, when they bought her restaurants, "Don't be standoffish. Get to know your customers. Treat them like family. Feed their souls, minds and stomachs, it's a winning combination."

"She eyed Sergeant Pedilla's smart outfit – black jeans, close-fitting white shirt, orange sneakers. "Love those sneakers! Oh, yes, in answer to your question, I carried a Glock for years when I would make my nightly after-hours bank deposits."

Detective Allison stood to the side saying nothing, drilling the five women, three of them leading edge Boomers, with her searching hazel eyes. Sandy could see she was very experienced and would discard any stereotypes about "little old ladies who wouldn't hurt a fly." Instead she would assess the likelihood of their capacity to murder and any clues she could deduce from their clothing, emotions and affect.

Allison let Sergeant Pedilla continue conducting the inquiries. Sandy caught a faint smile that tickled the corner of her mouth as Lizbet explained further about her Glock, her training, why she had carried a concealed weapon, her restaurants and her sons.

Detective Pedilla read from her notepad: Ms. Bobbi Power, Ms. Lizbet Sheridan, Ms. Phara Damour, and Ms. Cynthia Stagoff, tapping the page with her finger at each name while she eyeballed each woman.

"And you are?" Detective Allison pinioned Sandy with her flat gaze.

"Sandy Troux, I..."

Lizbet broke in, "Sandy is our friend, we've kn..."

Bobbi whispered, "Lizbet, let them..."

"So, Ms. Troux..."

Lizbet broke in again. "No, this is Dr. Sandra Troux. She's a...

"Troux, Troux," the officers glanced at each other and back at her with suspicion. "Weren't you just involved in an incident in Montclair?" Officer Pedilla asked. "In fact, two of you were involved. You, Dr. Troux and you, Ms. Power. And here you are again, now at the scene of a suspicious death.

Like Sandy, Bobbi had been very quiet, not wanting to draw attention to herself. She was not ready to be questioned about the break-in at the Lab, or the theft of her prototype pass card, or the computers that she prayed had not been tampered with. Better to find out the extent of the trouble and then, maybe, bring in the Newark PD. *It's such a delicate situation. And I can't have cops tromping around there. There's still too much top secret research underway. Well, I hope it is still top secret.* Bobbi groaned with worry and anger. Detective Allison asked, "Ms. Power, you OK? You look like you've got something on your mind. Want to tell us?"

Bobbi shrank back. "No, just upset." She looked down at the dead woman.

"Detective Allison, this may be unrelated, but earlier we were nearly sideswiped by a car. There might be video on our dashboard camera. And then I captured some video on my phone of another car that looked exactly like the first one." Sandy went on to explain about the near collision, their encounters with Cassandra Innocent alive and dead, the man behind the tree, and the mimes. Lizbet and Bobbi added details, but Cynthia, and especially Phara, said very little. "So you see Detective, we never really met the victim."

The park's street lamps flickered on. Dusk was falling, the balmy air chilling. All the women huddled together under the watchful eye of uniformed officers. The site was marked off with yellow tape. The ME examined Cassandra. An ambulance had arrived. Phara shivered, perhaps from the cooling evening, perhaps from her shock diminishing and melting into grief over the death of her dear friend. Lizbet wrapped her in the extra large scarf she always carried. Her motto being "You never know when…"

"Detectives, I think you need to look at this." The

ME pointed to Cassandra Innocent's back, covered by her blood soaked jacket. "It's hard to see because her blood and her jacket are almost the same color."

Allison and Pedilla crouched down, much as Sandy had done, and looked closely at Cassandra's body. "Was a suspicious death," Detective Allison murmured to Pedilla, "Now an official murder investigation. Likely stabbed to death."

4 Under Suspicion

SANDY PULLED THEIR PRIUS into a lot near the 22 Franklin Street Newark Police Department Headquarters and Major Crimes Unit. At precisely 10 a.m., Sandy, Bobbi and Lizbet were ushered into a grey reception room and told to wait.

"I'm still surprised they let us go yesterday. I thought we were going to end up in jail for sure! When they took our information and questioned why we were in the park, in Newark, in New Jersey at all, well…" Lizbet huffed, fretting at finding no words to express her conflicting feelings. She did the next best thing: she dug in her bag for a peppermint. She offered one to Bobbi and Sandy. "Fresh breath to meet the cops." She sat up straighter and patted her hair.

"Especially when those detectives looked at us cross eyed after putting you and me together with the Montclair pick pocketing, Sandy." Bobbi stretched and rotated her head. "Oh, I'm stiff. Too much tension. Too much worry. I'll probably have to go back to the lab soon." Bobbi started at her vibrating cell. She scooped it out of a pocket. "Message from John Simmons, my Deputy Director in charge of research." She read, "No new

43

developments. Scanning all programs for breaches. Your card confirmed used for break in. All seems secure at this point. Will check in later." She heaved a sigh of relief, temporary though it might be and groaned over the ramifications of her card being used. Then she changed the subject. "Tonight we sleep at my house and in my beds. Wonderful beds. Linen sheets. I got them special," her voice dropped and took on an intimate inward tone, "when I was in London at Christmas visiting Colin."

"Oooo ooo," Lizbet crooned in a teasing sing song voice.

"Cut it out, Liz. Down pillows, special cooling memory foam mattress. OMG! I'm babbling. Not like me to babble. I must be really, really nervous. I've never been questioned at a police station before. Especially in relation to a murder," she laughed uneasily.

"Now look, you two, if they thought we were responsible or really involved in some way, they'd have hauled us down here last night and given us the third degree. We'd have been stashed overnight in holding cells, cells with bars on them. Big thick grey steel bars. We've all watched enough *Law and Order*, *Rizzoli and Isles*, *Cold Case* to know that, right? Right? So don't work yourselves up into a tizzy or start picking at each other." Sandy's bracing words were belied by her warm smile and quick squeezes; and hid her own developing concerns. "Cheer up! We're not in the poky…yet!"

"Ha. Ha. Ha," Bobbi said sardonically, but clearly shaken out of her mental twist for the moment at least.

Lizbet hugged Sandy. "You're right, of course. Why

are you so often right, huh? Tell me that!"

"Just perfect, I guess," Sandy shot back, grinning at her two dear friends. A wonderful aspect of their long friendship was their ability to suss out when one or the other was getting tangled up in nonsense and then says just the right thing in the right tone of voice to check the slide into wild anxieties and fears. Each had their own. And each knew the others' inside out.

"I'm most concerned about Phara. She's a close friend of Cassandra. Was supposed to meet her. Seemed jumpy at the luncheon. Is she involved somehow? Does she know something special? Were her tears from grief or relief? Then she was awfully quiet while the detectives were questioning us. I had the feeling she was really scared. Was holding back something important. Knew something. What?" Sandy seemed almost to be talking to herself. She was working out some connections that were not apparent: linking some nearly invisible threads.

Cynthia Stagoff and Phara Damour, both frazzled and flustered from their late arrival were summarily ushered into the cold, hard room where Sandy, Bobbi and Lizbet had been waiting impatiently, waiting with worry mounting, waiting with questions accumulating. Nothing soft or colorful there. No pictures on the walls. Nothing human. Hard chairs, hard walls, hard floor – a severe message: here there is no nonsense. Here there is truth freely given or harshly extracted. Here is the business of murder.

Sandy's concerns about Phara seemed borne out as they waited for her to return from questioning. They had each been placed in a separate interview room. A central rectangular table with hand cuffs fixed at one end took up most of its space. The room was wired for sound and had an overhead camera to record everything that went on during an interview. A two-way mirror occupied most of one wall. The room was painted warm beige, and the chairs were padded and upholstered in a nubby maroon. That surprised Sandy. *Hummm…a ploy to get the suspect off guard?*

But what surprised her most was that no one came to question her. Ten minutes passed. Fifteen. Twenty. At half an hour, Sandy started knocking on the door. Another ten minutes and Sandy was taken back to the waiting room. Not one question. No one had even stuck a head in her room to say one word. And then one by one in quick order, Bobbi, Lizbet and Cynthia were brought back. *But where was Phara? Why was she being kept longer? Was she under suspicion?*

The experience had been so strange, chastening even. Were they being softened up and prepped for the real round of interviewing? "Any questions?" Sandy whispered. Three heads shook "No." *Why were they not questioned? Why was Phara kept so much longer?*

Cynthia checked her watch impatiently. "This has been a complete waste of time. I've got to get back to Montclair. I've got so many details t wind up for the concert.

"Listen, Cynthia," Sandy suggested, "when they let us go, why don't you leave? We'll wait for Phara. Actually, we're thinking of doing something here in Newark."

"Yeah," Lizbet added. "Leave her with us. We'll make sure she gets back for rehearsal....Oh, it's almost lunchtime. There's an outstanding Jewish deli just a few blocks from here. Hobby's Delicatessen and Restaurant, 'an old-fashioned Jewish delicatessen,' she read off her Smartphone, 'Hobby's still pickles its own corned beef in fifty-gallon stainless steel vats, and its potato pancakes are a must-have.' They also have salads, fresh fruits, gazpacho, fresh salmon, chicken fajita wraps, and more. OK, I'm sold. Let's go there for lunch and deliver her...you say when, Cynthia. OK, Sandy, Bobbi?" Both nodded in agreement.

"I was thinking the Newark Museum, too" Bobbi suggested, "that is, if we don't get called back into those little rooms. Gave me the creeps. One of my lab techs is a Buddhist, said the museum has the premier Tibetan collection in the U.S. And, the Dalai Lama has blessed the altar!"

"Those sound great...Well, I have an idea also!" Sandy paused for dramatic effect. "Why don't we go visit Nancy Drew's 'birthplace'?"

"What!?!" Bobbi exclaimed. "Here, in Newark?"

"Totally RAD," Lizbet chimed reverting to old slang.

"Yep, right here in Newark. Her creator, Edward Stratemeyer lived over on 7th Street." Before they could marvel over the 'hometown' of their childhood inspiration and the inspiration of thousands of women and girls for more than 85 years – Oprah Winfrey, U.S. Supreme Court Justice Sonia Sotomayor, journalist Diane Sawyer, Presidential Candidate Hillary Clinton, and scores more – Phara was escorted into the waiting room. She was ashen faced. Silent. Even more scared looking than when she had wept over her murdered friend.

"OK," Detective Allison said. "You can all go. But you, Ms. Damour, don't leave the state." And with that instruction and no further explanation by Detective Allison, they left as quickly as possible.

Sandy slid into her chair at Hobby's on Bradford Street a few blocks from NPD HQ, nearly moaning in delight and anticipation.

"OK, girls, what's it to be?" asked the gravelly voiced waitress.

Lizbet rapped out their orders: "Turkey, tongue and Swiss on rye with extra coleslaw and Russian dressing. Eggplant, roasted peppers and mozzarella on a roll. Old world tender pastrami on rye with mustard; and a slow roasted brisket on a hard roll with Russian. Then, we'll have an order of potato pancakes with applesauce and sour cream."

"That's what I like," their waitress said, fluffing the flowered hankie tucked in the breast pocket of her green uniform. "I like hearty eaters. Can't stand girls who're picky eaters. So, what's next?"

"Humm, soups." She ordered a variety including matzoth ball. "And a baby mixed green salad with roasted pepper and Portobello mushrooms. Put the balsamic vinaigrette on the side. Grated parmesan? On the side, too. Then an order of the black-and-white mini cookies. There are four, right?"

"Right." Evelyn turned to a third page in her order

book. She was chuckling now. "Hey, Joe," she shouted. "Tell the boys to get ready. I have an ORDER!"

Lizbet wound up with a Dr. Brown's Black Cherry, two Dr. Brown's Cream Sodas and a ginger ale. "And, lots of water. Sandy, anything else? Bobbi, Phara?"

Firm head shakes, "No!"

"OK, that's it. Well, we're going to need more pickles soon." Aluminum bowls filled with kosher dill spears were set on every table. Theirs was nearly empty.

Bobbi groaned, pushed her chair back from the table and mimicked the 1970s TV ad, "I can't believe we ate the whole thing! We *did* eat the whole thing."

"We did," Lizbet laughed.

"Oh, yes we did," echoed Sandy letting out a notch on her belt. But, Phara shrank down in her chair and said nothing.

While they nibbled on their black-and-white mini cookies, Sandy hitched her chair a bit closer to Phara and touched the back of her hand, inviting the unhappy woman to speak. "Phara, how can we help? What can we do?"

"Dr. Troux…"

Sandy stopped her with a light squeeze. "No, no, my dear, Sandy, please."

"OK, then," she gulped a bit uncomfortable calling this older woman by her first name. "OK…Sandy, there is so much that's wrong. Not just Cassandra's murder," she started crying again. Lizbet handed her a tissue. Bobbi signaled Evelyn for hot tea with lemon. "It's just everything. Everything that Cassandra was planning to give me. She had evidence about so much. She was going to tell me about the work she'd been doing and what she'd found out about bad things going on here. In NYC, Brooklyn really. In Haiti." Phara dropped her voice and looked around at the other diners to see if anyone had overheard her. Looked around to see if there was anyone suspicious. Though how she would pick out such people, she didn't know.

Sandy, Bobbi and Lizbet scooted their chairs closer – the legs scraping on the worn red and white linoleum tiled floor –forming a kind of protective circle around the younger woman. Dishes clattered, spoons clinked in soup bowls, cell phones rang. The lawyers, politicians and administrators who had their offices in Government Center, where the NPD, City Hall, the main PO, and the Federal Building were located, still did business while devouring their huge corned beef, pastrami and combo sandwiches; slurping their soups; and glugging their drinks. Once begun, Phara poured out her worries, suspicions and predictions.

Sandy's skin began to prickle. A sure sign that something was wrong. Someone was watching them, perhaps even recording Phara's account of horrible working conditions in Port-au-Prince in the T-shirt and dress factories that peppered the outskirts of the city. She told about the work Cassandra was doing: investigating slave labor, illegals transported from West Africa, the Middle East. Maybe being shipped in right here in Newark, in Port Newark. Her voice trembled. "I'm scared. What if they kill me, too? What if my sister and cousins in Haiti are killed? They know some people who have been locked up in a kind of work prison: local people and foreigners.

"We feared the Tonton Macoute when Papa Doc and Baby Doc ordered killings, but now, who are these bad people? Who killed Cassandra? She was my dear, dear friend. She was so brave." Phara was quietly sobbing again. "No one knows who these bad people are. Maybe it is only goods being shipped in and out. But Cassie thought she had a lead. There was clothing with some kind of new technology in the label that made it hard to steal." Bobbi jerked upright from her position. She had been leaning over the table better to hear Phara's soft tones. Sandy signaled, "Let her go on."

"The police questioned me about Cassie more than they asked about me. They seemed to think she was doing something wrong. Then they asked me about what kind of things I did. Was I involved with Cassie? 'No, I said, I'm a singer.' I don't think they really believed me." Phara stopped abruptly. "I need to go to Port Newark and see what I can find out. Can we go there? Right now? Can we go there and not to those other places? Dr. Sandy, can you help? Bobbi, Lizbet, will you help?"

Without a word, the trio got up. Phara's shoulders shuddered from relief at having support, shaking off her paralyzing grief and anxiety. "I feel so much better. I've been worried about Cassandra for weeks. Then she is murdered and then the police grill me for hours. They kept asking me about her work. What did I know? When was the last time I saw Cassandra? But they pounded me with questions about her and then they started on me. It was horrible." Phara's voice trailed off as the four women left Hobby's and walked toward the lot where the Prius was parked.

A man in a dark suit, a lawyer type, spoke into his phone, "Yes, Port Newark. I didn't catch everything. Something about papers. Uh huh, yep, got it." A black sedan slid up to the curb. He got in. The car idled until the Prius pulled out into Broadway. The Robin's egg blue sky took on a sinister greenish hue. Darkening clouds rolled up from the west. A chill wind tumbled street debris. The black car slipped into traffic a few lengths back, snaking in and out in and out of traffic. And never losing sight of the silver automobile, following stealthily.

5 On Dangerous Ground

PHARA CHOKED OUT HER WORDS, crying again, "Cassandra hinted she'd found out something really important. Something that was much bigger than she ever imagined. She was scared. She was really scared. And now she's dead." Shredding her tissue, balling and twisting it, Phara was still grief stricken. Sandy quickly glanced at the distraught woman in the rear view mirror while she drove south on Interstate 95 toward Port Newark. Fat raindrops spattered the windshield. Phara was hunched over in the back seat maybe even still in shock. She raised her head, and Sandy saw her expression change as if she had come to an important decision.

"You have something more you want to tell us?" she encouraged the singer.

Bobbi swiveled from the front seat of the Prius and gave her full attention to Phara. Lizbet shifted a bit closer to her in support.

"Well, it was more than a hint. She said she had names, places, quantities of goods, numbers of people, ship manifests, countries..." Phara hesitated. She still was unsure of these women. Her gut said yes, they were trustworthy, but she didn't know them. Her phone rang with a Haitian beat.

Lizbet blurted, "Why that's Leonise. I love her singing. I love that beat. I saw her on YouTube.

"You did? You know her? You know her music?" she was surprised.

Phara, smiled, distracted, acknowledging her comment, cheered by common knowledge, but engaged in the cell call. "She is? Really? Dr. Troux? Incroyable. Yes, I do remember that. They are? All three of them? And she is…" She looked at Sandy, Bobbi and Lizbet wide eyed. "Uh huh, I understand. I'll tell them when I need to be back. OK. Yes." And then she said, "We're headed for Port Newark. Wait. No need to be agitated and upset. You've just told me who I'm with. So I am safe with them. Now, you don't worry. I'll be there in time for rehearsal." Phara clicked off her phone and shrugged off a mountain of worry and fear. Her whole demeanor changed. She sat up. She relaxed her torso, shook out her shoulders and un-balled her hands. Her expression lightened and deeply etched anxiety lines smoothed out. Her eyes brightened and the smile flooding her beautiful face crinkled the corners of her eyes. "Now I know why your names were familiar…" She was relieved to find herself in the company of women she could rely on. She smiled even broadened and then chuckled. It was a wonderful release from the horror of Cassandra Innocent's murder, the police questioning, the troubles Bobbi was having. Lizbet chuckled along with her. Bobbi caught the laugh bug which began to "infect" Sandy, too.

"Don't want to put too much of a damper on you, but watch for the Port Newark exit." They passed exits 15, 14 and 14A – Newark Airport on the right. Huge "War of the Worlds" construction cranes on the left.

"Here, Sandy, Exit 13A. Get off this exit and then take the left lane up the ramp." Bobbi checked her GPS just to be sure. "Yep, this is it. See the big blue and yellow IKEA there?"

"As soon as I can, I'm going to find a place to park. We're going to have a real heart to heart. OK, Phara?"

North Avenue E. turned into McLester Street and curved around traveling north again. Warehouses, chain link fences and stacks of construction materials marched along on the left. At the Port Authority of NY and NJ, Sandy pulled into the headquarters parking lot and stopped under a spindly tree. "I was thinking that we might find some place secluded, but really, I think this is better. It's open. And we can see anyone…if there is anyone."

"And we can use the bathroom in the Port Authority building. What? What are you all laughing about? Well, we can," Lizbet insisted, miffed that her friends were smothering their laughter.

"No, you're right, Lizbet," Bobbi said mollifying her friend. "It's just that…"

"I know. We're on dangerous ground, and I'm talking about bathrooms. But don't you ever wonder in all those detective shows and those action movies what the main characters do about peeing? And what do the criminals do? Do they holler at each other, 'Hey, cops, hold your fire, I need to pee!' Talk about being caught with your pants down!'"

Now, they were all laughing so hard they were crying – this time from the sheer ludicrous juxtaposition of fictional criminals with their pants down peeing and the heavy and dangerous information Phara had been charged with discovering by her murdered friend. "Laughing clears the mind, and relieves the troubled soul," Sandy said. "And now, Ms. Phara, we need to hear everything you know so far." Even while she was laughing, Sandy noticed all the cars that passed by the Port Authority building. She was on alert for the black sedan that had been involved in two incidents. While the open spaces around the HQ made it easy to see any suspicious cars, the lack of shrubbery exposed their Prius. She was glad of the pounding rain which gave them a measure of protection.

"So," Phara concluded, "as I told you, Cassie was onto something big, really big. And really dangerous. And here's something I didn't say before." Phara still hesitated, "She was going to give me a flash drive with lots of very detailed information. Names, places, shipments, and Port Newark was one of the shipping locations. She said there were millions, maybe even billions at stake. She knew about this hi-tech lab somewhere." Bobbi and Sandy looked at each other. "She was getting ready to send a report to her organization *Sweat Free Communities*. She knew a lot. And it got her murdered." Phara's face crumpled.

"Do you have the flash drive?" Sandy asked.

"No. I don't. She hadn't saved everything when we talked last time. At least, she told me she wasn't quite ready yet. But, I wasn't sure. Maybe she had finished. Maybe she was just saying that, and she hid it somewhere. She said she was going to give it to me. And then she told me she thought she was being watched -- maybe even bugged. She did say something about a shipping company. The name was something with an 'S' and maybe an 'A' – I don't know, we had a bad connection. I got the feeling she was down here, looking around. Looking for this S company or this A company or containers or something."

"What about her apartment? Would it be there? Where did she live? Did she have a laptop or a tablet?"

"A tablet. She kept everything on her smart phone and on her tablet."

Bobbi quietly spoke to Sandy. "I didn't see either one. Her phone might have been in a pocket, but her tablet…nothing on that park table but papers."

"I didn't see either one. And I was watching those detectives search her body. Nothing was bagged. No flash drive either"

In the back seat, Phara went on with her story, "Cassie and I have been friends since we were kids. We both grew up in Cité Soleil."

Lizbet perked up, "Isn't that a really poor…"

"Yes, poor is not the word for it. It's an obscene place – worse than you can possibly imagine. We were both lucky. I could always sing. Cassandra was a brilliant student, and she got noticed. Some aid workers helped

Crystal Sharpe

her go to school. We are both so lucky, *were* lucky. We made a pact to do something about Cité Soleil, to help in some way. Cassie was working on this sweatshop investigation. I sing, raise money, help that way. Cassie's not lucky now. I'll have to be lucky for us both."

"We understand about pacts," Lizbet said. Both Sandy and Bobbi nodded yes."

"Can you tell us little more about Cité Soleil and her sweatshop investigation?" Sandy asked. This bit of information made her tingle. Here was a connection.

"Well," Phara began...

The rain had eased. A fog rolled in off the Hudson River as the afternoon waned. Mist curled around their tires and began to creep up the car's doors.

"I don't like this," Lizbet said.

"Me, either," Bobbi echoed.

Sandy's tingles turned to prickles. "Save it, Phara. I think we should leave." She turned on to McLester, driving north as it became Rangoon Street. The rain picked up again and splattered their windshield. Headlights crept up behind them. Too close, Sandy felt. She speeded up and drove north on Corbin. The headlights stayed right behind. She hung a right onto Fleet Street and then a left onto a narrow unmarked corridor between ranks of shipping containers. The headlights kept going past them on Fleet. Sandy slipped the Prius between two containers and waited, idling quietly. Then, she eased out and drove on, twisting and turning between containers. *I think we're being followed by that sedan.*

58

"Bobbi, where are we? Can you get your GPS working or the GPS on the car?'

Bobbi shook her head. "Nothing. The storm must have knocked it out."

Phara was shredding her tissues again. Lizbet sat forward in her seat, hand only on Bobbi's shoulder – for comfort or for reassurance. She didn't want to startle Sandy, who was anxiously peering through the blurred windshield.

"No signal. Something's blocking it."

Sandy slammed on her brakes. A man appeared out of the gloom, waving at them frantically. The drifting fog and driving rain were beat back by the wipers, swipe by swipe. He ran over yelling something. *I hope he's on our side,* Sandy thought. She let her side window down a few inches. *As if that would really protect us.*

The hairs rose on the back of Sandy's neck. In the rear view mirror, she saw the sleek flank of a black sedan slide past.

"Ma'am, stop. Stop! Don't go any farther. A few more feet, and you'll be in the canal!"

Lou Lombardi was a longshoreman who had worked on the docks in New York City and now at Port Newark for a lifetime. Lou's navy blue collar was turned up, and his silver-streaked black hair was streaming. He leaned into Sandy's window, taking in the four women. "I'm Lou. Look, I'm going to get my pal, Tony Marrara to lead you out of here. He's just coming off duty. It can be a real maze getting out of here, especially for anyone who's not in the know. Capicse?!? Cah-PEESH?"

"Capisco!" Bobbi said, chuckling before anyone else could answer. Her quick response made Sandy and the others relax.

"Sounds good, Lou."

"You all stay put while I get Tony and ask if he can help you. I'm sure he will." Lou pulled his hood up and trotted off to get his friend. Sandy got out of the car to stretch her legs and reconnoiter. They were indeed right at the dock's edge where a large ship was moored. Lizbet and Phara stared out of Lizbet's window. They could see brackish water trapped between the pier and the ship – churning with dirty foam, coating the ship's rusty bow. Bobbi shone her led torch first at the edge of the dock and then on the ship. Its name, Starlight Argent, was barely legible – the paint was worn and peeling.

"Get back in Sandy, you're getting soaked," Bobbi yelled over the roar of the rain.

Sandy got in and started the Prius. "I'm going to back up and turn so we're parallel to the canal edge. Lou's friend Tony can get in front of us." Just as she began to back up, the black sedan rammed their rear end. Their heads snapped forward and thudded back against the headrests, but Sandy reversed faster to counteract the force of the car that slammed them. Wrenching the steering wheel to the left, she spun rapidly to get out of the path of the sedan. It had backed up and was heading for them again. Sandy floored the gas and the Prius surged forward, gaining traction, almost leaping now, roughly parallel to the dock. At high speed, the black sedan shot straight ahead and screeched to a stop inches from the dock's edge. Without the Prius to act as a brake, it rolled closer as the weight of the car over balanced it. Its four doors were flung open and four large men jumped out and sprinted away into the storm and fog. The sedan eased forward again, teetered and slid nearly soundlessly into the gap between the ship and the dock.

Sandy and Bobbi jumped out of their car. Lizbet and Phara huddled in the back seat. Lou Lombardi and Tony Marrara came running to them. "Are you all OK? Everyone OK?" the men asked. "That was some fancy driving, ma'am. We saw that car ram you, and we thought you were goners." Lou ran his fingers through his hair in disbelief. "But here you are -- not a scratch. And that other car...salvage." Lou elbowed Tony and winked.

Tony grinned, winked back and nodded in appreciation.

Sandy said, "We'll stay until the authorities get here."

"No. No, don't you all worry," Lou said. "We'll get the Port Authority officers on the trail of those men. They won't get far, not on an evening like this." He looked up at the darkening sky, still pouring pounding rain on them all. He scraped the rain out of his eyes and pointed away from the dock. "They'll get lost in the phragmites."

Tony slapped his thigh, laughing at the men's stupidity. "Maybe, they'll end up like lots of people who run afoul of the Mob. They feed the fish and birds. Our very own New Jersey double-crested cormorants will love to clean up their bones."

"We'll handle everything here," Lou repeated. "It's

better for us. We'll get the salvage."

At the entrance to I-95N, Sandy pulled past Tony's truck. She tooted her horn and flashed her lights in thanks. Bobbi, Phara and Lizbet waved and called thanks from their windows. Sandy grinned, squeezed Bobbi's arm, and glanced back at Lizbet and Phara. "You never know when you will run into true gentlemen, do you?"

6 Time Out

BOBBI CLOSED HER EYES, taking in the sweet fragrance of spring flowers and blossoming trees and the soft caress of the early morning breeze off the Hudson River. "That's much better. I didn't realize how much the tension of the past few days had knocked me off center."

"You can say that again! I thought for sure we'd end up in the drink last night when that black sedan rear-ended us in Port Newark. Great driving, Sandy," Lizbet exclaimed. "Thank God for Lou and Tony! They showed up in the nick of time."

"Indeed, they did. And as Phara said last night when we dropped her off at Cynthia Stagoff's, we're getting closer to something, something dangerous.

"Anyway, thank you, Lizbet, for suggesting an early morning walk and yoga 'Salute to the Sun' in Riverside Park to get our minds off everything. I feel at one with my Qi again." Sandy stretched her arms back and rolled her neck once again.

"My pleasure!" Lizbet chortled. "Now, let's do our customary jog down to Eleanor Roosevelt's statue at the 72nd Street entrance garden and pay our respects. She was such an inspiration to America's women – no, the women of the world! After that, we've got to get back to Bobbi's brownstone toute de suite! I'm starving!"

"Surprise, surprise," her chums chimed in unison.

Fifteen minutes later, they were seated around the Gloster teak table in Bobbi's backyard pocket garden, enjoying a sumptuous NYC breakfast of fresh bagels and assorted cream cheese spreads (including a couple of tofu varieties), as well as smoked lox and whitefish salad.

"I'm so glad we stopped by Zabar's last night to pick up some of their fair trade coffee beans and chai tea. That fresh fruit and kale will make great smoothies. The veggie-based salmon, and of course, some Rugelach and Babka will top off our breakfast," Lizbet drooled. "It almost makes up for the loss of H&H Bagels to the neighborhood."

"I know, I know. Sophie and I were heartbroken when they closed their doors. No more intoxicating aroma of freshly baking bagels as we walked along Broadway on the way home from a late concert or movie."

The two friends chatted away, digging into their food while Sandy sat back into the deep-cushioned rattan armchair and sipped her chai tea. Deep in thought, she took in Bobbi's beautifully serene Japanese garden, with its stone lantern, koi pond, white stepping stones, cherry and Japanese maple trees, azaleas, and a stand of bamboo. She knew in her heart that the lovely life that Bobbi had created for herself and her daughter was about to change. And she was worried for her.

Bobbi had inherited the 19th century brownstone

from her Great Aunt Lizzie at the right time – just after her divorce was finalized and she landed a marketing position at Avon. Over the years, her career had taken off, and she had poured a lot of TLC into renovating each of the house's five floors. She had created a warm, inviting home that Sandy, Lizbet and their families had visited frequently. The Upper Westside of Manhattan had become very family friendly and upscale – abundant with green space, including the great urban treasures of Central and Riverside Parks and the perennials planted along Broadway's median strip. The Westside boasted the Museum of Natural History and Lincoln Center; and was resplendent with galleries, bookstores and restaurants of any and all cuisines. The neighborhood also featured a high concentration of adoptive families with children from all corners of the world. In fact, the international organization, Families with Children from China (FCC), had its roots in the Upper Westside community, enriching and supporting Bobbi and her daughter Sophie Rose and many other pioneering China adoptive families at every stage of their lives. Yes, it had been a good choice for Family Power.

But Sandy knew that dramatic change was on the horizon for them both. Sophie Rose would graduate from Stanford University soon and embark on her adult life – possibly not in NYC or even the USA. Moreover, she sensed deep changes in Bobbi, exacerbated by the events of the past week. Bobbi still loved all things New York, but she was finding more and more reasons to travel away from the City – either abroad or back to their Praireview home turf. The normally buoyant Bobbi was frequently tense and distracted. It seemed clear to Sandy that the "ageist" trend of corporate downsizing that left top, seasoned execs edged out of their expected career tracks was at work in Bobbi's company. She had seen it in academia as well, but not so aggressively. If so, the theft of the prototype security card could tip the scales.

"Hey, Sandy! Come back to us! Bobbi and I were just about to plan out our morning and early afternoon itinerary, but we need you too!"

"Yeah, and don't think you're going to get out of drinking Lizbet's high-octane fruit, kale, ginger root, and who-knows-what-else concoction…er, I mean, delicious smoothie. Remember, all for one and one for all!"

Their gaiety and laughter was short lived. Bobbi's cell vibrated loudly and insistently. "Oh, oh. It's my CMO calling. I've got to take this. Sorry."

Just as Bobbi stepped inside to answer her call, Sandy's cell buzzed, too. She recognized the number on the screen: "Oh, it's Phara. Maybe she has an update for us.

"Yes, Phara. How're you doing? What? Detective Allison wants you to come back to the Newark precinct on Monday? Something about your cousin in Haiti? Yes, yes. Of course, we will. Let's talk about it tonight after the concert. Don't worry. It's probably just routine. See you later."

"Sandy? What's going on? Do you think Phara's going to need a lawyer?"

"I don't know, Lizbet. But it seems her cousin,

Dayanne Mathieu, has disappeared near her boutique in Port-au-Prince. She had been working with local authorities on a case regarding some fashion labels she suspected were counterfeit. Phara thinks she had been in contact with Cassandra and is now in peril." *Why would Detective Allison be in touch with Haitian police? And was she implicated in some way? Why question Phara?*

Bobbi flung herself into one of the rattan chairs looking as white as a sheet. "I've been called down to our Park Avenue headquarters today for an emergency meeting with the top brass and our head of security, Emmett Brown. Emmet's a friend, and he told me on the QT that our CEO suspects an internal breach."

"You don't mean they suspect you?" Lizbet gasped.

"I don't know. I don't know."

"Look, Bobbi," Sandy interrupted. "They know the kind of sharp, honest and dedicated professional you've always been. You have a strong track record of problem solving and that's got to be why you've been called in. So relax.

"Let's all do a quick change and skedaddle out of here. Lucky we found a parking space for the Prius right here on West 83rd last night. Lizbet and I will drop you off at your office and then go down to TriBeCa and Wall Street as planned to check out those NYC UGRR sites. You can join us when your meeting is over."

Twenty minutes later, the trio was driving across the West 81st Street transverse to the East Side. "Just relax, Bobbi, and breathe in this glorious spring air," Lizbet gushed. "I just love Central Park. Do you know it was the first major urban park in the country and was designed by Frederick Law Olmstead and Calvert Vaux in 1858? They had to import more than 18,000 cubic yards of topsoil from New Jersey because the soil was so poor and rocky. Then they planted more than 4 million trees, shrubs and plants. The park consists of 843 acres, 7 manmade lakes and ponds, 36 different style bridges, 29 sculptures, 21 playgrounds, and miles of foot paths and roads for runners, bicyclists and cars. Oh, I could just go on and on! I love it so!"

Crossing 5th Avenue, they dropped Bobbi off at 277 Park Avenue. Sandy deftly guided the Prius downtown into the Park Avenue Viaduct, curving around the Helmsley and MetLife buildings and Grand Central Terminal, straight into the tunnel leading to Park Avenue South.

➳

Two men, wearing UPS uniforms and carrying delivery boxes, approached the Power brownstone on West 83rd Street. The taller man pulled out a cell-phone-sized receiver and pressed a button. A green light flickered and then held steady. "OK, Samuel. The alarm system is disabled. Go to it and be quick about it."

It took only seconds for Samuel to deftly disable the lock and gain entry through the door on the garden level, just out of view of potential passersby on the street. "Good thing she doesn't have a safety gate. That would've taken me ten seconds more to open," Samuel said with a grin.

"Yeah, right. Take a quick look around to make sure she doesn't have a cleaning lady or someone else hangin' around while I call in."

He pulled out a burner cell phone and pressed #2. "OK, boss. We're in. No problem disabling the alarm system. Yeah. Office on second floor front, bedroom facing back on the same floor – we'll check both and then do a quick sweep of likely places for a safe. Won't take long."

"Hey, Apollo, we're all clear," Samuel signaled from the stairway.

"Yeah, Boss, I understand," Apollo replied to the voice on the other end of the phone. "We'll open any locked drawers and safes and look for a report marked 'Operation Cheshire Cat' plus any flash drives with the same name on the label. You want us to take the report or just photograph the sections you wanted?" After a pause, he added, "Right, copy that."

He'd bounded up the stairs to the office. The lock on the desk file drawer was easy to open and so was the file cabinet lock. But no report appeared. They checked various boxes and cubby holes for flash drives but came up empty. *That's weird. Most people have a stash of used and new flash drives at the ready.*

"I found a safe behind a framed silkscreen above the bed," Samuel called.

It took no time at all to override the combination. Inside, they found a 3-inch thick report. The label on the cover read: "TOP SECRET: Operation Cheshire Cat."

Apollo DuBane was a pro. His years in a clandestine

government shadow operation trained him well. In less than 5 minutes, he had photographed the 20 most pertinent pages of the report – drawings, formulas, pass codes, etc. Then, he downloaded the photos into the secured Cloud-based drop box he'd set up.

By the time they reached the garden floor of the townhouse again, the files had been retrieved.

"Good work, Apollo. Now, I need you to go back out to New Jersey and find out if that Haitian singer received anything from the Innocent woman, like a flash drive or a DVD disc."

"Been there, done that. We staked out the house in Bloomfield where she was staying. We were there from midnight till 7 a.m. this morning. Nothing. She never showed. And she wasn't with the Power woman and her friends when we got here."

"Then she's got to have it with her. You know where she'll be tonight. I want that flash drive at all costs! I'll double your fee."

The two men retraced their steps and exited Bobbi Power's home, leaving no sign they'd even been there. They walked calmly and confidently down the block toward West End Avenue.

Across the street, 85-year-old Helen Pawlawski sat in the window seat that curved around her front parlor's bay window, sipping her morning tea. *How strange. I thought those UPS men just delivered those boxes to Bobbi. Why ever are they taking them back out? I must remember to call her later.*

7 Called on the Carpet

BOBBI STEPPED OFF the elevator onto the 30th floor executive offices. of her company. She swiped her company ID card to gain access through the glass doors. She turned left past the empty reception console, swiping her card again at the third door on the right. She entered her spacious office and came to a dead stop. The far end of her desk, adjacent to the bank of windows where her computer screen and keyboard normally sat, was empty. *What the…?*

A quick sweep of the room revealed no other anomalies. Her inbox held the usual memos about upcoming meetings and promotions, her issues of *Target Marketing, Fashion Market, Fast Company*, and a small stack of various fashion trade pubs. In the middle of the desk, Bobbi saw a small packet of invoices with a post-it note from her assistant Peter, asking her to approve and sign them. She glanced at the display case filled with awards – the five annual "Green Choice Sustainability Awards," the Women in Manufacturing STEP Ahead Award from the Manufacturing Institute, and numerous citations from the American Marketing Association for leadership in diversity and innovative marketing. She walked over to a cabinet in the far corner, taking out her key to unlock it. Much to her relief, the key worked, releasing the door. But, when she typed the combination to the safe inside (her parents' wedding date), nothing happened. She re-typed the code on the key pad. No luck.

"Don't bother," a voice called from the door. Bobbi turned to find her friend, Security Chief Emmet Brown standing there. "The code's been changed. And, as you've no doubt guessed, your computer has been confiscated – same for the computers of Hector Alberiz, Al Mackenzie and Stuart Ames. The top brass thinks one of you is responsible for the theft of the schematics for the programmable micro-lens technology as well as several prototype labels."

"Emmet, there's no way I'd betray the very security labeling program I helped to create, let alone the company, I…" Bobbi began.

"I know, Bobbi," Emmet replied kindly. "I've known you a long time. You have the highest level of integrity and dedication of anyone on the team – Hell – of anyone I've ever met!"

"Then why…"

"Because all four of you have had close and ongoing access to sensitive information throughout the R&D process. The fact that you each have top security clearance and have been working at Auguste, in one division or another, for roughly the same number of years, doesn't exclude you from suspicion. We're starting at the top to find the source of the security breach on Operation Cheshire Cat. Personally, I think the perpetrators are somewhere down the corporate chain from all of you, but we have to start somewhere. Consider it a process of elimination."

"What if the breach is coming from outside the company, or even the country – in one of the offices in Europe or elsewhere? Then what?"

"We don't have the people or scope of skills for a full-blown global incident, so we'd have to get help from the Police Nationale in Paris or international authorities, like Interpol. In the meantime, I have my security team in conference room A pouring through the copies of the Operation Cheshire Cat Report each of you had locked up in your office safes. They're looking for missing or replaced pages. The IT Surveillance team is in the Data Security department on the 31st floor running diagnostics on your computers and email records. I'll have to take your corporate cell phone to check your text and call records. Sorry, Bobbi."

Bobbi handed it to him without hesitation. "What's next, Emmet?"

"We join the others in the Board Room. Klaus Vandervoort, Chief Operations Officer (COO); Pierre St. Claire, Chief Marketing Officer (CMO); and Harvey Steinberg, Chief Financial Officer (CFO) have been put in charge of this preliminary meeting. They flew in last night. M. Etienne D'Arsenault, our very concerned CEO, is joining us via Skype from Paris in about two hours. We've just been waiting for you and Al Mackenzie who's on his way from the Newark Lab where he pulled an all-nighter developing a new program for the micro-lens label prototype.

The Board Room was thirty feet down the hall from Bobbi's office, so they were there in a matter of minutes. Bobbi entered first, with Emmet close behind her. There were already six men seated around the long oval-shaped mahogany table. The panel of executives leading this investigation sat at the far end of the table, flanking the 60" LCD screen that hung on the wall – all media systems ready to connect with the Paris office.

Two of Bobbi's colleagues were already seated on the long side of the table facing the door. Hector Alberiz, executive vice president of manufacturing sat diagonally across from the COO, while Stuart Ames, executive vice president of finance was directly in front of his CFO. Emmet Brown excused himself to check on the whereabouts of Al Mackenzie, and Bobbi reached across the table to shake hands with her CMO, Pierre St. Claire. "Bonjour, Pierre. Il est bon de vous voir. It's good to see you although I wish the circumstances were different."

"Oui, I agree, Bobbi." He replied with a worried look on his face. He and Bobbi worked well together, and while he knew she would be an excellent choice to succeed him at the end of the year when he retired, he knew the chances were very slight. *They will likely select one of the younger, up and coming French candidates being groomed for executive growth. Quelle dommage.*

Emmet Brown returned with Al Mackenzie, the company's executive vice president of R&D. He sat next to Bobbi, leaning over to tell her that her suggested solution had worked, and they were well on their way to a stronger prototype. "I even succeeded in adding a new failsafe mechanism. I think those felons actually helped us," he added with a grin.

Before Bobbi could respond, the meeting was called to order. The atmosphere in the room quickly became heavy and uncomfortable. Once again, Bobbi was the sole woman in a room packed with powerful men, but she knew full well she could hold her own, especially when she turned up the volume of her own brand of "Power" energy. Still, it was frustrating that all the work she and others had done to diversify the company and extend opportunities to all had barely cracked the glass ceiling at the top level. *We've lost some ground, but change WILL come.*

"It looks like all of you, at one time or another, have signed out confidential reports on the Cheshire Cat project, presumably to work on it at home," COO Vandervoort began. "Two of you – Bobbi Power and Al Mackenzie – still have last month's feasibility study. We will need to retrieve them from you today and have some assurances that they have been adequately secured. Al? Bobbi?"

"It's locked in my desk at home in Hoboken. I'll bring it in on Monday."

"No, we will retrieve it from you today. Emmet, please arrange to have him accompanied home this afternoon. I want his copy examined by your Security team as soon as possible."

"My copy is locked in my safe at home, and I have a very sophisticated alarm system with video surveillance. I assure you it is secure. No one but me has had access to it. I take it you'll send me home with someone from Security?"

"I'll run up to your brownstone with you myself after the meeting," Emmet Brown interjected. "I think we can trust that your precautions have been thorough."

"Bobbi, you still have to answer for why you took your new prototype security card with you to a public place," CMO St. Claire declared. "Can you enlighten us? Have the local police found the thief yet?"

"I knew I was coming back to the Newark Research Center that night or early the next day," Bobbi replied. "It didn't make sense to check it in with Security, especially if I returned after hours. And, no, there's no sign of the perpetrator of the crime. The Montclair police are still on the case."

"But were you planning to return to the Newark Lab? Weren't you in the middle of taking some vacation days? Please explain why you thought it was acceptable to take some personal time before we were ready to launch the new program," a gruff CFO Steinberg questioned.

The interrogation continued over the next hour, often directed towards Bobbi and not restricted to the matter at hand. By the time, the company's CEO, Etienne D'Arsenault, joined the meeting on the LCD screen, Bobbi was feeling singled out – and most uncomfortable.

Sandy and Lizbet emerged from the Icon parking garage at 299 Pearl Street and walked downtown toward Fulton Street. "I'm so glad we took the time to check out those UGRR sites in TriBeca," Lizbet said. "Even though some of them are only survived by commemorative plaques, it was exciting to retrace those historic steps. The plaque at the corner of Church and Leonard Streets marked the first location of the Mother A.M.E. Zion Church, which was known as the 'freedom church.' Not only was it a station on the Underground Railroad, but it was also the center for black social activism of the time. Why, Frederick Douglass, Sojourner Truth and Harriet Tubman all spoke there! Gives me chills to think about it."

"Me, too," Sandy agreed. "There were other AME churches in lower Manhattan and in the Boroughs where the leaders of many social movements of the time gathered. I've read that the famed Broadway Tabernacle Church that stood near here in the early to mid-1800s at Worth Street and lower Broadway provided a platform for many of the early leaders of the abolition, civil rights, women's rights, and temperance movements. Boy, would I love to go back in time to listen to their impassioned speeches!"

"You can say that again," Lizbet chimed in, thinking of one of Douglass' most impassioned speeches and wishing she could have heard it in person.

∽

The crowd cheered, some stomping their feet, others jumping up and clapping in sheer joy. As the great Frederick Douglass – fervid abolitionist, orator, writer, social reformer, former slave – walked to the center of the stage, a hush fell. You could hear a pin drop now in the center of the Broadway Tabernacle Church. It was July 5, 1853 and Frederick Douglass was about to repeat the speech he'd given the year before in Rochester, New York.

"What, to the American slave, is your 4th of July? I answer; a day that reveals to him, more than all other days in the year, the gross injustice and cruelty to which he is the constant victim. To him, your celebration is a sham; your boasted liberty, an unholy license; your national greatness, swelling vanity; your sound of rejoicing are empty and heartless; your denunciation of tyrants brass fronted impudence; your shout of liberty and equality, hollow mockery; your prayers and hymns, your sermons and thanks-givings, with all your religious parade and solemnity, are to him, mere bombast, fraud, deception, impiety, and hypocrisy -- a thin veil to cover up crimes which would disgrace a nation of savages. There is not a nation on the earth guilty of practices more shocking and bloody than are the people of the United States, at this very hour...

"Whether we turn to the declarations of the past, or to the professions of the present, the conduct of the nation seems equally hideous and revolting. America is false to the past, false to the present, and solemnly binds herself to be false to the future." No one in the crowd of several hundred people, ever forgot his impassioned message."

≈

"It's too bad the David Ruggles Home and Boarding House that used to be at 36 Lispinard Street in TriBeca was demolished. Dad wrote an article about David Ruggles for the *New York Times* years ago. He was a free Black man born in Connecticut who moved to NYC in 1827 as a 17-year-old. He became the editor and printer of the first African-American magazine, *The Mirror of Liberty*. The Ruggles house was a hub of African-American activism and intellectual culture as well as an UGRR station. More than 600 freedom seekers passed through there, including Frederick Douglass. Dad'll be happy we walked past the site to show our respect."

"At least we did get to visit one of the old stations," Lizbet added. "Wasn't it lucky we bumped into Rabbi Rachel Fein in front of the Bialystoker Synagogue? She was so gracious to give us a tour of what had been the Willett Street Episcopal Church until 1905. She brought us through the women's gallery to see the old UGRR passage way. Can you imagine the number of runaway slaves, er, Freedom Seekers, who climbed that old wooden ladder up the narrow shaft to a chamber with more wooden ladders leading to the high loft attic? How many people hid there until they were rested enough to continue their dangerous trek north through Long Island and New England to Canada."

"There were hundreds, no thousands, on that journey for sure," Sandy added. "Remember Bobbi telling us about the network of Quaker Meeting Houses and A.M.E. churches throughout Brooklyn, Queens and Long Island that were part of the Underground Railroad? Her Mom's old alma mater, Flushing High School, is only a couple of blocks from the Quaker Meeting House on Northern Blvd. that's now the Bowne House Museum."

"If only we had time to visit it and Bobbi's parents' old stomping grounds in Whitestone before they moved to Prairieview," Lizbet sighed. "This security card theft and corporate shenanigans sure put the kibosh on our plans!"

"Speaking of Bobbi, we haven't heard from her," Sandy frowned. "I'll text her and see if she's free yet to join us for lunch."

"Lunch," Lizbet said longingly, suddenly realizing she was hungry. "Tell her we're right by the Fulton Street Market where there're lots of food choices."

Sandy's cell phone chimed an incoming text. "Meeting still going...really bad...will text when can."

The two friends picked up some salad and iced tea from a Bean Sprouts vendor in the Fulton Street Market building and sat down at one of the outdoor tables in the square. The events of the last few days had certainly put a damper on their "carefree" vacation tour. And they were both worried about the third point of their triumvirate, Bobbi.

"Well, let's make the next stop our last one, and then see if we should head back uptown to pick up Bobbi," Sandy proposed.

"Agreed. We can always schedule a future tour of historic lower Manhattan sites another time. I'm sure not in the mood now to visit the African Burial Ground National Monument at Duane Street and Broadway today."

"So, let's take a short walk over to the corner of Wall and Water Streets where the first official Slave Market in 18th century New Amsterdam was located," Sandy suggested.

When they arrived, they were disappointed to see no

demarcation for the site. Lizbet referenced her research notes, which she had tucked into her bag. "Oh, I forgot," she sighed. "The marker won't be in place until June! The NYC government is planning to hold a ceremony on 'Juneteenth' or Freedom Day as it was known after slavery was abolished. That's on the 19th of June. There will be a freestanding commemorative maker installed in that pocket park on the corner across the street."

"Well then, let's walk over to it, sit on one of the benches, and you can take us both on a journey back in time."

Moments later, they were sitting in the small park, facing the approximate location of New Amsterdam's first Slave Market. The Dutch first brought slaves to the New World in 1626 and by 1700, the population of 5,000 included 750 slaves. Lizbet went on to explain that the Slave Market, which was in operation from 1711 to 1762, was essentially a wooden building with open sides built on a pier along the East River at Wall Street. The current real estate the two women had walked on was landfill built up over the years. In the 18th century, ships from Africa and the Caribbean would moor at one of the piers and unload their cargo of Black men, women and children captives. Often, captured Native Americans would be added to the population of enslaved laborers that ultimately built the great city of New York and helped fund the forerunners of companies like Aetna, New York Life and JP Morgan Chase, among others.

"Wow," Lizbet stopped a moment to ponder, "the responsibility for the horrors of slavery can't just be laid on the doors of Southern Americans."

"Can you imagine how terrifying it must have been for the people thrown into this market – and others in the colonies?" Sandy mused. "Charleston and New Orleans were supposedly the worst." She closed her eyes in an effort to block out the images she couldn't help conjure up.

᳀

"Git up there, git up there you lazy brutes!" The whip cracked again across his broad shoulders as Osner climbed onto the platform in back of the St. Charles Hotel in New Orleans, which housed the biggest slave market in the city. His feet were shackled together, and he was connected to the men ahead and behind him by chains linked to a tight metal ring. It greatly limited his ability to move as fast as he was ordered. That didn't matter to the men about to auction them off to the highest bidder.

He did not regret his fourth attempt to escape the whip of his Master's overseer. He knew freedom was there for the taking…if you were strong enough, brave enough, stubborn enough. This was his punishment for "not knowing his place," his Master said. He was to be sold away…sold away… from his family…from the only life he had ever known. He knew his mother and many others had traveled before he was born on a ship over rolling seas from Hispaniola to the hot, humid sugar cane plantations of Louisiana. He longed to go to that island, that free island. He had been raised a house slave, taught to read, write and factor numbers until he was twelve. Then his independent spirit and sharp tongue had sent him to the fields, and to the whip.

Osner stood proudly before the crowd, his chest slathered with *oil to make him appear healthier and more muscular. The auctioneer and prospective owners poked and prodded him, examining his teeth and his privates for any sign of disease. Oh how he longed to flatten them all...and run. The bidding started...and then...sold! Sold to Henry Fleetwood Abbott for $1,000.*

∽

Sandy shook herself out of her reverie and looked at her watch. "It's nearly 2:30. Let's head back to the garage on Pearl Street, retrieve the Prius and see if we can rescue Bobbi, shall we?"

"Aye, aye, ma Capitan," Lizbet chimed in an attempt to lighten what she perceived as a heavy mood threatening her chum.

Before they reached the garage, Sandy received another text from Bobbi: "Proceed to Montclair without me...Security taking me home to get documents...will follow when I can."

8 Missed Cue

BOBBI TURNED OFF her cell phone after texting Sandy and poured a cup of lemon de-stress herbal tea. She settled into the sectional in her ground floor family room to calm herself and reflect. Emmet had left with her copy of the feasibility report under his arm, reassuring her again that everything unfolding was routine protocol and not to worry. They both knew differently.

Although it was not at all unusual for a top executive to check out classified documents relevant to one of their own projects, she alone seemed to be under suspicion. Never mind that she was fully vetted and bonded. Never mind that all the men at today's meeting had signed out copies of the same report at one time or another. Never mind all the years of above-reproach work and "Exceeds Expectations" job performance reviews at Auguste and before that at Avon. Bobbi was angry and more than a little hurt.

Then, the call from her neighbor Helen. Something had not felt quite right when she opened her safe for Emmet. Knowing now that strangers had been in her home gave her chills. In addition to wrinkled pillow and after a careful sweep of each room, she found a few other things slightly off and called her alarm company. Nothing appeared out of the ordinary from their end, but they promised to do a priority check of all systems and report back to her by the next day – best they could do on a weekend.

Bobbi noted the time – 6 o'clock, the height of rush hour. She reached for her land line and arranged to have her car service pick her up at 7:20 p.m. She'd be late for the concert, but she needed a good long soak in the tub.

Sandy and Lizbet stepped out of Raymond's, a chic, family restaurant on Montclair's charming Church Street. It was a cool spring evening but several restaurants had already resumed alfresco service with café tables and chairs set on the wide sidewalks. The block-long pedestrian-friendly street reminded Sandy of many she had visited in Europe. It was a narrow one-away lane flanked by sidewalk cafes, blooming trees and plantings, comfortable benches, and eclectic shops that drew townies and visitors alike. A stage at the base of a huge fir tree anchored one end where area musicians performed during warm weather, and township residents gathered for winter holiday events.

Lizbet gushed about their dining experience, filtered by her years as a restaurateur. "I loved the friendly, neighborhood ambience, the diner-like décor with its white subway tiles, distressed mahogany booths and red banquets. The service was spot on. They sure keep everyone happy and well-fed, yet move diners in and out without making them feel rushed. The simple, American fare was great! I loved my vegetarian chili, garnished with non-dairy cheese and tofu cream. The braised collards and key lime pie were just like my Aunt Madge used to make. Yum."

"Lizbet, dining with you is always a delight, especially when you put on your professional chef demeanor and schmooze. You really know how to bring out the best in anyone who works in the restaurant business. By the way, before you ask, my pan-seared salmon with French lentils and arugula fennel salad was great. The brownie sundae was out of this world."

The two continued their short walk, crossing South Park Street, stopping across from the white church set back from the road at Church and Valley. They crossed over to the home of the Unitarian Universalist Congregation of Montclair, which was co-hosting the Sixth Annual Concert for Haiti with Outpost in the Burbs, a non-profit organization dedicated to building community through music and cultural events.

They'd stopped at the church before dinner to see Phara, bringing her up-to-date on the day's happenings, and wishing her the best for the evening's performance. The interior of the church had been alive with activity. Lighting and sound equipment were getting final tests; musicians were warming up; volunteers were adding rows of folding chairs in front of the pews in anticipation of a large turnout. Cynthia Stagoff was a whirl of activity, checking and rechecking every aspect of the venue to ensure everything and everyone was in place.

"I'm so happy you're here for the concert," Phara had said. "Cynthia has been most kind, inviting me to stay in her home last night so I wouldn't be alone. I had a restful night, and this morning, her delightful children kept my mind off this terrible week." Then, she looked around and added, almost in a whisper, "I must speak with you after the concert. My brother JanJak called me from Haiti this morning with alarming news about the investigation into my cousin Dayanne's disappearance. Will you come backstage after the performance?"

Before Sandy could reply, Cynthia had ushered Phara to her "dressing room" in the minister's office to change.

Now, as Sandy and Lizbet made their way to the front of the large nave of the church to claim three seats, Sandy was thinking about the expanding circle of seemingly unrelated incidents – the murder of a sweatshop investigator in Newark; the kidnapping of a fashion designer in Port-au-Prince; the theft of a prototype security pass in Montclair; and possible corporate espionage and theft of proprietary anti-theft labels in Newark and New York. *But what did they all have in common? Fashion? Was that enough of a thread to tie them all together? And what about the theft of the letters and Civil War diaries? How did they fit in?*

"Sandy, let's take these three seats on the aisle at the end of the second row," Lizbet said, breaking Sandy's reverie. "I'll put my shawl over the aisle seat to save it for Bobbi when she comes. When do we expect her again?"

"She just texted that the car service picked her up, and they're about to enter the Lincoln Tunnel," Sandy replied. "I'd estimate she'll get here by 8 p.m. if there's no traffic."

"Hope she doesn't miss Phara's performance. Anything else? Any more clues about today's meeting?"

"Nope. You know Bobbi. She'll tell us when she's ready."

Sandy's cell phone buzzed; she recognized her father's number. "Hi, Dad. We're at the Haiti Benefit Concert. It'll begin in a few minutes, so I can't stay on long. What's up? You found part of a letter to Great Aunt Babby dated 1962 mixed in with the older ones? From Greensboro? What was the name? I don't know. That would be too much of a coincidence. Could be a common name, with different spellings. But I'll ask her...sorry, Dad, the concert's about to start. We'll ring you back at intermission. Ciao."

"What was that all about, Sandy?"

"Tell you at intermission. Cynthia's about to speak."

"Good evening," Cynthia Stagoff, the concert's lead organizer, began. "Welcome to the Sixth Annual Concert for Haiti. The Montclair community is revving up its commitment to the people of Haiti, still recovering from the devastating aftermath of the earthquake and tsunami that struck this small country in 2010.

"We have an exciting and diverse roster of musicians to entertain you at our annual fundraiser for the Edeyo Foundation, Lamp for Haiti and the Haitian Education and Leadership Program (HELP). All three of these organizations embody the commitment the Montclair community has made to help provide better access to food, clean water, education, and social programs for Haiti's children. More about them later.

"Our program tonight will resonate with rockin' music in a number of genres – from reggae, jazz and a little bit country to Haitian and Latin rhythms. This year's headliner is Haitian singer-songwriter Phara Damour, whose spirit and phenomenal voice shine brightly on the international stage. Her original songs combine elements of native Haitian konpas and twoubadou ballads with jazz, pop, meringue, and samba. She has performed at jazz festivals and concerts throughout the Caribbean, Europe, Canada, and the U.S., as well as her native Haiti.

"We're also excited to have with us once again the groups Big Mamou, Zing Experience and Oxygen Box Band, as well as the award winning Jazz House Kids, Montclair High School's Passing Notes a cappella group, and a quartet of singers from Temple Ner Tamid.

"Without further ado, let me bring out Big Mamou to lead off our program!"

Moments later, the church was rocking from the exciting rhythms of reggae and invigorating beat of rock Krèyol. The audience was out of their chairs swaying, jumping and clapping to the music. Sandy felt someone tap her shoulder and turned to see Bobbi. "You made it!" she shouted over the din of music. Lizbet nearly tripped over a chair to join them in a three-woman hug. "So glad you're here!"

The set ended to tumultuous applause, and Cynthia stepped up to the mike to announce the next performer. "I'm very pleased to introduce our special guest, the renowned Phara Damour, who will open her program with what I'm told is a zouk-love song, 'Plus Près de Toi' – which means 'Closer to You.' Phara Damour!"

Phara glided onto the stage, resplendent in a beautiful salmon gown created for her by Haitian designer Maelle Figaro David. Phara followed her opening number with the love song "Se Pa Pou Dat," celebrating childhood love come full circle. She then switched to a sultrier samba-inflected song before ending in a unique jazz-rock rendition of "God Bless the Child." The audience went crazy!

After Passing Notes sang two numbers, "Bewitched," and "Bohemian Rhapsody," Cynthia announced a ten-minute intermission. The interlude gave Sandy, Lizbet and Bobbi time to catch up a little. Bobbi wouldn't say much, except that the day had been very draining, and a full scale investigation had been launched. "I really need to take a break from it all, so please let's not talk about it now."

"I feel badly that you were going through such an ordeal while we were taking our historic tour," Lizbet said kindly. "It wasn't the same without you so we'll just have to schedule another visit when everything blows over. It *will* blow over, Bobbi. Count on it!"

"Can we get some snacks?" Bobbi asked. "And I need a bathroom break."

"Me, too," Lizbet added, as they threaded their way up the aisle to tables in the front where brownies, water, coffee, and tea were on sale. CDs of the various performers were being offered as well.

Along the way, a young woman, apparently videoing the event, bumped into Lizbet. "Oh, I'm so sorry," she said. Lizbet noticed she was wearing a name tag that read, Lisa Tan, Edeyo Volunteer.

"That's OK. I see you're from one of the organizations benefiting from this concert."

"Yes, I'm actually working on a video project for their website. I might even expand it some for YouTube. Oh, excuse me, I have to catch someone."

"I'll be back in a few," Bobbi said, "really need the loo."

Lizbet turned to Sandy. "Now, before the concert resumes, what was that call from your Dad about a 1962 letter?"

Before Sandy could answer, the lights flashed, indicating the concert was about to resume. Robert D. Jackson, the Mayor of Montclair Township, was introduced by Cynthia and invited up to the podium. After acknowledging Cynthia and her fellow concert planners, including the township's previous mayor Robert Russo, he directed the audience's attention to the three non-profit organizations that would channel the proceeds of the event to improve the lives of Haitian children. Leaders of each one provided brief presentations of progress made over the last year.

The concert resumed with a promise that Phara would close the program with one of her own compositions, followed by the Haitian national anthem, "La Dessalinienne" or in Haitian Creole, "Ladesalinyèn."

Oxygen Box Band, Jazz House Kids and Zing

Experience had everyone up dancing and singing again. After a delightful medley from the Temple Ner Tamid quartet and a reprise from Passing Notes, Cynthia returned to the microphone. She re-introduced all of the acts, inviting them to line up behind her for the finale.

"Now it's my great pleasure to invite the incomparable Phara Damour back to the stage to sing us home. Phara Damour!"

Everyone's attention turned stage left as the pianist played a few introductory "ta da" notes. No Phara. "OK, once more with more feeling. Presenting the Fabulous Phara!" Phara still did not emerge.

Cynthia had Sandy in her direct line of sight and her look said, "Help me out here."

The lead singer of Big Mamou stepped forward and said, "Let's all start the anthem and Miss Phara will hear and join us!"

Sandy, Bobbi and Lizbet slipped quietly toward the door leading "backstage" on the heels of Cynthia. She opened the door to the minister's office and found it in total disarray, with one chair overturned and makeup, clothing and music sheets strewn on the floor.

They heard a groan and saw a foot move on the other side of the desk. "Phara, Phara, are you OK? What happened?" Cynthia cried out.

Sandy and Bobbi helped Phara up and into a chair. She was holding her head, clearly in pain. Her cheeks were red and swollen.

"Two Montclair police officers I know are in the audience. I'll go get them," Cynthia said, thinking clearly.

"And I'll get some ice from the kitchen," Lizbet said, making a quick exit.

"Phara, can you tell me what happened? Who attacked you and what did they want?" Sandy asked.

"There were two men, both tall, all in black, wearing ski masks and white gloves. They demanded I give them the information they said the 'immigration woman' sent me. They had to mean Cassandra. I told them I had nothing, had received nothing. They tore through all of my bags and started throwing everything all over. One of them rifled through my shoulder bag and said, 'Found something.' The other one hit me over the head and knocked me out."

Cynthia returned with two off duty police officers who'd been in the audience. "Excuse me, I'm Detective Sam Roberts, and this is Officer Kevin McNally," the taller of the two said, flashing his badge. "Thank you for your help. We'll take over now. Please don't touch anything. This is an active crime scene. Miss Damour, those are nasty bruises, and your head is bleeding a little. Did you lose consciousness?" When Phara nodded, he directed the other officer to call an ambulance. When Phara started to object, he said kindly, "You've had quite a shock. And we have to be sure there's no concussion."

A uniformed Montclair police officer appeared and spoke with the detective for a moment. "Did they get a plate number? Good. Put out a BOLA with the car description and the partial number."

He turned to Cynthia. "You've done your usual great job with this concert, Cynthia. Due to the circumstances,

I suggest you tell the audience that Ms. Damour has taken ill and won't be able to perform again. Then, see if you and your staff can quietly usher everyone out. I don't think there's any need to keep the audience for questioning. Two men matching the description I overhead Ms. Damour make nearly hit an elderly couple crossing the street when they sped off in a black sedan. They gave us a good description. But if any of the other performers or volunteers heard anything, I'd like to talk with them."

"Detective Roberts, Phara said the thieves took something out of her shoulder bag, which is still on the floor near the door. None of us touched it," Sandra assured him.

"Kevin, bring it over so she can see what's missing from it."

Phara checked the bag and looked puzzled. "My money, credit cards and return ticket to Port-au-Prince are all here. The only thing missing is a DVD disc of my music that I was going to give Cynthia. It wasn't labeled. Perhaps they thought it contained what they wanted."

Turning back to Sandy, he asked, "Are you and the others here friends of Ms. Damour? Did you see anything that might be helpful?"

Sandy introduced herself as well as Bobbi and Lizbet, who had returned with ice for Phara. She repeated what Phara had told them about the attack and filled him in on the murder of Phara's friend and the Newark police's investigation.

"Thank you. If you think of anything more, please call

me," he said, handing Sandy his card. Officer McNally will take down your names and numbers, in case we need you.

McNally started to write down their information in his pad and stopped. "Wait. I recognize your names. Weren't you all robbed by a pickpocket at Applegate Farms on Monday? I hope you don't think ill of Montclair. We really are a safe community."

A few minutes later, as the three friends were leaving the church, Sandy's cell rang again. "Hey, Dad. Sorry I haven't had a chance to call you back. We've just…"Sandy began. "Say again, Dad, while I put you on speaker."

"We need you all to come home right away," Dallas said, sounding grim. "We've found some shocking information in one of the letters that we need to discuss face to face. What's more, we had the feeling we were being followed all day today. And just an hour ago, someone tried to run us off the road!"

.

9 A Secret Made Plain

"DAD! ANNA!" Sandy Troux rushed into her father's arms and then pulled Anna Greene Troux in, hugging them both. She then held them out at arm's length scrutinizing their faces. "I couldn't bear if anything happened to the two of you. We've been sick with worry." Bobbi and Lizbet bustled in with hugs and kisses for Dallas and Anna. Sandy flung her arms around two of the most important people in her life. "We took the red eye. We couldn't wait to see you were all right. What's wrong? Why did you call us home?"

Anna, ever the organizer said, "First things first." She got "her girls" settled in their rooms. "Dallas sweetheart, can you set out lunch?" Anna called downstairs to her husband. She came with Sandy, Bobbi and Lizbet to their rooms, chatting along. "We have so much to talk about. We'll tell you all about what happened that prompted us to call. Plus, there are Aunt Babby's letters. We want to know everything from you – you understand me? No holding back! I've got some surprises for you three. Wash up and come down quickly." She turned and quickly went downstairs. "Her girls" could hear Dallas and Anna in the kitchen giggling like teens and rattling dishes and pots.

"Whatever it is, they seem safe and whole," Sandy said turning into her room which had been her childhood haven, now redone and expanded into a spacious suite. She had a sitting room/office; a large bath with a Jacuzzi and shower; and a light airy bedroom. Her bedroom was hung with some of her mother's best works – from her early days as a fashion photographer for the Emile Auguste Salon, precursor of Bobbi's company to her later career as an ethnographic and war photographer. She and Dallas had worked together often. Sandy was still inspired by her mother, dead many, many years, and she was grateful for Anna who had been her "mother" after Simone. But her most precious photographs were those of her daughter June, son-in-law Tim, and granddaughters, Kat and Charlie. She loved waking up to her favorite of Joaquin's abstract period paintings: *A New Day*. When she viewed that painting any new day was filled with promise.

Sandy's office was lined with built in book and display cases filled with artifacts from her years as a working anthropologist. The shelves were crammed with her own publications, Dallas' collected articles, books and journals of her colleagues and students, now professors and working researchers themselves. She was deep in her current project: writing up the two international mysteries she, Bobbi and Lizbet had solved. *We're at the beginning of another one. There are so many unrelated happenings. Well, they might seem to be unrelated, but I think I see a faint outline. The murder of Phara's friend. The black sedan. The break ins at*

Bobbi's house and lab…

Bobbi called from down the hall. "Hey, you two, you have to come see what Anna has done to "my" room. Sandy came back from her reverie. She and Lizbet sat down on Bobbi's new king sized bed. Anna had quilted a special cover for Bobbi. She had scraps from Bobbi's childhood clothes and made a story quilt for her, marking key events in her life. Bobbi choked up. "I can't believe she's done this for me."

"You think that's something, you've got to come to MY room," Lizbet tugged them. Sandy and Bobbi crossed the hall and there on Lizbet's own new huge bed was her own story quilt, again telling important events in her life sewn from her girlish clothing. "Now, I'm going to blubber."

"How did she get our clothes?" Bobbi and Lizbet were mystified. Sandy clamped her mouth shut and ducked her head.

"You rat!" Bobbi grabbed Sandy while Lizbet pulled her down on her new bed. "You knew."

"No," Lizbet said, a light clicking on, "she's complicit! She helped Anna." The two of them mock threatened her, a time honored method they had used to make Sandy talk since they were girls.

"OK, OK, I'll confess! When we were helping you both clear out your parents houses, I took some of your things. Anna was taking a story quilt class and wanted to make quilts for you both. She wanted you to know that this is always your home. She wanted to do something really special that would ease your sorrow over losing your parents." Her friends stopped tickling and sat on either side embracing her, all three sniffling.

"Come on down, you whippersnappers, lunch is ready," Anna called tartly up the stairs. "No delay, my cheese soufflé will fall. And I can't have that happen."

"Well, that's the first time I've heard sixty-something women called whippersnappers. I think I like it!! She's just too much." Lizbet shook her head in admiration. "Anna is something else. Something wonderful."

After a towering cheese soufflé, a baby greens salad (the first of Anna's spring garden), fresh baked 7-grain bread and non-gluten corn bread, rose petal and hibiscus iced tea, topped off by peach cobbler, everyone pushed back from the table happy in body and soul. "Those peaches were canned last summer; they're Elbertas – the best and tastiest peaches ever and my last jar 'til the end of this summer."

Dallas cleared the table and wiped it down. "These are only a few of Aunt Babby's gift to me. There are years of letters. We're going to sort them and transcribe them. Anna, tell them what you've planned."

"So, like Dallas said, we plan to sort them by year. Then we're going to transcribe all of them. We're going to scan all the originals so that we have both digital copies and the transcribed ones. Those will be easier to read. Some of the letters are just scraps. Some are written on very thin paper front and back and cross wise as well...really hard to read. On some, the ink has faded. We'll do our best. And Lizbet, I'm going to do a Greeley genealogy. Also one for Troux, and one for Abbott. I've got some new software – just learning it, makes family trees. It's supposed to be easy."

Sandy picked up a letter at random. It was dated August 25, 1861 from Amaelie Fleurie Abbott to her sister Lillie. "Look at this." Sandy held a thin paper gingerly on her flattened hand. Bobbi and Lizbet crowded close looking over her shoulder. "This is the same name we saw in the letter at *Applegate Farm*. And in that scrap of letter at the New Jersey Historical Society. Dad, Anna, so much has happened that I totally forgot about Amaelie and the extraordinary way we *met* her." She explained how and where they had seen letters that mentioned her. Sandy read out loud the letter she was holding.

August 25, 1861
Storeville, SC
Ma Chere Soeur Lillie,

We are sweltering here. The weather is especially hot and heavy today. I feel if I could stretch my vision far enough, I would see Him, my dearest husband, riding home to me. If only there were some word or something. It is terrible to be so shorn of my dear one. I keep looking for a letter from Fleetwood. I plan to take the buggy and drive over to the store to see if a letter has arrived.

His regiment has been gone since the end of June. Oh, my dear, you should have seen them: so gallant, banners waving. High stepping horses. Fleetwood looked so handsome on Annie. He said he named her for me; her chestnut hair is the same as mine, he said. 'So when I stroke her flanks I will dream of you,' the last thing he whispered to me. Oh, my dear, I shivered in delight and cried and cried. My darling will win this dreadful war for us and be home soon. They all think it will be over in a few months. Kiss your babies for me.

"Here's another." Sandy picked up another thin sheet with no date. It seemed as if it were a last page. "Anna, once you and Dad get these letters sorted, we can follow their lives throughout the war before and after."

...Oh, Lillie, whatever would I do without Osner? I have come to depend on him in the fields as I depend on Minette in the house and with the children. Georgiana is walking now. We must run after her every day. She is such a spirited child and oh so sweet. Henry Fleetwood is a stalwart big brother. He talks of going to join his daddy in the fight. I pray it will be over soon. They all say it will. Hezekiah Jackson is my little trickster. The boys both adore their sister. Oh how I love my children so! And I miss Fleetwood more and more each day. I will him to come home. Things are not the same. Life is harder and sad here.

Please write soon. We get so little mail or news these days. I haven't seen a copy of the Anderson Intelligencer in weeks. No one seems to know anything. Do you know how the War is progressing? Are we winning? Some of the boys are coming home. Their injuries are dreadful. I still don't know what happened to Fleetwood. There are some bad men around. Bummers they call them. They are deserters.

I remain your affectionate sister,

Amaelie Fleurie Abbott

A

In a shocked tone, she said, "They were slave

owners!" Sandy blanched. Bobbi looked down, embarrassed to witness this family secret revealed. Slave owners. Her dear friends Sandy and Dallas descended from a family of slave owners.

In a small voice, Sandy said, "My nightmare; my worst imaginings about our family. I knew we had southern roots somewhere, but I fooled myself that members of our family were only dairy farmers and nothing more. I feel so responsible. Dad, did you know? What did you know? I feel sick to my stomach." She turned to face her friends. "Now what do you think of me? Are you changed? Am I changed? What am I to do about this?" And Sandy, who was calm in most crises. Who was level headed; who could think in the most extreme situations; who had consistently pulled Lizbet and Bobbi out of tricky and even dangerous circumstances since they were girls: Sandy put her head down and cried: mortified, horrified, and shocked to the core. "I always feared it, dreaded it. And now it's true."

Her friends sat on either side of her again, as they had done a few hours ago. Again, they embraced their dear friend. This time there was no laughing or communal sniffling. This time there was only silence and love telegraphed by their warmth, because what could they say.

10 A Briefing and Debriefing

SANDY, BOBBI, Lizbet, Anna, and Dallas gathered in the Troux library. The mood was subdued. Sandy especially was troubled. Bobbi restless. Lizbet perplexed. Anna on alert. Dallas tense. "Murder, pick pocketing, thefts, attacks, assaults, stalking, police investigations, stolen letters, break-ins, corporate intrigue, imperiled jobs," Sandy recited the major incidents. "Some kind of international crime. And now real slavery – in our own family." She sighed, disconsolate.

"Look, right now you can't do anything about that past. It is past. So, so we'll deal with that later." Bobbi gave her the squint eye: guaranteed to snap her out of the funk Bobbi could see Sandy was edging towards. We've got enough to concern us right here in the present!"

Anna stood up. "Lizbet come with me." She crooked her finger beckoning Lizbet. Dallas started to rise, "No, your daughter needs *you*. But *I* need help getting lots of fuel for the troops. I can see this is going to be a long serious afternoon. We'll need sustenance while we debrief."

Lizbet and Anna were busy planning a feast as they went to the kitchen. "What do you think about tuna salad sandwiches?"

Anna added, "Good, tuna salad with some of the baby greens: easy, quick, filling and lots of good protein. I've got more of that barbequed tofu -- made it especially for you. We'll use the left over breads. I have oatmeal cookies and early strawberries and a dark chocolate dipping sauce. Did you like that herb tea?"

Their voices faded.

"I knew there was something nobody wanted to talk about," Dallas said. "I did know that. And there were some hints, but nothing directly expressed. We never went south. I mean South Carolina south. We sometimes visited Aunt Babby in New Orleans, but that's not south...not the way Georgia or South Carolina are south. And there were certain subjects that just, well, seemed off limits. Your grandparents were committed to the Civil Rights movement and so was I. It was important; still is. I did wonder where their intense involvement sprang from. Just figured, they were good people and saw injustice and the need to rectify those injustices. But I agree with Bobbi. We'll deal with that past later. Now is the time for the present."

Sandy was comforted by her father's kind voice, his effort to explain something that was unexplainable, but she paid only surface attention to what he was saying. *It's like a huge jigsaw puzzle with many of the pieces missing and no edges. We've been here before. In the middle of confusion in China and Russia, we worked through. The parts all came together in the end. Now, again, all these disparate elements. All these elements on different sections of the periodic table. What kind of chemistry is at work: a surprising solution? An explosion?* She sat back in her favorite wing back chair and tucked the lavender mohair throw over her knees. The weather was mild, but she felt cold. Or maybe she was just chilled by the gravity of the current issues and, yes, chilled by the horror of that specific past: never-mind-how-much-she-wanted-to-push-out-of-her-memory past, an impossibility: it was there forever; now and forever a family reality: her reality. Her belief in another impossible, in total justice, left her with an unyielding, unwieldy, tormenting sense of culpability. *Did they ever know they had done wrong and lived through that wrongness? But how did that wrong, still wrong, still wrecking millions of lives today, connect with all the jumble of events of the past days?*

Sinking lower in the enveloping chair, tucking the throw, her mother's favorite lap robe, in her mother's favorite color lavender, more tightly around her, the irony of place did not escape Sandy. A mystery ago, Anna had sat here in this very wingback chair, shocked and shivering. Dallas had sat near her in the companion wingback chaffing and warming her chilled hands. Anna had been tucked up in the self-same throw and comforted by Sandy and Bobbi while Lizbet got hot tea and chocolates. Now Dallas patted and stroked his daughter's chilled fingers. "OK, you're both right. I'll put that aside for the moment. But it is connected to the present in some important ways beyond my wish that it maybe, just maybe, is not true."

Bobbi considered the connection Sandy had made. She paced the library restlessly. "You're right. Otherwise, the letters and diary from that Union soldier, that Natty Crane soldier wouldn't have been stolen at the New Jersey Historical Society or that letter copy you had." She raked her fingers through her hair and turned her usually smooth shining cap into a punk rock do – spikes standing on end.

"What do you mean, Bobbi?" Dallas asked.

"Let's wait 'til Lizbet and Anna get back." Sandy started to get up to help.

"Nope, dope, sit." Bobbi pushed her back into her chair. "I'll go."

Bobbi rushed out of the room as if she were fleeing from some nasty imp nipping at her heels. Sandy watched her closely. She knew Bobbi's "signs" as well. She had lived through Bobbi's awful divorce, step by anxious and painful and destructive step. She knew her friend held it all in. That she practiced self-restraint to a degree that was dreadful. Sandy had been at the end of phone calls when Bobbi was at the end of her rope – defending her daughter against a neglectful, almost phantom father, against racial slurs while fighting her own way forward in a company that had then favored men. She had watched Bobbi fight – successfully – for better company practices towards its employees and its production processes. Successful gender sensitivity programs, successful diversity programs, successful community awareness programs. She had supported Bobbi while she pushed – successfully – to open the first tech lab in the enterprise zone in Newark – the very lab that had been invaded. She knew these positive contributions to Auguste Fashion

Marketing had saved the company millions of dollars and netted positive public opinion internationally, boosting a previous faltering bottom line.

Now Bobbi was pressing for a new green program that would transform the company once more and bring it to the forefront of best practices: "the environment is the economy; the economy is the environment" Bobbi's slogan, adapted from Interface founder Ray Anderson's talk. So very exciting. And for her dear friend a coup, another coup in the making and perhaps achieving that long desired corporate corner office. *Huh, I'll bet she throws out the old corner office status thing and makes some new physical and financial arrangements that foster and draw on all the creativity of all the employees.* One crisis after another had piled up in the last day or so: Bobbi getting called in to HQ, the problem at her house. They didn't really know what had happened. Then the attack on Phara and their red-eye flight to Dallas and Anna. They had scarcely had time to go to the bathroom, much less talk about anything. But something was seriously wrong with Bobbi and why not? She knew her normally sartorially kempt friend was in trouble when she started doing the hair raking thing.

Anna and Lizbet bustled in with trays of food. Bobbi had a tray with a cut glass pitcher of iced tea and floral etched tumblers. "Dallas, pull that little table over here, darling. We'll set up a little buffet and help ourselves."

Bobbi banged her tray down on a side table so forcefully the glasses jumped and so did everyone else. "Bobbi?" Sandy grabbed her wrist. "Bobbi, you have to tell."

Again raking her fingers through her hair, Bobbi took a deep breath and let it out in an explosive burst. "Everything is wrong, everything. We were in the office for hours and hours. They went through all my digital and paper files. Not just mine, but Al, Stuart and Hector's as well. And I understand they're going to do some sort of forensic analysis of my budget." Bobbi threw herself down on the love seat under the window. "I had some really funny feelings when we were all in the morning meeting."

"What do you mean?" Anna asked.

Sandy turned her full gaze on her friend. "Yes, what do you mean?" she asked.

Lizbet sat beside Bobbi and took her hand. Dallas frowned as if to say, I don't like this.

"Well, when Hector was asked a question, he kept looking at me. It was really strange. Then when I was asked about why I'd kept the last version of the new label feasibility report in my safe at home, all three of my peers, I thought my friends, looked down or away. They didn't look at me. The worse thing was that Al had taken home a copy of the same report, and they didn't question his motives."

Uh oh, that's not a good sign. Sandy scooted forward in her seat. "Didn't or wouldn't?" she asked gently.

"I don't know. I just know it was strange and different – made me really uncomfortable. I just felt so alone."

"Well, you aren't!" all chorused in unison and then laughed. That laugh broke some of the tension; Bobbi seemed a little relieved.

"But then...I got a call from my neighbor. That's what I told you. She saw something strange. She saw two UPS men delivering two packages and then ten minutes later coming out with the same packages." Bobbi jumped up and began pacing restlessly again. "First thing, why would it take them ten minutes to deliver packages? I mean you go in, you set the packages down. You tuck the notice in the mail box and you leave. Two minutes tops? And where were they delivering them? They would only have access to the vestibule where the two mail boxes are. They wouldn't deliver anything to the garden entrance, or step inside my home. What were they doing? Why would they leave with the same packages? I didn't leave any to be picked up. And my tenant Sally Soames told me she hadn't scheduled a pick-up." Sandy was leaning forward concentrating intently. "When Emmet arrived with me earlier, nothing seemed wrong or out of place. I opened the safe. You know, the one over my bed that I had installed over my head board instead of the common closet location most thieves would know? The copy of my company's Cheshire Cat feasibility report was exactly where I had placed it. Nothing was different. I gave it to Emmet, and he went back to the office with it.

"After Helen's call, I retraced my steps and rechecked everything. In my bedroom, I found a tiny depression in one pillow that I'd missed because I was so distracted when I opened the safe earlier. That's just not me. I never leave any wrinkles. I'm sort of obsessed about having my bed perfectly smooth." Sandy narrowed her eyes and her lips slightly as if to confirm something she was thinking.

"I re-checked the safe, but nothing was missing. Nothing anywhere was different, except the depression on the pillow. But I called the alarm company anyway."

"Good," Sandy murmured.

"And the worst: not what they found, but what they didn't find."

"Like the dog that didn't bark in the night," Lizbet said.

"Yes, Sherlock Holmes says in *The Hound of the Baskervilles*: the dog that didn't bark in the night. What wasn't there that should have been." Sandy leaned back again. She seemed energized, even somewhat cheered. Here was a mystery she could grasp in the here and now, rather than a moral abyss – an obscene pit of history. Something straightforward, a linkage to events that were pointed towards Bobbi. Why she felt they pointed to Bobbi was still a mystery, but that there were multiple events were plain facts. They were pointed towards her friend and that was something she could not tolerate.

"Yes," Bobbi said, pacing again. "Yes, what the alarm company found was not what should have been there; it was what was missing. There was a ten-minute gap in the surveillance recordings; no time stamps; no audio; no record of locks opening; no record of the safe being opened. Nothing. Well, an alarm company is supposed to alarm you. I am duly alarmed." She sat down, exhausted.

Anna busied herself getting Bobbi a fresh glass of tea. Lizbet sat close, looking out the front windows. The doorbell rang. "I'll go." Dallas started to get up.

"No, Dad. Rest yourself. We have lots more to share. And you and Anna still have to tell what got you so freaked that you called us home."

Sandy got up and walked to the front door.

Lizbet shook Bobbi's arm, "Do you see that car? It's been there for a long time."

Anna bent down to see what she was talking about. "Dallas, that's the car that was dogging us. Honey, look. Sandy," she started to call her almost daughter as the car slipped around the block.

From the library, they heard Sandy, a joyous Sandy, exclaim, "Ray!"

11 Framing the Puzzle

"DO YOU HEAR what I hear?" Lizbet asked.

"I don't hear anything," Bobbi said.

"No, nothing. We don't hear anything. Another non-barking dog?" Anna and Dallas smiled and agreed.

"That's what I mean…I don't hear anything either." She slapped her knee and laughed. She called Sandy and Ray, "OK, you two stop smooching and get in here. We have lots to talk about and lots to figure out."

A few minutes later, Sandy appeared in the library door flustered, rosy cheeked and smiling. Ray stood behind her smoothing his hair. "Look everybody, Ray!"

Anna pulled a side chair into their cozy circle beside Sandy's and motioned him to sit. "Sandwiches, cookies, tea?"

"Um, this looks delicious. Thanks." He loaded a plate and began to eat – ravenous. "I'm really glad to see you all. But, I haven't had anything since yesterday, I think it was yesterday. I was in Ghana, Sri Lanka and then Haiti. Was it yesterday? Maybe it's tomorrow! I've been back and forth across the International Date Line so many times in the last few weeks; I may have arrived here before I left! So let me just sit, eat and listen. Then I'll tell you why I'm here."

"So," Sandy began, "Let's go around and share what's been happening. Agreed? No objections?" Everyone agreed. "So let's get started." Sandy had regained her center and her direction. "Dad, do you have that old chalk board? We need an investigation board like on *Law and Order* or one of those other detective shows.

Anna left the library and was back in a few minutes rolling a large white board from the store room. We just got this."

Dallas added, "We thought we'd need it while we sort and organize Aunt Babby's letters. You know, note names, dates, places, cross list similarities and connections; create some order and meaning. Things like that."

Sandy nodded. "Exactly. And exactly what we need to see if we can begin to make sense of these disparate elements. First, let's start with the pick pocketing incident."

Over the next four hours, the group shared details and ideas about all the events of the last several days: the pick pocketing, the theft at the NJ Historical Society, the murder, the police investigations, the black sedan that had appeared three times, and then how the four men had jumped out of it just before it slid into the water. They went over the details of the attack on Phara at the concert. The disc the thieves had stolen that was filled, not with the secrets they hoped for, but with Phara's music. Bobbi recounted the break-ins at her company's lab and her home, and the suspicions raised by her senior management. Anna said, "Don't forget the letters. We haven't even begun really to look at those."

Lizbet wrote "Aunt Babby's Letters" in caps on the board.

Sandy said, "Write 'Dad and Anna's stalkers'."

"And, Lizbet, 'Sandy's little rectangle', the little rectangle you peeled off your shoe back in Military Park." Bobbi said. "Which we haven't even seen, much less figured out what it is."

"Very sharp, Ms. Power!" Sandy fished in the pocket of her black jeans and brought out a folded napkin that was wrapped around a small rectangle. It was fabric and looked like a clothing label. It was an iridescent black with curving letters woven into the background – 'S' and 'A'. These letters had a strange shimmer to them. "Bobbi, do you have your replacement lab pass card. Can I see it?" Bobbi went out to her purse, which was on the hall settle. She got out her green leather date book and opened it to the card slots. She slid out her Auguste Labs replacement security card and returned to the library.

"Here, Sandy. What are you thinking? What do you see?"

Sandy took the card and stared at it for several minutes. Then she held it beside the label. "What do you see, Lizbet?"

"They both have 'S' and 'A' capitalized. But the names of the companies are different."

"OK, Bobbi?"

"Same as Lizbet. And there is a shimmer in both."

"Anna, Dad?"

"Yes, the initials and the shimmer."

"Ray?"

"I'll pass for the moment. I'll explain why in a minute."

"Well, Sandy, you?" asked Bobbi.

"Certainly, the lettering. And the names are similar, but not exactly the same. Also, remember the initials on the ship that was docked where the thugs rammed us? The ship was named the 'S'tarlight 'A'rgent. The shimmer reminds me of the anti-counterfeiting strip in the Norwegian kroner bill that was stolen from my wallet at Applegate Farm. Reminds me, but is not exactly the same. So, Bobbi, can you talk about the anti-theft technology that your lab has been developing? Or is it still too top secret."

"The secret is out now, because those criminals have my card. What is unique about our anti-theft technology for the labels and some of the fashion items in our new SA Elite clothing line is our use of a combination of the latest security devices and software. Al Mackenzie, our EVP of Research & Development, has re-programmed our software and added more forensic authentication techniques, taking it up several more levels that we don't think can be penetrated. And he's now exploring other enhancements. I can't talk about any of our new, ongoing research, of course.

"What I can tell you is that we've combined micro printing with special fluorescent inks as well as holographic security foils similar to those used in the new Norwegian kroner currency. These techniques employ

115

micro lenses, so tiny you can't see them with the naked eye. It's the same technology used to create holographs and lenticular graphics with alternating images you sometimes see in consumer packaging and some toy products. We also employ DNA taggants in our fabrics – similar to the kind currently used in forensic authentication for pharmaceutical and cosmetic product packaging worldwide. It's all quite exciting."

"That brings me back to Cassandra's murder and the attack on Phara at the concert. Those guys wanted something they thought she had – probably that missing flash drive."

"Flash drive?" Dallas asked.

"It's supposed to be loaded with names, dates, ships, buyers, and sellers connected to illegal activities." Sandy saw Ray's attention sharpen. "Sweatshops – here in the States: in Brooklyn, at Port Newark, as well as Haiti, other places globally." Sandy paused. "Are you ready to tell us why you're here now, Ray?"

"Well, first of all, Dallas called me. You know we talk often. He told me about the incident in Montclair and..." Sandy wrinkled her brow. "Now before you get all twisted up and think your Daddy is calling your boyfriend to come to your rescue, just relax. You, too, Bobbi and Lizbet. We do all help each other out when we need it. And I need it. In fact, Cassie was helping me."

"Cassie? You mean Cassandra Innocent? The murdered woman we found in Military Park? That Cassie?" Bobbi was astonished. Lizbet's mouth opened and closed with no words emerging.

"Since you're working on something that has taken you from Africa, to Asia and to the Caribbean in the last few days, it has to be big. You've been flying around so much you don't know if you're coming or going. What is it, Ray? Some sort of international human trafficking supplying sweatshop labor?"

"But that's modern day slavery!" Anna burst out.

"You're right, it is modern day slavery of the worst kind," Ray said.

"Makes me shiver, any kind of slavery, back in the bad old days or here in the present, makes me sick to my stomach." Lizbet actually clutched her stomach as if she were going to throw up.

Sandy's face fell. Then she shook herself and said, "Ray, so Cassie was helping you?"

"Yes. She was on to something big. And she was working with two of my men down on the docks at Port Newark."

"Don't say. They were Lou Lombardi and Tony Marrara, right?"

"Darling, nothing, not a thing gets by you. Ever. Not ever," Ray said, beaming.

Before he could continue, Lizbet said still thinking of past slavery here in the US, "Anna thinks she has found some connection to my ancestors on the Greely side. We were talking about that in the kitchen." She gave Sandy a sympathetic glance. "Slavery. I don't get it. Why would you, how could you own other human beings? I mean *human beings*?"

"People do it all the time and have done so

117

throughout human history." Dallas took out his reporter's notebook. Even retired as long as he had been, he still did research for his network of colleagues and friends. "I was saving this for you, sweetheart," he told Sandy. "Thought all of you would be interested since you're on, or were on, that Underground Railroad Tour. Are you still on it?"

"Sort of, Dad. We got really side tracked." She paused and got that far away look they all knew so well. "Maybe we haven't been side tracked at all. It's just that our train has jumped the tracks from one century to another a century and a half later. What did you find out?"

"This is not pretty. I searched these numbers on the ILO, the International Labor Organization website. 'Almost 21 million people are victims of forced labor – 11.4 million women and girls and 9.5 million men and boys. Private individuals and enterprises exploit about 19 million people.' Wait a minute. I'm looking for a reference. Here it is. Business using forced labor generates US$ 150 billion in illegal profits every year. Manufacturing is one of the biggest sectors.

"And here's some info from your organization, Ray." Dallas flipped through his notes. "Wait a minute, ummm, hummm, OK, I found what I want. 'The second most common form of human trafficking is forced labor, although this may be a misrepresentation because forced labor is less frequently detected and reported than trafficking for sexual exploitation'."

"My God," Sandy shuddered. "I think we've found a global labor trafficking ring."

12 Voices from the Past

AS I SEE IT, we're dealing with slavery in two eras. But I still don't understand why, Dad, you and Anna were being stalked. And are you sure you were?" Dallas, narrowed one eye. "OK." Sandy quickly withdrew her question "You were being stalked. What happened?"

"We were at the library doing some research," Dallas said.

"You know I'd promised Lizbet I'd help her find out more about her Greely family roots," Anna interjected.

"So it was the strangest thing. Almost all of the letters in Aunt Babby's collection were written before, during and after the Civil War. But Anna found one from the 1960s from a Mrs. Mason in Greensboro, North Carolina. It mentioned something about an accident involving a family named Greeley. Spelled with an L-E-Y. Anna wasn't sure about the spelling, but she thought it sounded like the story your birth mother Ae-Sook told you about your birth father, Lizbet. What do you think?"

"It's pretty unlikely, but eerie," Lizbet said. "The spelling's close. My birth mother spelled it without the last E, but that could be a translation thing. She did say my birth father's parents were killed in a car accident. She didn't know much more except that it happened in the Carolinas, and that he never found his little sister afterwards. Was there anything else?"

"Just a reference to a newspaper article enclosed in the letter, but Anna hasn't located it yet. She's scanned the letter. And she plans to keep looking for the article. But why this letter would be in Aunt Babby's collection is a total mystery."

"So anyway, we left the library. We were planning to get a bite at that cute little fish restaurant on River Lane that runs by that sweet pond, and your father noticed a car shadowing us. Well, first we thought it was just kids. You know how they want to get to where they're going before they've even started. So, move over grandpa! That's what we thought. So we pulled over and slowed down to let them by, but instead, they just kept coming and coming closer and closer and almost ran us off the road and into Pink's Pond. We were really shook up. I insisted your father call you and tell you girls to come home to help us."

Lizbet was still focused on the unlikely connection between her ancestors and a letter from a Mrs. Mason in Greensboro, NC and Sandy's Great Aunt Babby. What was that all about? "Anna, can I see the letter?"

"Sure, honey. I'll print out a copy for you." Anna went to her office. They could hear her printer clattering.

"Ray," Sandy said.

"Yes, sweetheart?"

"Do you feel the same about me now that you know I come from a slave holding family? I don't know how I feel about me. I'm feeling dislocated. You think you know who you are and then something springs out and knocks you off your feet, spins you around, and you are a different person."

"Sandy, you're not a different person. Your family history is different, but you're not. And yes, I feel the same and more intensely that ever."

"Thank you, Ray. Thank you." Sandy leaned her head against his solid chest and sighed with relief. "OK, I think I'm ready to know more."

"Lizbet, Bobbi? Dad?" Sandy sifted through stacks of letters. Here's one from the end of 1861. It seems to be about First Bull Run."

Anna came back with Mrs. Mason's letter for Lizbet. She sat down to listen as Sandy read the 1861 letter.

Ray commented, "That battle was fought on July 21, 1861 at Manassas Junction in Virginia. It was horrible, and there was a huge loss of life. The Confederates took that day."

Sandy began reading.

We carrye on. That is the best I can say now. John Martin came home on furlough. He is in Fleetwood's company and Regiment, the S. C. 4th. He cam to see me carryeing word of Fleetwood. I am destroyyed. Fleetwood is noe more. He was mortally wound at Manassas, July 21ˢᵗ. He was shote in the upper arm and died on the field. John does not know where he is buried. That paines me almost more than his death. John has brought me the Keowee Courier for July 27. This is the first acount I have seene. I'm tolde the Anderson Intelligencer has ceased for the duration. I prey that will be short.

Here is what the newspaper said: "The Battle was a terrible one with great slaughter on both sides. A great battle has been fought at the Stone Bridge on Bull's Run. It is impossible to estimate the number of dead and wounded. Gen. N.G. Evans of South Carolina led the Brigade into battle. Among the Southern forces engaged were Col Sloane's 4th Regiment and others. In Col. Sloane's Regiment, the loss of life was greater than other regiments."

Lillie, my heart is broken. I am dede with my dearest husband. He is among the glorious fallen of Col. Sloane's Regiment. John recounted the day for me. He was beside my dearest one on the field and only the hand of the Almighty protected him. Would that the Almighty had extended his hand a bit wider and saved my precious one. John sayes, The heat was unbearable. Uniforms already stinking and filthy from the inside and outside – no baths, no clothes washing in nearly a month and now July 21, 1861 dawned. We took waggons, walked, or rode our farm horses and mules to the railroad station. Little sleep since we entrained on the cars from Columbia. The SC 4th Volunteer Regiment Co C Captain's Deans's Company mustered in late June. On the 21st We marched advancing towards the stone bridge over the small river called Bull Run. Birds twittered in the pinking light of early morning. A slight breeze stirred and cooled our sweating browes. Fleetwood said he was thinking of you. that Dawn was your special time. Yours and hisn. We recruits cautiously advance. He sayed the were fearfull, but brave. theye picked thru a thick forest snagging and stumbling on tangled undergrowth. We cheered ourselves onward with encouragin, but we crawled silentle like we were out squirrel huntin at dawn. John said he herd Fleetwood saye "Look, through there, Boyes." He ws excited. We all was, we was screered,too. happy, oh, we was

mixed up, he told Henry and me, "I sees them. I sees them." We crepted closer and there at the mouth of Stone Bridge over t'her side on the east side of Bull Run the first Yankee soldiers stepped up onto the roadwaye.

Then he tolde me Muskets roared. Gray and Blue felle. Blood flowed. Screams pieced the morning peacefulness. Bodies layed there groaning. Bodies layed ther stilled forever. Fleetwood and Robert Henry was crumpled together. He tolde me thay was Friends in life. Friends in death. "Look at us..." He sayed Fleetwood gurgled blood draining his life awaye. "No one will look at..."

"The other pages are missing."

Anna said, "We haven't sorted all yet. They may still be mixed up with other pages."

It was hard to come back to the present: Amaelie's account was so potent and her distress so intense. Grief over her husband's death at First Bull Run, barely a month after the regiment had ridden and marched off so gaily and so confident that they would be home in a few months. And now "Amaelie must have been on her own, managing the farm and the Negros as well as three small children. Wonder if Fleetwood's parents were some help. Perhaps they were struggling as well. Their sons were all gone and their Negros were no doubt running off as fast as they could." Sandy seemed mesmerized by Amaelie's plight.

Lizbet picked up another page. "I think this one is from some time in 1862."

Mme. Lillie Fleurie Troux
Troux House, New Orleans, La
Dearest Sister,

We have gotten word that the Congress will take large portions of our crops. Yes, we will cast in our property to swell the current that will waft our Ship of State to glorious Nationality. I praise the facte tha we have the stor. The store has beene our saving gracre. Even before the War we were struggling sum. My dearest was not the beste farm manager. I am sorrye to saye this about my poore dead one, but it is the truthe. Verily it is. And then we have the Greeleyes. Thaye is so good to us. Thaye send over help. Sometime s the send over Little Luke. He is young but big and strong and a grate help.

"My God, Sandy, did you see Greeley's on the next farm! And one named Luke." Lizbet nearly collapsed into the sofa. On the next farm! Greeley's living side by side with Abbotts. And it just hit me – Amaelie's sister Lillie's married name is Troux? What does this all mean?"

Ray picked up the page she dropped and continued reading,

Many of the Negros has run off. Osner is our biggest helpe. He is faithfule and I manage everything now with his helpe now that Fleetwood is no more. I am learning too. Life is not as it was when we was girls at Daddye's. I had to put awaye all my sliks and fineries a long time ago. Homespun is what we wear, it weares strong. We get along. The babies are strong. My heart's desire is to see you and holde you clos, my dearest sister. It is a lonly life with no one of my own familye here. I dread that I may never ee you in this life againe. Writ me. Writ me. Write me.

Ever your affectionate sister,
Amaelie Anne Fleurie Abbott

"Do you think she ever did see her sister again?" Bobbi asked.

Dallas shook his head. "I don't think so. The name Fleurie is in the family tree, and I'm not sure, I think my great-grandmother's name was Lillie. But, there were no hints about a sister, or her whereabouts, that ever filtered down in the family stories. She seems to have been erased – just totally written out of the family history."

"Well, it's easy enough to find out," Anna said. "You keep looking at the letters. I'm going online to check the census data for the 1830, 1840 and 1850. With my subscriptions to ancestry.com and *Family Tree Magazine,* it shouldn't take me long to scan for a Troux/Abbott connection in Louisiana." Anna went back to the office to power up her desktop, while Dallas' eyes smiled after her. "Boy, I love that woman."

"You know, Dad, it makes no sense," Sandy murmured, "Why would a family, ours or anyone else's, have done that? Erase a beloved sister from a family tree? From the letters, the sisters seemed to have been very close. Unless she had done something that was against the code of the day." Sandy looked at her friends, Ray, Anna, and her father. "Dad, any hint why she was just erased from all those family stories you told me?"

"No," he replied.

"Well," Bobbi said, scanning first one then another letter that seemed to be stuck to the first one. "Listen to this, and we know why. It's explosive, so everyone sit down."

> *Bishop James Holly*
> *Holy Trinity Episcopal Ch*
> *Port-au-Prince, Hayti*
> *12 Septembre 1868*

Mme. Lillie Fleurie Troux
Troux House, French Quarter
New Orleans, Louisiana, America

With great respect, Mme. Troux,
If you would be so kind and convey this leteer to your deer sister Madame Amaelie Fleurie Abbott.

> *With Appreiciation,*
> *Osner Mathieu*

Mme. Amaelie Abbott, my deare,
I write to you to saye that I am alive and safe from harm. I am a free man. I am a citizen of my mama's country. I am a free Haytien man.

I rode that ole mule you give me as long as he let me. We rode all night slept in woods and bushes to hide at daylight til that olde mule up and runned away from me maybe he got back too yoo maybe he got eat up. all the ground was black nothing growing all burnt up houses along the way closer I gote to Colombia was all burnt up glass blowed out of winders stuff drug out and left lying on the blacke grond. bones animals sticking up like they was Butchered on the spot and meat carried away with the yankees sum white

126

*people women and childrens looking like theyed been Pole axed. I
rekon theye beene.*

*I saw the fires the Yankees made of Columbia Blaze so high
could see fore miles and miles Hard times for all sade time too i
dropped in with Bunch of Negroes thay was walking behind
Yankees A grate train of yankees and negroes. and I followe them.
We marched behind old General Sherman's army north. Sum of he
Negroes call himour second moses. Thts a good name. one daye I
heerd his riding by talking to his men he sayed this is hard war total
it is sure total wesee Sherman neckties. Railroad rails ired up and
wrapped around trees. Thay saye down savannah waye forty
thousand free negroes come along with his armye.*

*And lots going to git 40 acres of farm and maybe even a mukle
to plow with. When we got to north Carolina I peeled off. Some old
boy tolde me that I need to hed to Wilminton to get on a ship I took
out alone to the ocean Sum lumbee people hiding out in the swamps
from jonny reb helped me git corss a big river named Lumber when I
got to another big one called cape fear, get on a little boat with some
negroes and that took me far way to wilminton. Amaelie, was
feburary with itook up with Gen Sherman. I nearly forze to deathe,
but that freedon claa kep me warm and looking on your sweet face
in the locket. I see it now   W walked swum throu swamps, and
rode rivers for nigh onto a month till I git to Wilmington.when I
smelled th ocean it was the s thesweetest smel the scent of freedom. I
hired out to a French ship captan takin cotton, sugar, corn and
beans to Hayti. We run blockade through Blue and Gray ships. It
took 2 months to git here .. to git here to Port o Prince in Hayti. I
am in the land of my Mama and her family. 'member that mr. holly
we heard about. That freeman who went to hayti with his mam and
family and lots of our people to set up hous. Make a church. Make*

127

schools and all I found him he helped me ther help me I found mama's folks I take their name as mine – Mathieu. I am Osner Mathieu. I work for my Mama's uncle on his Farm.

I followed your Wishes that I should go and I should be free to live. My feelings for you never Change. I have no sorrow for what happened but that it keeps me from you i am Free like you asked me. Am i a pa? I do hope so. If you… is born healthy and strong? A Girl child or Boy chile? kiss our Baby and_____ about you.

I miss you. I wish you to cum and live Free with me in Hayti. bishop holly help yoo too. Writ to him Episcopal church hayti.   I remain your friend with great affection,

Osner Mathieu

The room was silent. No one spoke.

Anna came into the room quietly, sensitive to the change in mood. "Dear ones," she began ever so gently. "We are reading about members of the Troux family. It is all there in the census. Dallas, my love, your great-great grandparents were Marie and Jacques Pierre Fleurie. They had several sons and two daughters – Lillie Elise and Amaelie Ann. Lillie was your great-grandmother, Dallas, and Amaelie your great-great aunt."

"That makes Amaelie…what? My great-great-great-aunt? And a slave owner who dallied with someone she considered property? This is too much!" Sandy exclaimed emotionally.

"There's more we should all know," Bobbi said and began to read on.

Bishop James Holly
Holy Trinity Episcopal Ch
Port-au-Prince, Haiti
4 Avril 1872

Deliver to Mme. Lillie Fleurie Troux
For Mme. Amaelie Fleurie Abbott
Troux House, French Quarter
New Orleans, Louisiana, America

Dear Amaelie Abbott,

My sweet Amaelie. I think of you always and hope you are well and that the child is well. I dare not hope you will write Back and live to hope you will one day.

I am safe and well and free in Hayti. It took many months to march and ride to cross many miles of Carolina. I saw Columbia burn and wept for the Poore women and childrens. But Exulted for my people now Free... Cruel life was in chains. Bishop Holly says God loves even the Master. Perhaps.

I marched with all the Negros who Left when Old Sherman and His troops burned our way to Freedon we went with Yankees north. I left them when we came to Nort Carolina. I walk more going east to sea. Sweet smell of free seas calls me never mind I never smelled it until I did. I could smlee real freedom calling me. It took months to git pass all fightn an' killn to git to sea at Wilmington. the Lumbee people help me in the swamps where they hide out from the conscriptors. Jonny Reb just takes and takes.

I hired out to a Frenchman who sailed past navy ships to deep water then down to Hayti. Took 2 more months to git to my mama's island. She was a fighter and made me into one. Tolde mee about hayti a free nation where all black people free and citizens.

Lit the light of freedom in me. Never Forgot. Now I am free man in my Free country.

Bishop Holly helped me and I come from the Farm to help him with the school and church and all he does, A Grate man. Helped me Find my family. I now work for my mama's uncle. He has a small farm where we grow cassava and grind it to musa and boil it to make meal and bake cassava bread to sell. I take care of it for him as he is too old now.

All my heart's desire that you and our child here with me. Even thou I have not rec'd a letter from you in all these years, I know you had our child. I know you wont leave your other children. Write me soon and take good care of yourself goodby my dear.

I remain your friend with great affection,
Osner Mathieu

"Well, now we know. They must have cut her off. The Troux family, I mean." Dallas looked down and clasped his fingers. Anna reached over and laid her hand on his. "She and her slave, well, technically not her slave, Fleetwood's slave, unless he left a will, maybe he did, probably he didn't in the flush and excitement of the WAR! And they were in love with each other and perhaps she had a child. Osner hopes she has. We don't know yet. But to have a love affair with a slave: brave, foolish, rash, transgressive. Flies in the face of all the stories of Black slaves and White masters. So maybe you have Jefferson and Sally Hemmings, but that is still white man and black female slave, and he never freed her. This is white woman, disenfranchised herself, in love with black male slave who she sends to freedom. Extraordinary."

"I really don't know what to think. It is extraordinary, almost unbelievable. But there is the evidence right before us." Sandy turned to her friends, "Lizbet, Bobbi, what do you think?"

Bobbi was slow to answer, "She was brave, that much is clear. And she must have loved him deeply to send him away. To send the second man she was 'married to' away, both into danger. The first to fight for the new nation that would keep the second one enslaved. The second one into danger to find his freedom, and he did. Yes, Dallas as you said, extraordinary."

"And what if she was pregnant, what became of that child? In fact, what became of all the Abbott children? Dad, do you know? What became of Amaelie? And who are the Greeleys?" Sandy asked her family, but no one had an answer.

"Yes, Boss, they've been reading some old letters about some woman who was screwing her slave. Sorry, Boss. Before that, they might have figured out something about your factories. That Troux bitch, oh, sorry Boss, woman was talking about sweatshops. Huh! Those people should be grateful they are getting any jobs at all. Anyway, that Ray Morgan showed up. He seems to have a thing for the Troux woman. The Sheridan woman is all twisted up, maybe finding something about her black family." He stopped, "Un huh, OK. I see, you want to fix her up real bad." He laughed a really nasty laugh, "Sounds fun. Gonna make her come back to New York and get them to throw the book at her. OK, Boss, you're the man! What do you want me to do?" he paused again and listened on his burner phone. "Yes, I see, but can't I mess with those old geezers some more? You've got all you wanted to know about them. Well, if you say so. Keep on the trail of that Troux bi, um woman. Will do." The big man tossed his phone in a dumpster. "Yeah, baby, I'd like to keep on your tail, ummmm, trail," he said to his partner, jabbing him in the ribs smirking. They downloaded the data from their distance listening and recording device and sent it to the Boss's cloud. "Well, time to hear what else is going on."

13 Treachery

THE NEXT DAY, everyone in the Troux home was rather quiet and circumspect. After a delicious lunch, courtesy of the culinary team of Anna and Lizbet, everyone settled into the family room at the rear of the house for coffee, tea and a few nibbles.

"You've all had quite a time, my dears," said Anna, smiling tenderly at her three honorary daughters. "With all the tumult of the week and yesterday's shocking revelations, it's no wonder you all slept in this morning."

"There's been a lot to absorb," Sandy admitted, nestled cozily in Ray's arms on the love seat. She directed her gaze at her two BFFs. "How are you two doing? Any thoughts, questions or observations you'd like to share?"

Lizbet looked pensive, and Bobbi distracted. Neither looked her straight in the eye, which hurt her.

Bobbi was about to say something when her cell buzzed a steady vibration. She looked down and murmured, "There's an email coming in from my office. If you don't mind, I'll go into the library to check it."

The mood in the room was uncharacteristically low key as they waited for Bobbi to return. "Anyone care for a brownie?" Anna asked. "I made it from scratch this morning with the Belgian dark chocolate baking callets Alix sent from Paris."

"Has anyone spoken with her lately?" Sandy asked, glancing at Lizbet. "How's Rini liking the American School of Paris and the class she's auditing at the Sorbonne?"

"They're fine," Lizbet said a bit flatly. "Alix and I are halfway through writing our international Veg Fest cookbook. We're…"

Bobbi marched in looking angry and upset. "I can't believe it! I've been ordered back to New York for a 2 o'clock meeting tomorrow. Ordered! The email from Carol Atkins, the executive assistant to the president of our U.S. operations, was pretty terse, so I called her. All she'd say — this woman I've known for ten years, encouraged to go for the position, and counted on as a friend — was to tell me how disappointed she is in me. For what? It feels like I've been convicted of a crime without the benefit of counsel!"

"Bobbi," Sandy said as she rose and took three long steps to her friend, resting both hands on her shoulders. "Calm down, my friend. Breathe. You know, and we know, you've done nothing wrong. Don't read anything into this summons until you know the facts."

"Sandy's right," Dallas added, rising from his recliner. "I've never known you to cave under pressure, and you won't now. Whatever is going on, you've got to walk in with confidence, with your head held high. So, think what you need to know before you get to your meeting."

Bobbi gazed out the bay window overlooking the

backyard garden and focused on the blossoming peach tree while she collected her thoughts. "It's hard to know who to trust. I had the feeling Pierre, my mentor as well as CMO, was playing it safe during Saturday's meeting. I think the only people in the room that I can rely on is Al, my partner in the label project, and Emmet who's an old friend as well as head of Security."

"Bobbi, if I were you, I'd be a little cautious around anyone who's involved in your project," Ray interjected. "When it comes to this kind of corporate skullduggery, people tend to watch out for themselves. And anyone in Security would have to keep neutral. Isn't there anyone else you can depend on?"

She thought for a moment. "Oh, of course. There's Betty Wilson in HR. We've worked very closely on a number of diversity and community outreach programs. We always have each other's backs."

"Great. Call her then," Sandy added. "I agree with Ray. You've got to be sure you have an ally on the inside, someone you totally trust."

"Dear, why don't you stay another night and get a good night's rest with all of us who love you. You can fly out to New York in the morning," Anna suggested.

"No. Go tonight," Sandy countered, "so you can meet with Betty and scope things out. You have to be ready for anything and everything."

Ray, who'd been on his cell, announced that he'd been called back to New York for a meeting in the morning. He'd just made arrangements with someone he knows at Delta to get Bobbi and him on a 6:00 p.m. flight from O'Hare to LaGuardia Airport. "Make your call to your friend and then get your things together. Sandy can take us both to the airport, right Love?"

❧

After Bobbi, Sandy and Ray left, Anna turned to Lizbet with an invitation. "Care to join Dallas and me in the library to sift through Aunt Babby's letters? We'd like to resume sorting and organizing them so we can begin cataloging. Who knows what else we'll find?"

"Absolutely!"

They spent the next two hours poring through the letters, arranging them in date order, separating the ones written Amaelie Abbott to her sister from the ones from Lillie Troux to Amaelie. They set aside any that were written by other parties.

"The year and month are blotted out, but see Amaelie is in Charleston now with someone," Anna pointed to the upper portion of the letter Lizbet was holding.

> *14 187*
> *80 Flower Street*
> *Charleston, South Carolina*

Mm. Lillie Fleurie Troux
Troux House, New Orleans, La.

My beloved sister,

We arrived. Terrible time coming here, but as you advised, we could not live back in the old place. The little one is my heart. She shines with his spirit. I dare not name exactly what I mean for fear this letter may fall into

Lizbet flipped the partial page over to see if anything else was written on the reverse. "Who is she talking about? Who is 'we'?"

Anna handed her another partial page. "I think this is from the same letter."

My girl is clever with the needle. Already she can stitch so small you must hold the piece to the light to see them. Mrs. Whipper is going to school her. I will do sewing for her and Mrs. Whipper will educate my girl. She says my little one is going to be bright about her books. She sits at my knee and comforts me. 'Tis a hard life, but the red shirts do not trouble us here the waye I feared them back home. Some of the old Negro folks back home were burnt out and one old fellow was hanged. Lillie it was the terriblelest thing you ever saw. I feared they would take my little one. My only child left to me. My precious one. Her softest cheek like the old days of café au lait with our beine..

"Where is the rest of the letter?" Lizbet scrabbled through the piles that were sorted. "Does she name this child? Who is she talking about? 'My girl' she says. 'My only child,' who does she mean?"

The next morning in New York City, Bobbi was sitting in the office of her friend and colleague Betty Wilson, senior vice president of human resource management. She glanced at the digital clock on the credenza: 8:00 a.m., Tuesday, May 5. *Only a few more hours before they commence my Inquisition.*

"Want more green tea, Bobbi? It'll soother your nerves a little."

"Sure, although right now, I could use another week at the New Age Health Spa up in Neversink. Remember how great their Pranayama Yoga program was?"

"Yeah, when this all blows over, I say we head up to the New York Catskills for another retreat, this time just us. Last year's program there with the company's Rainbow Diversity Group was the most successful planning session we've ever had," Betty said with a smile. "But we digress. Let's get back to the problem at hand: how to best arm you for your meeting this afternoon.

"As I said last night on the phone, there's definitely something going on – an undercurrent of distrust and fear, and some really questionable decisions by management regarding key appointments. There's been an attempt to undermine some of the progressive diversity and succession programs we put in place last year. There've been people rightly due promotions that were inexplicably passed over in favor of others not as qualified. In at least two cases I know of, our standard vetting procedures were circumvented by someone apparently very high up."

"Did any of them involve the classified label program I've been leading in the Newark Innovation Center?" Bobbi asked.

"Yes, there's been a very significant shift in personnel over there," Betty replied, frowning. "Key industrial designers and computer technicians have been transferred to different locations without explanation, or even much notice. They've been replaced by newcomers from outside who don't seem as knowledgeable or as experienced."

"Haven't you questioned this? What does Al Mackenzie say about it?" Bobbi asked.

"Of course, I've questioned it, and so has Harry Simmons, the HR manager for that location. All we get is 'the Board wants it done.' Al claims he's being stonewalled, too."

Bobbi looked puzzled, wondering to herself why Al hadn't told her of this problem. They were supposed to be partners in the new label program. She ticked through in her head the team members she knew in Newark and realized there were three or four she hadn't seen for awhile, and some new faces too.

"Listen, Bobbi, whatever is going on, we need to get you prepared with a strategy for your meeting in the executive corner office this afternoon," Betty declared, pulling Bobbi back from her thoughts. "I think you can expect some intensive grilling."

"I have nothing to hide, Betty," she said a bit defensively. "If they question my integrity after all these years…"

"Now don't get your dander up," Betty cautioned. "You have to have a plan. First, be on guard, but not obviously so. Be confident, not cocky; decisive but not defensive; knowledgeable and committed about the project, not yourself, etc. Remember, Lucio Veigas only moved here from Buenos Aires to head the U.S. operations six months ago. He doesn't know you well enough yet."

"I know. He strikes me as a strict numbers man too, not a people person."

"Add to that, the cultural differences and a bit of a machismo attitude. I don't think he knows how to relate to a strong, independent woman like you."

"Sounds like a cake walk," Bobbi said, with a sardonic grin.

"That being said, you need to arm yourself with whatever tools you have at your disposal."

"That's easier said than done, Betty. All my techie communication tools were taken away from me on Saturday. This morning, Abner automatically passed me through the ground floor security station to the elevators, and Peggy buzzed me in at reception with her usual cheerful smile. No problem. It wasn't until I tried to open my office door that I discovered my ID's security strip no longer works. When I tried to log in at Peter's computer, it didn't recognize my pass word or encryption codes. The message – big and bold on the screen – was DENIED ACCESS! Seriously? Just since Saturday?"

Betty lowered her voice, almost to a whisper. "I was afraid that might happen. That's why I took the precaution to bring in my personal laptop from home," she said, pulling it out of the lower draw of her desk. "Here are the pass codes I use to get into the company system from home, plus another code to access the personnel records. Most of them are sealed, but not the most recent hires. And if you use this encryption code," she said as she handed Bobbi a post-it, "you can open your own file to see if anything dire has been added. I didn't want to invade your privacy by looking myself."

"Thank you Betty. I know you're taking a real risk here."

"What are friends for, after all? I'm going to take a walk down the hall to brief my NYU intern on the project's she's to work on the rest of the month. Lock my door when I leave. I'll buzz you from Loretta's desk in about thirty minutes so you can let me back in. OK?"

"OK 007, OK."

Bobbi walked into Lucio Veigas' outer office ten minutes before the scheduled meeting and greeted his executive assistant with a smile. "Hi Carol. How are you? How was Michael's track meet on Saturday? Did he bring home another medal?"

Carol Atkins looked up from her computer monitor with a judgmental, almost hostile, look on her face. "You're early. Sit down," she said, nodding toward the two club chairs along the glass wall opposite her desk. "He'll buzz when he's ready for you." She returned her gaze to the screen without further comment.

Wow. That's cold. Guess she's another "ally and friend" I can tick off the list.

Harvey Steinberg and Klaus Vandervoort walked in, barely glancing Bobbi's way. "He just called us."

"Pierre's already with him. Go right in," she said with a smile. Next, Al Mackenzie entered the office. "Good afternoon, Carol," he said – totally ignoring Bobbi.

"Wait a sec." She picked up her phone's handset, depressed the intercom button and said "Al Mackenzie is here. Do you want him to wait? OK." She nodded toward the door, and he proceeded inside.

Really? They're treating me like some kid called to the principal's office. I will NOT let them get to me. My name's not Power for nothing! It's obvious I'm being set up for something.

She thought about what she'd read in her personnel file that morning in Betty's office. Everything – her first quarter review that had been deemed "Far Exceeds Expectations;" her upcoming second quarter bonus and new stock issues; her request for a new Marketing Associate in the Boston office; her promotion recommendations for Peter and Julianne (her administrative assistants in NYC and Newark) – had been labeled either "On Hold" or "Under Indefinite Review." ALL of her security access codes had been suspended.

Much worse, the usually super punctual, never-out-sick Peter was not in the office, and Julianne hadn't checked in at the Newark Lab that morning.

Carol's phone buzzed. "Yes, sir." She gave Bobbi a steely gaze. "You can go in now."

Bobbi walked into Luis Veigas' large corner office, which had a bank of windows on two sides overlooking Park Avenue and West 47th Street. The president's large antique mahogany desk and red Corinthian leather executive chair was set back on the left. An original painting by Brazilian artist Beatriz Milhazos hung on the wall behind it. To the right, two cushioned chairs and a leather sofa were arranged around a coffee table for informal meetings. Across the room, in Bobbi's direct line of sight, Veigas was seated at the center of the long, oval conference table, flanked by three chief officers of the company. Al Mackenzie stood to the left, shifting his weight and avoiding her eyes.

Bobbi held her head up, smiled and approached the executives. "Good afternoon, gentlemen. I presume you have more questions for …"

Luis Veigas interrupted. "This is not the time for more questions or explanations, Ms. Power. The Security and IT teams are still auditing your files for the proprietary label project that has been compromised. They are also examining all programs you have managed in the last three years. Harvey has put together a team of forensic accountants to review your budget for the project as well as the Newark Innovation Center. I have authorized them to extend their investigation into your department's financial records."

Bobbi was shocked and barely managed to respond, "I assure you there's nothing improper in my work for this project or any other. I'd like to know what evidence of wrong doing you believe you have. My records over the past 15 years have always been precise and transparent. It's something I've insisted on with all of my staff.

"Pierre, you know this about me. When have you ever doubted my integrity or my commitment to the company?" She looked squarely at Pierre St. Claire, long her mentor and her champion. His eyes appeared sympathetic, yet his face was ashen. He shrugged his shoulders slightly. "My hands are tied, Bobbi, until the investigation is complete."

That was a personal blow. So was the embarrassed and oddly suspicious silence of her colleague and co-author of Auguste's Eco-Loc label and security program for the new SA Elite brand. Bobbi and Al had worked day and night developing this project and establishing the Newark center. Now, when she needed him to back her up…nada! Nothing!

"There is ample evidence that you have been, at the very least, negligent and sloppy during the developmental period of this project, Veigas continued. "You have been frequently absent on personal business, missing important meetings, taking credit for the ideas of others. Your own assistants have come forth with complaints about your treatment of them and your work ethic. What's more, after carelessly allowing proprietary information – which should never have left our facility – to be put at risk and stolen, you dared to take credit for a new program to safeguard it."

"What? None of these allegations are true," Bobbi countered vehemently. "If you'll allow me to examine this evidence and face my accusers…"

"No. This panel is not prepared to hear any more testimony until the company completes its investigation."

"If I may, Lucio," COO Klaus Vandervoort interjected. "Bobbi, if the results of our investigation warrant it, we are prepared to hold a tribunal at which you will be able to respond and dispute whatever evidence is presented, including any criminal charges that may be deemed necessary. If it comes to that, I strongly recommend you have a lawyer present."

Now it was CFO Harvey Steinberg's turn to address Bobbi. "Of course, we hope to avoid such unpleasantness. That's why we are prepared to offer you two choices. You may resign and take an early retirement, with a reduced pension and cancellation of any stock options or profit sharing for this calendar year. Or, you can accept a demotion to Marketing Director at a 40% salary reduction and no profit sharing plan. All medical benefits will remain intact, of course."

"If you accept the second choice, you will no longer report to Pierre St. Claire, who is going to announce his retirement at the end of the month, instead of remaining in place for the entire calendar year," Lucio Veigas added. "You will instead report to both Al Mackenzie here and to your replacement as co-director of this project, Lena Morris."

Bobbi was so shocked, she couldn't help blurting out, "Lena Morris! Why? She has half my experience, no advanced degrees and has never been in charge of a program of this magnitude. She's…"

"She has our complete confidence and has been highly recommended by Al as well as both Stuart Ames and Hector Alberiz," Veigas continued. "They were cleared yesterday of any indiscretions concerning your project, Bobbi. We respect their opinions."

Pierre St. Claire finally spoke. "Bobbi, I have suggested that you be given time to weigh your decision on what I consider to be a Hobson's choice. You're being given a week to determine your course of action. And you'll remain on full salary – your *current* salary, I may add." It did not escape Bobbi that Pierre turned to look directly at his colleagues when he reassured her about her compensation. She knew for sure that he was being forced out and that was why he had not backed her up. But it still hurt.

"There is one more matter," Vandervoort said. "Regardless of your decision, you are required to spend a month training Lena Morris on all the marketing aspects of the project. You'll be joining her in South Carolina as she wraps up the site selection for the Eco-Loc pilot program."

Bobbi was truly speechless.

Luis Veigas looked her coldly in the eye and said: "That is all. You may go."

Bobbi had walked out of the Park Avenue building feeling as if she'd been run over by a Mac truck. Regardless of all her preparation with Betty that morning, and the deep to her core knowledge that she had made the right decisions and had operated as always with the highest degree of professionalism and integrity, she could not believe how helpless she had felt in that corner office. She – the powerful Power woman who had faced and overcome so many of life's curve balls. The feeling of embarrassment – no, shame – that was sweeping over her was almost too much to bear.

Somehow, she managed to flag down a cab and get

herself home. Now, as she lay soaking in a hot tub, inhaling the scent of lavender that should have calmed and renewed her, she felt betrayed and utterly defeated. She wanted to cry, she wanted to scream, she wanted to rant and rave and smash something breakable. But, she couldn't.

She thought of calling her daughter Sophie Rose in California for some TLC. Or ringing up Colin, her more-than-friend-friend in London. He was so good at getting her to laugh at herself when she took life too seriously. This was one of those times she wished she could pick up the phone and call her Mom.

The cell phone she'd left on the chair next to the tub vibrated. She reached over and there on the screen was a text message from Sandy. "Just landed in Greensboro. Text about meeting. When are you coming?"

That Bobbi could do. That she could do.

14   Piecing It Together

ENROUTE TO DOWNTOWN Greensboro, Lizbet pointed at her friend, "Your ancestors owned my ancestors. Not logical, I know, but I feel, I don't know, betrayed by *you*. As if *you*'ve been lying to *me* all our lives. *Your* ancestors owned *my* ancestors. Can I ever see you the same way again?" Lizbet leaned her head against her side window, tears sliding down her cheeks.

Sandy reached tentatively to touch her dear friend. Lizbet pulled her hand away. "I don't know, Sandy, It's all so strange and horrible. It's like you said earlier, it's something you've dreaded all your life and now it's a reality. Your ancestors were slave owners. Mine were slaves. And *yours* owned *mine*. I don't see how we reconcile that. Are you the same person? Am I?"

Sandy drove on, her mood reflecting the lowering clouds and the rain beginning to tick tick tick on the windshield. She was chilled to the core. Her best friends were wrapped in their own concerns. No Simone lap robe or fatherly caress to comfort and warm her. All three friends disconnected in a way they had never been in all the long years of their friendship. Lizbet was weeping. Bobbi was brooding in the back seat, isolating herself.

Sandy was disconsolate. On Route 40, she headed towards Joseph M. Bryan Blvd. and downtown. She and Lizbet had planned a visit to the famous Woolworth's where the four young students had initiated the 1960s lunch counter sit-ins. That entire building had since been transformed into the International Civil Rights Center & Museum. There would be no time for a visit, lunch and Lizbet's important meeting with Mrs. Mason.

What had begun as a shower was now a powerful storm of driving rain – a real gully washer. Eighteen wheelers roared by, flinging up torrents of water so dense it was as if they had driven under a waterfall. The wipers could not keep up with the rain that was as thick as fog. There was zero visibility. Cars pulled off the road waiting out the storm. A freak hail storm began pounding the second Prius Sandy had rented at the airport with stones the size of golf balls.

The foul weather exacerbated the tension in the car. The hailstones drummed on its roof; the rain pounded and huge trucks roared. "Sandy, do something, I can't bear this. I feel like I'm freaking out," Bobbi yelled from the back seat, barely making herself heard. As if the sudden violent storm had loosened the violent feelings she had been bottling inside, Bobbi burst out. With Lizbet still weeping, now loudly and Bobbi yelling, kicking the back of Sandy's seat and yanking her seat back, and the storm; Sandy knew she needed to park somewhere and quickly. Up ahead, she saw a highway overpass. She pulled over in the narrow space between the overpass wall and the road. Suddenly, the rain and hailstones stopped, and while the trucks still sped by, at least there were no cascades of water. The noise level dropped dramatically. "I can't stand it," Bobbi said, suddenly quieter herself. "I've got to get out of here. I need to walk. I need to go somewhere. I can't talk about it. I've got to get away." She flung her door open and thrust herself out into the right hand lane.

"No, Bobbi, no!" Sandy yanked her door open as well and reached for Bobbi before she dashed into the oncoming traffic. "No, screw them. Whatever that company did to you, it's not worth getting hurt."

Lizbet grabbed the steering wheel and dragged herself over the console to Sandy's open door. "Bobbi, come back. I need you. We both need you. Oh, God, Sandy, be careful. Get back, both of you. Look out. Truck!!!" she screamed.

Sandy seized Bobbi's arm and pulled her back to their car. She shoved her in the back seat and plastered herself against the car as another 18-wheeler roared by, flinging sheets of rainwater on Sandy and whipping her hair in her eyes. "Move over, I'm getting in back here." She clapped her hands to her face, sluicing away the wet and revealing outright fury. "What the hell do you think you were doing? Are you crazy? Oh my God, jumping out into that traffic. Have you lost your mind?" Sandy grabbed Bobbi's shoulders and gave her a fierce shake, so hard her head rocked back and forth like a bobble head toy. "What if something had happened to you? Bobbi, we love you. Let us in."

Lizbet climbed over into the back seat as well. "OK,

Bobbi, you have to tell us. Everything."

"Everything," Sandy echoed. She and Lizbet scooted to one end of the backseat and faced their friend. "You've got to get over bottling everything. Look where that swift move brought you. You almost got both of us killed."

Forty minutes and half a box of tissue later, Bobbi said, "So that's it. Take a demotion, turn over my project and report to Lena. To Lena! MY PROJECT! OR get out. All these years, all the projects I have successfully created and managed. All the money saved and made for the company. And it's report to Lena or get out." She took a deep, deep breath and blew it out. "OK, I'm better. I'll do better, I promise. No more bottling and stewing. I'm done with that." She opened her purse and took out her comb and small mirror. She smoothed her hair. "Not quite my regular shiny self, but closer – and better than in many, many days." She took out a wipe and cleaned her hands and face. "Lizbet, here." She handed over another wipe. "Wash your face. Stop blubbering. And stop blaming Sandy for something she didn't do, didn't even know about and clearly feels terrible about. And Sandy, cut out the mea culpa crap. I mean, you're not even Catholic! That's my trip. OK, we good? We all over our tantrums? We bonded again?" She jabbed Sandy in the ribs and shook Lizbet's foot. "Are we good? Huh?. Are we good?"

The storm had cleared the humidity and left a cloudless blue sky. The emotional storms that had brewed and burst cleared away the tension as well that had plagued the old friends. Lunch had never tasted so delicious. Lizbet mimed slathering a huge fluffy biscuit with butter. "And I'll have the buttermilk pancakes loaded with pecans, sliced bananas and chocolate chips. I know, no need to say a word, but these biscuits are only here and after the rough times we've been through, I *need* pancakes." She punched out that last word, just challenging Sandy or Bobbi to chastise her. The Smith Street Diner was famous for its biscuits and all day breakfasts.

"I'm going to have country steak, collards and fried okra. Large iced tea. No sugar. Lots of ice and lemon. Oh, yeah, cornbread. I'll think about dessert later. And I'm with Lizbet, no dirty looks about my choices."

"Looks like, I'm the only one who's ordering something remotely healthy. OK, that was sneaky. Withdrawn." Bobbi scrutinized the menu and then told the server, "I'm going to have the bagel and Ducktrap smoked salmon plate, cream cheese, sliced tomatoes and red onions. Coffee and lots of it – hot."

"Food and friendship for the soul and stomach. Peace?" Sandy asked.

"Peace," Lizbet and Bobbi said in unison.

Sandy located N. Church Street and parked in front of an old two-story house with a sagging front porch. The street was lined with a mix of styles from the late 1800s to the 1960s. They sat across the street from a sidewalk bordered by a twenty-foot wide park. On the other side, there were railroad tracks. "Do you have an address for Mrs. Mason, Lizbet?"

"No, just on N. Church where the railroad tracks are

across the street. It has to be this house or one of the others on this side." Lizbet made her way up the front walk and rang the bell. "I don't think anyone is home." Sandy and Bobbi followed her. She turned away quickly, relief washing over her face – wanting to meet Mrs. Mason and nervous about meeting Mrs. Mason. "Maybe I got the date wrong." The front door opened behind her.

A genial and quizzical face appeared. "Yes, ladies? May I help you?"

"We're looking for Mrs. Alice Mason. Is this her house?" Lizbet asked.

"Oh, no, my dear," the older gentleman replied. "She's in the blue house two doors up the street." The man chuckled as he came out on the porch. He was a slight man, with crinkly brown eyes topped by an aureole of white hair and anchored with a full white beard. Dressed in grey work pants held up by red gallowses and a worn denim shirt, he might have stepped right out of the previous century. He slipped his thumbs behind his suspenders, rocked back on his heels and chuckled even more. "I thought you were treasure hunters. You have a minute? Oh, I'm Mr. Bill Trotter. But everybody around here just calls me Mr. Bill.

"You're not treasure hunters, are you? Even if you are, but you're not, right? Well, even if you are, come with me. I'll show you something." Somewhat mesmerized by Mr. Bill's charismatic manner, they followed him across the street to the long narrow park that lay between the sidewalk and the tracks. "See that railroad? Jeff Davis and much of his Confederate Cabinet took the last train south of the Piedmont Railroad when they were escaping the Yankees. People here in Greensboro were pretty pro-Union, so they got a cool reception. The entourage had goods, political papers and possibly even the Confederate Treasury with them. Maybe the Treasury got looted, maybe it didn't. Nobody knows. Old Mr. Jeff slept in a boarding house. Cabinet members used a leaky boxcar as their bedroom and meeting room. Anyway, people thought they had the Confederate Treasury in gold with them. People still think that gold is here somewhere." He laughed again, "That's why I didn't answer the door right away. I thought you were going to ask if you could use metal detectors on my yard. Anyway, Mrs. Mason is right up the street in that blue house. Stop by and see me again if you have time. I'll take a break from writing." He waved and toddled across the street.

Mrs. Alice Grace Greeley Mason slowly rocked on her porch. A colorful quilt was spread over her knees. Lizbet with Sandy and Bobbi behind her, hurried up the front walk a little late for perhaps one of the most important appointments in her life. Mrs. Mason waved her visitors welcome gesturing towards rockers set close to hers. Her house was a two-story frame dwelling clad in pale blue clapboard with white trim. Her spacious porch wrapped the house on two sides and was set with slat-back wooden rockers painted crisp white and small white tables. Generous baskets of magenta and hot pink bougainvillea, trailing salmon-colored geraniums hung from the porch eves. White moonflowers twisted around porch posts and through its fretwork. Huge pots of maiden hair ferns flanked the front screen door. The porch ceiling was painted a warm sky blue.

"You're Lizbet. And these are your friends, Sandy and Bobbi?" Lizbet was taken aback. How did this elderly woman know her friends' names? "I can see you're surprised, sugar. Well, you see, I knew Sandy's Great Aunt Babby."

It was Sandy's turn to be surprised. "How?"

"Quilts, dear. Quilts. Babette and I met in New Orleans in the 1950s. I was in my 20s. I was working at Café du Monde making beignets. But we met in a little store that sold old clothes in the 9th Ward. We were both looking for old cloth. I was just getting really interested in the craft, the art really. She'd been quilting for years. My mama, Grace, was a quilter. This is one of hers." Mrs. Mason smoothed the pieced quilt she had spread over her knees. Babette and I bonded over a piece of hand-dyed indigo homespun cotton from the mid-1800s!" Her laugh crinkled her cheeks and turned her eyes into half moons. "We both became story quilters. Mine about lynchings, hers about slave owners. Our ways of bearing witness."

Amanda Mason backed out onto the porch pushing the screen door open. She was carrying a tray laden with pink lemonade and pralines. "My daughter, Amanda Mason. Amanda, this is Lizbet Sheridan. Her biological dad was also named Greeley." Mrs. Mason recounted how she knew about Sandy, Bobbi and Lizbet. "Sugar, remember my quilting friend Mrs. Babette Troux Scott? Sandy is her great niece. And Babby always kept me up-to-date on all you girls' doings. You're surprised? Well, that's what we friends do; keep each other up-to-date. But you didn't come see me, Lizbet, to hear about quilting or old ladies' gossip, did you, sugar?"

Lizbet shook her head. "No, Mrs. Mason, like I said on the phone, I'm looking for my birth father's family. I have the letter that you wrote to Mrs. St. Denis in 1962 telling her about a clipping of your parents' car accident. How they died in 1932 when you were just two. "I've got the letter here." She handed Mrs. Mason a copy of her letter, written fifty years earlier.

"I remember this letter like I was just writing it. Look, you can see where I shed a few tears." She pointed to some dark stains on the page. "I never knew what happened to them, until a cousin sent me an old clipping that reported the accident."

"Your letter said the clipping was included, but we couldn't find it."

"Never you mind, dear; Amanda made a copy of it for you. My cousin sent me two, and I kept one and sent one to Babby." Mrs. Mason leaned back in her rocker and closed her eyes. Her hand fell to her lap, and the letter fluttered to the porch floor.

"Is she all right?" Lizbet looked stricken. "Have I upset her?" she asked Amanda.

"No, she's just a little tired. Wait a few minutes, and she'll wake up, but never admit she fell asleep. You watch. She'll claim she was just resting her eyes."

Bobbi was riveted at this unfolding and unlikely tale. Sandy had that far off look. In a few minutes, Mrs. Mason opened her eyes and resumed rocking.

"I was just resting my eyes and thinking about that long time ago – that sad time. Well, here is what happened. My parents were wonderful people, my aunt and uncle told me – hard working, God fearing and just plain good folks. They managed to get back some land in Anderson County, SC that came to the family after the Civil War. They were making a good life for me and my older brother. They bought a car, a 1930 Ford Model A Coupe." She trailed off. Amanda handed her mother an embroidered hankie. Mrs. Mason dabbed at her eyes. "Still sad." She sat quietly for a moment, holding tightly to the rocker's arms.

Lizbet held her breath. Sandy and Bobbi each clasped one of her hands. Perhaps, at last, she would have a clue as to her birth father's family.

"And then one day, a truck came around a curve and smashed into them. They were both thrown from their car and killed. Amanda, will you get that clipping for Lizbet? I left it on the hall table under the glass rabbit paper weight." Amanda opened the screen door and stepped into the front hall. In a moment, she was back with the clipping and handed it to Lizbet. It was dated June 6, 1932 and was a tiny notice in the Obit section of the *Anderson Independent and Tribune*. 'Mr. and Mrs. Luke Greeley who met an untimely end by automobile accident. They will be buried in Welfare Baptist Church Cemetery in Belton, SC on June 9. All are welcome to come and pay tribute to this family'."

"Mrs. Mason, you said you had an older brother. What was his name?" Lizbet whispered. "Was it

Benjamin?"

"Why yes, sugar. It was."

"Mrs. Mason, Aunt Alice, my birth father's name was Ben Greely." She rocked forward, grasped her aunt's hands and broke into a radiant smile that lit up the shady porch.

With tears and smiles, the rest of the story emerged. Alice revealed how the children were farmed out to different branches of the family. Alice was sent to an aunt, a sister of the children's mother Grace and her husband. They had no children, lived in Greensboro, and Alice grew up in the very house she now owned. "But I never found out what happened to Benjamin."

Lizbet took over the story. "My birth mother told me what Benjamin told her." She related Lee Ae-Sook's story. How Benjamin was sent from one family to another and finally to Greeley relatives who went north in the Great Migration and settled in Harlem. How they, too, lost touch with Alice's guardians. How Ben grew up and enlisted in the Army. How he met and married Lee Ae-Sook in Seoul during the Korean War. How a daughter, named Lee Bong-Cha Alice Greely was born on December 24, 1951. How Ben was killed at the Battle of Pork Chop Hill in the spring of 1953. How Ae-Sook had been forced to leave her daughter at the Seoul Children's Home because they were starving. How she was adopted by Robert and Delores Sheridan from America and became Elizabeth Lee Sheridan. How she grew up in Prairieview and became friends with Sandy and Bobbi. "And," Lizbet concluded, "she told me that Ben Greely and his family were in a terrible car accident when he was little. His parents were killed, he woke up in a hospital, and his baby sister was lost to him."

She reached into her bag and pulled out an old B&W photo of two children. "She gave me this photo that he'd left with her. Here he is, at 5 years old with his little 2-year-old sister Alice Grace. That must be you."

Mrs. Mason let out a sigh of joy and delight and broke out in a huge smile. "Now she is found. Now you are found," Mrs. Alice Grace Greeley Mason pronounced, eyes glistening a little. She rose majestically from her rocker. "Come here, Sugar, let me love your neck. Amanda, meet your cousin. Lizbet, meet your cousin." The three encircled each other in a long hug.

Sandy and Bobbi looked on, quietly taking in the tender scene and happy for Lizbet.

Sandy's cell vibrated, breaking the mood. She glanced at the text message. It was from Lena Morris, inviting her to become a member of the Board of the new Eco-Loc label operation for the SA Elite brand in South Carolina – Bobbi's pilot program. She passed her phone to Bobbi whose mouth turned down. Her brows drew together angrily. "You're not going to accept, are you?" she mouthed.

"Yes, I most certainly am."

Bobbi looked stricken and betrayed. "How can you?"

15   Et Tu Sandy?

SANDY JUMPED THE PORCH STAIRS to the sidewalk and took off after Bobbi. "Bobbi, wait, wait. You don't understand."

Bobbi looked around: *where could she go? This was the final betrayal. Her job gone. Her integrity besmirched. Her dearest friend a traitor.* She looked around for something, anything, familiar. Her eye fell on the white-haired writer. He sat in a weathered wicker porch rocker sorting his mail, a tall glass of iced tea near to hand. She stumbled up his front walk.

"Ms. Power, isn't it? Won't you sit for a minute and join me for a cool drink?" Mr. Bill could see she was terribly upset. Sandy edged into his yard. "Dr. Troux, will you sit with us, too?"

"No, not her: I don't want to see her two-faced face." Bobbi turned her back on Sandy.

"Mr. Bill, I'll just sit here on your steps if that's OK." In the guise of telling the writer a story, Sandy touched on the highlights of Bobbi's plight. Bobbi turned back towards Sandy a tiny bit as if she were eased by hearing her troubles told as someone else's story and told to a virtual stranger.

Mr. Bill sipped his drink and rocked. "I see," he murmured soothingly from time to time.

"So, finally, this Lena texted me just a little while ago and asked me to join the Board of the very project that Bobbi created and has been dumped from. The whole thing has been so weird. And just wrong. Really wrong." Bobbi stiffened again, but seemed to be listening attentively. Something in Sandy's tone drew her a little out of her misery. "So, I said yes."

Bobbi jumped up and glared at Sandy, "Et tu, Sandy? Et tu?" She dropped back in her rocker and burst into tears.

"Bobbi, do you really think I would betray you? I said 'yes' to get an inside angle. All this stuff happening to you is WRONG! You know it. I know it. But how do you prove it? Even your records have been doctored. You said so yourself. You have to believe me, I said 'yes' so that I can find out what's really happening. I mean all of it, right from the beginning – the theft of your pass card to being called on the carpet – it's ALL WRONG, and I'm going to find out who is behind all this and what's really going on.

Sandy walked quietly over to Bobbi, sat down in a slat back side chair, and spoke gently so as not to startle her. "I think everything is just smoke and mirrors. Diversions. Red herrings, if you can call murder and false accusations red herrings. Something deeper is happening." She got up and went to the porch railing. She picked at a flake of peeling green paint. She turned it over and over, examining it as if one side or the other were encrypted with the answers she sought. "I can feel it." she said slowly. "It's like smoke that keeps flowing between my fingers, so to speak, and I can't exactly put one finger on the main point, much less grab hold of the threads with both hands and weave them together."

"Sandy," Bobbi jumped up out of her seat and grabbed her. "I'm so sorry, Sandy. I do feel out of my mind. Everything has made me crazy. I'm not really myself. One minute, I'm calm and logical and the next, I'm flying off the handle – accusing you of betrayal, suspecting all my friends, even that my long term colleagues are in league against me."

In reply, Sandy squeezed Bobbi's hand, but looked thoughtful again.

"Ladies, if you will allow me to interrupt this *touching* moment…" This sardonic interjection brought a smile to Sandy's and Bobbi's lips. "If you will permit me a small observation…perhaps your dilemma is simpler than you think. Dr. Troux, you spoke about slavery and sweatshops, aren't they both about labor, free labor, forced labor? I have just published another book about slavery and the Civil War..."

"Another?" Sandy asked.

"Yes, and several others, but never mind that. My point is that slavery, whether in America, or other parts of the world is all about free labor. I visited Haiti some years ago. I was struck by some similarities, past and present. Disney had factories there with conditions little better than the plantations of the past."

"Yes, you've put your finger exactly on the right point. That's exactly what we think as well. So, it's really very simple, isn't it, when you look at it from that perspective."

Mr. Bill nodded, "Yes, it is."

"Now we just work backward. We assume we have the right motive: free labor for maximum profit. So rather than weave every thread together to see the whole, we assume we have the whole and now we pick apart the warp and weft to see how the threads are woven to make a false pattern. That's it. Thank you for your hospitality and that confirmation."

Bobbi crossed to the author, "Mr. Bill, I want to thank you, also" she took his hand and gave it a warm squeeze, "thank you, for everything." She crossed to Sandy, "I can't promise that I won't fly off the handle again, I'm really on edge, but for the first time since Applegate Farm, I feel that perhaps, just perhaps, things might turn out all right."

"You've made your decision then?" Sandy asked.

"Yep. I'm gonna eat some crow – go back to New York, tell them I'm accepting the 'demotion' and feed you whatever Intel I can."

❧

CFO Harvey Steinberg, COO Klaus Vandervoort and Bobbi's partner on the anti-theft project, Al Mackenzie, tipped back in Steinberg's high backed leather office chairs and put their feet up on his conference table. "Cigars, Gentlemen?" Steinberg asked. He opened a three stick package of Cohibo Esplendido and offered each man one.

The office filled with aromatic smoke, and the men smiled lazily at each other, "So, that went well, didn't it?" Vandervoort chortled between puffs of smoke. "Veigas slayed that girl: Bobbi Power is Bobbi Powerless, right? Ha ha ha ha. As she should be. That girl needed to be cut down to size, and Veigas did it. And he bought it all hook, line and sinker."

"And the best part is Lena," Steinberg. "What a babe and she knows it. I especially like it when she wears those whadda you call 'em, some kind of heels?"

"Stripper heels," Al Mackenzie supplied.

"Yeah, stripper heels: 'Hey Baby, put on your stripper heels, and give me a lap dance...' heh, heh, heh." He reared back in his chair, brushed back his silver hair, patted his flat belly, and roared with laughter. "So, next, we send Mzzzzz. Lena to South Carolina to set up the new operation. Put her in first class and Little Miss Bobbi Powerless in coach. What Stripper Heels doesn't know won't hurt her..."

The office door swung open quietly, and Lena Morris stood there outlined against the light, looking at the senior officers, men she thought of as "The Boys," but gave full deference to, shrouded in thick blue cigar smoke. "Gentlemen, you wanted to see me?"

❧

"I'm sorry, Bobbi," Lena said leaning over Bobbi's coach seat, "I tried to get you into first class, too, but those guys just wouldn't go for it."

Bobbi clenched her teeth, "I understand, Lena." She plastered a weak smile on her face. She'd come back to New York to get clothes, her papers, close up her house, and tell her neighbors and tenant that she would be on business in South Carolina for an unspecified time. She asked Sarah Soames to water her plants and take in the mail while she was gone. Then she took a cab to LaGuardia Airport to meet Lena for their flight to the Greenville/Spartanburg Airport in North Carolina.

"I just don't understand what happened – why they seem to have it in for you. You didn't do all those things everybody at the office is saying about you. Did you?" Lena paused, but Bobbi was silent. "Well, I don't believe a word of it." Lena patted her on the shoulder. "Don't worry, Bobbi, we'll make it right. I'll help all I can."

The flight attendant passed by, "Miss, you need to return to your seat. The captain has turned on the fasten seat belt sign"

"OK, I'm going." She straightened up and turned to head forward in the cabin. "Bobbi, I'd better get back to my seat. Have a good flight. We'll work it all out."

"Thanks, Lena. I appreciate it." Bobbi leaned her head back and sighed. *Support comes from unexpected quarters sometimes.*

Lena accepted the flute of champagne the flight

attendant offered. She lifted it in a silent promise. *Yes, we'll work it all out.* A slight smile crossed her lips and then she drained her champagne.

"Sandy, look at this flyer Aunt Alice gave me. She's showing some of her quilts at a new museum. It's mostly a story quilt exhibit in South Carolina at the Abbott House and Farm Museum. Abbott House, Sandy! Abbott House! We've got to go. Little Luke Greeley helped Amaelie Abbott. The Greeley place must have been nearby," she said excitedly.

"Of course, Lizbet," Sandy replied evenly, as that far away look came into her eyes.

16 A Telling Story

SANDY AND LIZBET parked under the bright pink Crepe Myrtle trees that ringed the Abbott House Farm & Museum. The museum was located in the South Carolina upcountry near the small town of Iva in Anderson County. It consisted of the main farm house; a large red barn; smaller "out buildings" that housed the chicken coop and small animals; and two rows of small wooden frame shacks separated by a sandy path. Slave quarters.

Two hours earlier, Sandy and Lizbet had landed at the Greensboro/Spartanburg airport, rented a car and driven down the busy Interstate 85 highway. The Interstate cut a swath through one of the fastest growing industrial corridors in the region, termed the "Boom Belt of I-85." Major companies in the automotive, energy, metal products, and textile industry were moving their R&D and manufacturing operations into the area, attracted by the low cost of land, labor and materials as well as proximity to the research center at nearby Clemson University.

They'd taken the exit onto SC Route 29 toward Anderson City, planning to stop at the City Hall Annex on South Main to check land records for the location of the Greeley farm. About two miles from town, Lizbet's cell phone rang with a bluesy jazz beat. The caller was her newly found cousin, Amanda Mason.

"Hi, Amanda," Lizbet answered. "I didn't expect to hear from you. What's up? Aha, really? (pause) Aww, that's disappointing. I was hoping to visit and see if I could fill in more gaps in our family's history. Did she tell you anything more, like how long ago it had been sold? And what happened to it later? Or where exactly it was located? (pause) Well, that's at least something. Yes, yes. I'll call and tell you what we learn at Abbott House. I'll take some photos of the quilts for you and your Mom, too. OK, great. Thanks for everything. We'll talk soon. Bye, now."

"What was that all about?" Sandy asked.

"Well, first we don't have to stop in Anderson City. We can drive straight to Iva. I'll check for new directions with my Google App in a minute," Lizbet replied. "My cousin Amanda – I still can't get over the fact that I suddenly have an American cousin and an aunt! After growing up without any cousins and then discovering that I have a huge family of relatives in South Korea, and now America…well, it's beyond cool!"

"It is, Lizbet, it sure is," Sandy said, with a smile. "Now, tell me please why we're driving through Anderson City and not stopping."

"Well, Amanda decided this morning to do what she could to help, so she called the Anderson Economic Development office and started to ask questions. After being transferred to three departments, she finally found someone who was happy to help. A woman named Mary Sue Rankin, who's apparently a history and genealogy buff, was quite taken with the family story. She checked the land deed records and cross checked them with census records. It seems there was a 400-acre farm, or maybe a small plantation, that was owned by a Greeley family from the 1840s until about 1935. It was auctioned for back taxes and has had four or five owners since then. Now...get this. It's part of the Abbott Redevelopment Zone that runs from Generostee Road to the Savannah River. And it's only about 5 miles south of the Abbott House Museum!"

The two pals continued along Route 29 out of the city, eventually turning southeast onto Route 81-S. The countryside in this part of South Carolina's upcountry was beautiful – lush, verdant, flowing fields with pockets of woodlands, and well-watered with many brooks and small rivers. This part of the state had been rich Cherokee hunting lands until the mid-19th century. It was still populated with fields, now tamed with various food crops.

As they drove along the route, Lizbet took in the view from her side window. "If you squint and block out the few power lines and those little signs at the road intersections, I'll bet it looks almost the same as it did 150 years ago. Eerie. Except of course, there are no slaves working the fields. I wonder, though, if the people we can see over in that field are locals or migrant laborers, even migrants forced to work for their papers. So, maybe nothing's changed."

"It's possible, Lizbet. There's a lot of human trafficking happening in our own country – forced laborers in the sweatshops up North are only part of the problem. If there are migrant workers in the fields of California and Florida being victimized, why not here in the Carolinas?"

They came to a flashing red light and saw the sign pointing toward the left fork, marked Generostee Road. In another 3 miles, they had spied another sign with two arrows pointing in opposite directions:

← Abbott House Farm & Museum
→ Abbott Industrial Development Zone

They turned into the parking lot of the museum.

"Saddle bags? Natty, look alive!" Clyde Van Vleck ducked low behind an overturned wagon. Natty Crane hoisted bags of loot over his shoulders while he ran for cover following Clyde. Flames soared to the sky. Houses crumbled, leaving only brick chimneys standing. Runaway horses and mules screamed as they escaped burning stables. Terrified residents cowered against the advancing blue-uniformed troops. Columbia, South Carolina was being destroyed: by retreating Rebels, by advancing Yankees, perhaps by accident, perhaps with purpose. Historians will never agree. A soldier with General Sherman's Army wrote after the war that what happened to Columbia on February 17, 1865 was "the most monstrous barbarity of the barbarous march."

Barbarity fell on this beautiful city and burned it to the ground. Its populace was seared by the hot winds of fire and the hard war tactics of Sherman: white, black, free, enslaved, rich, poor, men, women, and children alike. General Sherman hated Columbia and determined to wreak vengeance on the city and on South Carolina. It was the center of many railroad lines, which stretched up into the fertile and fruitful agricultural district in the south. The city contained the largest printing establishment in the Rebel states. Manufacturers of power, arms, cloth, and other materials were there. Columbia, therefore, was a richer prize and more important capture than any city in the South. Columbia was also important to Sherman, his men and the North for another reason. South Carolina was viewed as "the cause of their woes" and thoroughly deserved destruction.

Nathaniel "Natty" Crane and Clyde Van Vleck's New Jersey 41st regiment had seen much battle since forming in Newark June 6, 1861. Now part of a shock force of Union soldiers, they had marched right in step as part of General Sherman's troops on Atlanta, down to Savannah, and now up to Columbia. But no more. "Clyde, I can't go no more," the younger man cried. "I'm tuckered out. I'm sick of all this war. I got to quit, no matter what." After the devastation of Atlanta and the surrender of Savannah, Sherman's armies had turned north in an easterly direction. More than sixty thousand soldiers in two wings left "waste and a burning track behind it of 60 miles width," as one post-war writer put it. Natty and Clyde's army was supported by 2,500 supply wagons and 600 ambulances.

Sherman had issued orders against foraging, but few soldiers, including Natty and Clyde, complied. Bummers foraged and raided farms and plantations, terrorized locals leaving them hungry and demoralized. Soldiers were forbidden to attack citizens and perhaps few whites were harmed. But attacks on black women raised such a threat level that many black male slaves stood guard outside the cabins of slave women. Clyde especially thought the South deserved everything it got, and he and Natty deserved everything they could get. And they were getting a lot – jewelry and silver not the least of it. More than one black woman found herself violated and beaten in their wake.

"Natty, get that chestnut," Clyde, a sergeant used to ordering his young companion, barked. Natty zigzagged in the road, avoiding blazing sparks the size of fists, and grabbed a runaway horse's reins. It tossed its head, backing and bucking, eyes rolling, and slobber drooling from its mouth. "Quick, tie him up. Let's git one more and git outta here while the gittin's good."

∽

"The Abbott House Farm was a bequest from Hezikiah Fleetwood Abbott to his middle son, Henry Fleetwood Abbott in 1858, the year before he married Miss Amaelie Ann Fleurie of New Orleans," the museum's vivacious college intern and guide, Lucy Benedict began. "They had about 15 slaves to help farm the land. They grew indigo, a little cotton, and various crops like soy, corn and sorghum to sell. By 1861, when the Civil War began, they had three children: Henry Fleetwood II, Hezikiah Jackson and Georgiana Belle. Tragically, Henry Fleetwood Abbott was mortally wounded in the First Battle of Manassas (Bull Run), leaving his young wife a widow. She farmed the land for about five years after the War ended. Then it reverted to her husband's family because he left no will."

"That's so not fair," Lizbet exclaimed.

"I totally agree," said Sandy. "Back then, women had it tough. They couldn't work outside the home, or vote, or have any say in their own future. And in this case, without a will leaving the farm to her, she could be tossed out of her home at anytime."

"She had it very bad," Lucy said, turning back to her script for the tour. "During the 'War between the States,' some of her slaves would've run away, leaving her and her children to work the land. People starved and were in constant danger of robbery from Yankee bummers and scalawags. Some who lived closer to Columbia also had to be on alert to attacks from Sherman's Army."

"But this museum isn't about the Civil War, is it?" Lizbet asked, starting to feel oddly uncomfortable.

"Well, no," Lucy replied. "It does show what farm life was like in that time period. You can tour the grounds and see typical farm equipment and visit the old slave quarters. Here in the museum itself, we have a section with an exhibit of old daguerreotype portraits of the day. One of them is of Amaelie and Henry Fleetwood Abbott on their wedding day." Sandy paused a moment to look into Amaelie's face to see if she could pick out a family trait. *There it is. The shape of the eyes and the way one crinkled just a little…that's so Aunt Babby, and so Dad.*

"Here in our main room, we have our first major exhibit: *Story Quilts of the Carolinas.* They're incredible pieces made by some of the leading craftswomen of this art form."

"Yes," Lizbet interjected. "Two of them are part of my aunt's 'Lynching' collection. She's Alice G. Mason.

She has story quilts in the collections of the American Craft Museum in New York and the Museum of Fine Arts in Boston."

"OOOh, how exciting!" Lucy exclaimed, clearly impressed. "You know, story quilts first depicted historic and political views that women couldn't otherwise express. There were quilting patterns called 'slave chain' and 'Underground Railroad' – see this one by another noted quilter, Faith Ringgold? Later, many illustrated issues related to the Reconstruction period and 'Jim Crow' laws, like your aunt's lynching stories.

"And here's a doll quilt that was made by a young girl who grew to be an early expert in the craft. It's embroidered with the name, Lilianna G."

"Sandy, that has to be Aunt Alice's grandmother, er- my great-great grandmother, Lilianna Greeley," Lizbet said, her eyes glistening a little. "I'm so proud to be related to two of these incredible artists."

"I know, Lizbet. And you should feel proud," Sandy said, putting an arm around her dear friend. "You know, it seems that all of these quilts are like pieced fabric paintings."

They read the description on the wall plaque. "Each quilt features a story appliquéd in the center panel and surrounded by two fabric frames. The inner frame has the text of the 'story' written or embroidered on it. The outer one is like a border of fabric patches."

"Yes, and the colors chosen sometimes carried a message," Lizbet added, as she read the descriptions. "A black square identified a 'safe house' for escaping slaves on the UGRR."

Lucy directed them to a patchwork appliquéd quilt near the window. "Here's one of our own treasures. We found it in a small oak trunk hidden under floor boards in the sleeping loft when this house was renovated last year. The small water color painting hanging next to it was found in the same trunk. It has the initials AA in the corner, so we think it was painted by the original occupant of the house, Amaelie Abbott. She probably made the quilt herself from old scraps of fine fabrics and homespun cloth. See the appliquéd flowers in the center? They're like the flowers in the painting. The quilt's an unusual combination of silks, brocades, linen, homespun cotton, and muslin. That tells its own story.

"But the best part was her old diary that our curator found hidden in the batting inside. It's right here in this glass case."

Sandy and Lizbet bent over the case and read the fragments of the diary that was still readable:

"...I so miss having yur strong arms round me ... life .... Hard ...difficult to keep the little one fed and safe. She is a joy dear O....how ...ish you c..ld hold h...My love ..ife...my Osner...Yr A....ie"

"What? Wait. There's that name Osner again!" Lizbet said, turning to Sandy.

⤚

It was a hot, muggy night. Amaelie had buried the family jewelry and silver to keep it safe from the rumored bummers wandering through the county. And what if Old Sherman came this way? She had wrapped it up in a worn out quilt and loaded it on a wheelbarrow, cut through a field far away from the house and the Quarter and buried it in the little woods by Bear Creek. She'd made a notch on several trees. There were several really big rocks nearby. These would help her find the place again. Her bodice was soaked with sweat and her skirt and petticoat were dripping wet with dew from the field, her boots muddied. She slipped out of her clothes down to her linen chemise and washed herself, pouring cool well water over her hot skin from the tin bucket and ladle. Minette had taken the young ones to Fleetwood's Mama for the night. Their grandma missed her grandbabies even more in the years since her favorite son had died. It was quiet except for the chirping of the cicadas. She sat in her rocker, patching the seat of Henry Fleetwood's pants, drowsing, worried about how to keep her boy in clothes, and waiting for Osner. Her Osner, her love. Their time together in the dead of night till dawn filled her with joy. Tonight her body ached so to have him inside her. A floor board outside creaked. She rose with a smile and crossed eagerly to the door and opened it. She froze.

"Well, lookie here Natty. Our welcome committee. You go fetch whatever's got value an' come back fer some." *The younger man hesitated a little.* "Clyde, it's no good goin' after a white woman. Her men folk'll…" "You see any men folk round here?" *He ripped the gold chain and locket from the woman's neck and threw it to Natty.* "Now git!" *He turned back to the woman who was slowly backing away toward the parlour table. He grinned and licked his lips with his tongue as he approached her.* "I ain't had no white woman in a long, long time…"

❧

While Sandy and Lizbet were touring the museum, Bobbi was not far away. She and Lena had driven down Generostee Road from the opposite end after touring two possible sites for the Auguste pilot program near Abbeville. Now they made a left turn onto the newly paved Greeley Road, passing the sign announcing the Abbott Industrial Development Zone. About a mile down the road, they turned into a driveway, edged with low, verdant box wood hedges, leading to a flat-roofed warehouse. They stepped out of their rented Honda hybrid to survey the outside of the building.

"This one already looks like a better possibility than the two we saw in Abbeville, Bobbi," Lena said with a smile. "We sure don't want to put our new sustainable cooperative program next to a Walmart, like the one they're building at the last site."

"That's for sure," Bobbi replied. "If the roof of this one is sound, we could fit it with solar panels and maybe add some wind power or RECs (Renewable Energy Credits) from the Anderson County Eco-Electric Company to keep our energy use totally sustainable. Let's take a look inside."

So far, so good. Lena's been pretty supportive and sensitive to my change in status. I may have misjudged her.

They walked toward the office end of the building and met their realtor June McIntire. "Hey, you must be Lena Morris and Bobbi Power from New York City! I'm the realtor for this property. You can call me Junie," she said, extending her hands to both women in a simultaneous hand shake.

"Let's go inside, and I'll give you a tour of the interior. Then, we can walk around the property. Mind if we just use first names? We're pretty neighborly round here."

The realtor rarely stopped talking about the attributes of the building, the new park-like industrial zone, and surrounding area as she took the two women through the building. She continued rattling on as she drove them around the complex, pointing out brooks and stands of trees under which the developers plan to create small park-like picnic areas for company employees to use. They even had a recreational facility planned, complete with day care center, cafeteria and gym. Companies would only have to pay a nominal annual fee to give their employees full, free use.

As she continued her exuberant sales pitch, Lena looked around the landscape and noted some geographic markers. *Yes, I think this is it. The map Granddad tore from the old soldier's diary matches this area. The old house we saw on the other side of the road must be the old Abbott farmhouse. There were acres of fields for two contiguous farms that ran between that house and the river. Yes. The marker on the farm where they buried their loot must be here somewhere. I'll have to come back tonight. Alone.*

"Well, what do you think, Miss Lena?" Junie McIntire asked. "The county's ready to give your company some mighty attractive tax incentives."

"We'll have to confer first, Junie, and then prepare a report for..." Bobbi started to answer, but was cut off by Lena.

"Oh, I think this is the right place," Lena interrupted.

"I'm sure Harvey, Klaus and Al will agree if I like, I mean, if WE like it."

"What about housing and schools for our employees?" Bobbi asked, feeling undermined by Lena's attitude.

"Oh, we've got lots of private and multi-family properties in this area, and the best schools with a 77% rate of kids goin' on to college! And there's a new mall goin' in just10 minutes south of Anderson City with some high-toned retailers plus a Target's movin' in."

"Well, we really should drive around the area to see for ourselves, don't you think, Len?" Bobbi nudged her "partner."

"Sure, Bobbi, sure," she said with a false sweetness that could curdle milk.

The hairs on the back of Bobbi's neck stood at attention with an old familiar message: Watch out!

Sandy's cell rang. "You have what? More pages from those Union diaries. Natty Crane's and Clyde Van Vleck's?" Sandy nudged Lizbet and put the call from Oliver Trichenor, director of the New Jersey Historical Society, on speaker. They stepped outside the Abbott House Museum. "Oliver, can you repeat what you just said? Lizbet Sheridan is here with me."

"Yes, Sandy. Hi, Lizbet. Nice to talk to both of you again. So as I was saying, Mrs. Pennington found more pages from the Van Vleck and Crane diaries. She just brought them in a few hours ago. I haven't deciphered them completely. There're lots of pages, and they're all mixed up. Some are unreadable. Some blotched. Ink on some pages looks like it was washed away. Some pages are torn and so partial. Anyway, as I was saying, oh I said that, ha, ha. Anyway, I think these dairies have something to do with what you were telling me at the luncheon. Natty's talking about something really bad that happened at some place in South Carolina to some woman whose last name is Abbott. So, that made me think about that letter from Amaelie Ann Abbott that was stolen along with the diary pages. Do you think that could be the same woman?

Sandy and Lizbet looked at each other. And then Sandy said to Oliver, "Yes, we think it's the same woman, and she's definitely connected. She was my great-great aunt!"

17   Secrets Unraveled

"LIZBET, IT'S ALMOST UNBELIEVABLE. Here we are at the Abbott House Museum where my Great-great Aunt Amaelie lived and to whom, according to Oliver, maybe, it sounds like, something bad happened. He's been wonderful to scan and fax pages to us here."

Lizbet took Sandy's arm as they went back inside the museum. "OK, we're going to ask the museum director if we can examine the entire Quilt Diary. I'm sure she will understand once we explain."

In a small side room, Sandy and Lizbet put on the white cotton gloves Lucy had given them and turned on the bright reading lamp. The diary was, for the most part, amazingly well preserved. "The dry air and darkness in the floor space and then packed away carefully so long ago preserved both the quilt and the diary." Taylor Rice leaned over between Sandy and Lizbet, pointing out each characteristic as she described the differences and methods used. "As you can see, this diary was made by someone. This was not a store-bought booklet. Different types of paper were cut to roughly the same size and then stitched together to make this little booklet. Paper was really hard to come by during the Civil War. So people used anything they could get. Some of the paper was not good quality and has virtually degenerated. See this page? Other paper – see this really brown sheet – probably was lighter originally, but over the century and a half has darkened beyond readability. We'd need a forensic lab to recover the writing, maybe at Clemson. I'll leave you to it. If you need anything…Must call Jerome in the Clemson Anthropology department forensics lab, yep…"

Sandy and Lizbet set to work, carefully turning pages. They could decipher a word here, a phrase there. *"…rely on sweet Georgiana…churn...butter..,"* *"another hot day in the fields with my boys…planting, planting…hope for a better harvest this year."* *"Minette….godsend…"*

Then they found a full spread with a long, legible entry.

Shocked. Not Osner. Some crude Yankee. Smelling, filthy, stinking of drink. Looked like a devil, slobbering, red bulging eyes. "No, no, no, noooo." I backed away as the Yankee grabbed at me. I stumbled; fell backward. He was on me in a minute. Then he called, "Natty boy, don't go far, you'll want some of this. She's a pretty filly, well, not a filly, a mare. She well filled out. Got some meat on her in all the right places." That Natty told him, "Clyde, don't do it. Don't." He ripped my chemise right down the middle, leaving me naked and exposed and helpless. He laid on me and crushed. He twisted one breast and pinched my nipple.

I screamed, but Clyde clamped his hand over my mouth. It smelled of dirt and something rotted. Such an odd thought to have. I have to stay calm. Osner is bound to come soon.

He told me, "If you want to get through this, best be quiet. I

*cain make it right hard on you. harder than you can think." He
laid his arm deliberately across my throat. The rough wool of his
jacket sleeve scratched my neck and the buttons cut into my throat. I
heard the other one, the one called Natty searching in the chest of
drawers, blanket box, linen press, corner cupboard, Fleetwood's
desk bookcase, the sugar flour press, the pie safe. Clothes went
flying, food falling, dishes breaking, tin ware clattering. Then the
badder one called, "Hey, you Natty boy, keep it quiet. Ain't
nobody here in the house, but maybe one of the niggers might can
hear something and come see." The badder one grunted when he
called out to one called Natty. Grunted each time he thrust into me.
I groaned. "Thas right Miss Mare, you groan. Bet you're hungry.
Bet your man gone off and left you. Bet you gonna love everything I
can give you and that youngun, Natty can give you."*

*Each thrust pushed me further along the floor towards my
rocker and my sewing basket. A little notion bloomed in my mind.
My scissors. Help him get me closer to my sewing basket. I love
those scissors. A wedding gift from a family friend who had traveled
to Italy and brought back many wonderful items, not the least my
scissors, her dagger scissors, Samuel called them. I had such
strangest thoughts. Time seemd so slow and I thought of how
Samuel had told me, "You keep these near and nobody can harm
you Miss Amaelie." They had sharply pointed iron blades that
undulated, a brass grip with short quillons palmed at the ends, and
tortoise grip scales. They were beautiful and deadly.*

*The badder one thrust and I helped him. let the thrust shove
me backwards untill flung my arm back and it struck my sewing
basket. "Now, we'll see." The next and Clyde's last thrust knocked
me against the basket, over turned it and its contents spilled out, its
secrets unraveling, as balled yarn rolled away and my dagger scissors*

touched cold and deadly against my hand. Now we'll see, I thought. I gave one last groan. "Ha, I tole you you'd get good stuff out of me." Clyde himself groaned deep in his throat with pleasure, his eyes squeezed tight, mouth in a rictus of ecstasy. And then groaned even deeper as I as Amaelie thrust her dagger scissors into his back and that rictus of pleasure turned into a rictus of horror as Clyde realized his death.

Natty stuck his head in the great room from my bedroom. I heard him speak low, "Oh my, now you gone an done it." He heard boots from the back of the house. "Oh, now I'm for it." I saw him sling a bag over his shoulder and make for the porch. Running for his horse, I expect. Running for his life.

Osner stepped into the front room and saw...everything.

He picked me up from under that beast. Kicked that beast aside. Bathed me. Washed off the blood and sweat stink. Put me to bed. Gentled me. Sat with me. Took that beast's body away. Never told me where. Never asked what happened. Smoothed my forehead. Held my hand. Told Minette for me. Sorried for coming too late. Told me again and again of our loving the night before. Wiped out the hurt from my mind with the loving of us. Helped the hurt in my body. Made me whole. Went away. Oh, my Osner, my Osner.

Sandy and Lizbet sat silently, looking at the diary and at each other. Taking in this passage. Taking in that Amaelie was raped. Taking in her bravery and quick thinking. Taking in the incontrovertible proof that Amaelie and Osner were lovers...no, they were more than that... they were each other's beloved.

꙳

184

"Bobbi, I have to take this call. I want you go with Junie and look at potential housing and schools for staff we'll transfer to the facility. I need your findings for my report to the 'Boys' in New York." Bobbi frowned, puzzled. "You know who I mean." Lena chuckled conspiratorially to her, "you know, Klaus, et Al!" Turning away, she began speaking before Bobbi was out of ear shot. "OK, I see, Klaus, you want us on a fast track: Haiti before the end of the week. Yes, and get this report in ASAP." Bobbi stopped in surprise. *These changes are not part of my work plan, at least not at this point in the program development. What's happening?* Lena waved her away peremptorily and walked toward one of the proposed workshop production building sites.

After Bobbi and Junie drove away, Lena slipped her phone in her slacks pocket and pulled an antique paper out of her boot top. She unfolded the document, an aged hand drawn map. She walked over to a temporary picnic table set up for the construction workers and smoothed the paper, rotated it this way and that until she had lined up Beaver Creek with the current Google earth map on her phone. She compared various aspects of the old map with the bird's eye image, showing the same land and corresponding what she could see with her own eyes. "Really unbelievable; the topography and built features look almost the same. Nothing seems to have changed since this map was drawn. Creek where it should be, that wood lot, fields, Abbott House buildings, Greeley big house still standing. Oh my God! I might really be able to find the stuff. Incredible."

Her phone rang for real this time. "Uh huh, OK. What progress? You got the place? I see, down near Starr." She listened intently. "Now look, I don't want any excuses. I want that building, and I want everything in place just like I told you. Things are heating up in DR and Haiti." She tapped her foot while listening. "No, it's a good opportunity. Yes, they did good work there. We can get a lot of them cheaper than cheap. You got it?" She clicked off her phone and got her Google earth map on the screen. Checking back and forth between her phone map and the hand-drawn map, she started pacing off distances.

Natty led the chestnut away from the farm and the woman and Clyde. Dead, Clyde. When he reckoned he was out of hearing, he mounted and rode hell for leather west and then turned northwards toward the mountains that he could see faintly in the distance. The dawn broke and the sun rose as he found a narrow pathway up that wound around the skirts of the mountains and took him higher and higher into dense forest and by spilling waterfalls, through narrow chasms. He was far away from the bloody wretched scene in the house before he discovered he had taken Clyde's horse, saddle bags, and an extra coat, a jacket Clyde had stolen off a dead officer. It had Clyde's own pocket notebook in it and was slung over the saddle pommel. Through the mountains going north and north. From time to time he stopped at a cabin in a holler and begged some corn pone and beans. Sometimes he worked for his meal. Sometimes he came across bushwhackers who took him in and tried to take everything from him. Sometimes he came across folk who wanted the

Yankees to win and so were "Glad, glad, glad" to see him. He was glad to see them and glad he had that extry coat of Clyde's – cold in those mountains. It was late March before he got to Virginia and turned east again. Started looking for other Yankees. Hoping he could join up again. Hoping he had waited out the last of the war in the mountains. "I ain't no coward," he'd told lots of mountain folk. "I just cain't do it no more." He arrived in central Virginia the first week of April. Word going round that it was to be soon over. He made for a place called Sailor's Creek to help out and hoped he was not being real ignorant and get himself killed. Some fool had to be the last one dead. "Not me." He helped round up seven thousand Johnny Rebs, they said. And more got captured at High Bridge. And those poor boys were so starved and ragged he seemed like a fat rich man by their side.

In later years, he told his grands, who called him Grandpa Windy, some of the day at Appomattox on April 9 in the year 1865. They weren't much interested. They had things to do. He did write a lot of what happened at that farm and to that woman and to Clyde and what he done to her and what she done to him, and all about the running away and keeping some stuff they stole and leaving stuff they buried and the map he brought back and about the locket wrapped up in a piece of paper he snatched off the desk. That paper turned out to be some sort of letter or something. And then when he died, the Clyde diary and his Natty diary, and the wrapping paper for the locket went off somewhere and ended up in a yard sale, cause nobody really cared about that old stuff. Only liked the jewelry and the other good stuff they could turn into money to help them out in hard times. This Crane family wasn't like the other rich Cranes. His Cranes always seemed down on their luck, even when one of them married a Van Vleck. The locket came down the generations until it rested with one of the girls who thought it beautiful and kept it for her own.

Back in Praireview, Anna found a letter that would unravel another secret, another piece of an old puzzle that would change and enrich all their lives. "Dallas, Dallas," she called. "You have to hear this."

> *20 November, 1879*
> *80 Flower Street*
> *Charleston, South Carolina*

Mm. Lillie Fleurie Troux
Troux House, New Orleans, La.
Dear Madame Lillie,
My name is Lilianna Fleur Abbott Greely. I am the child of your sister Amaelie Abbott. I writ you with sad newes. Brakes my heart to saye Mama's gone into the bye and bye. The chest fever took her in the night too weeks last. Please tell Mamas other Abbott childrens Fleetwood Hezikiah and Gorgiana I took good care of our Mama. She raized me right and loved me. Taught me to read, write and cipher. She taught me all the good ways with a needle. I love her all my heart and I cry every nite for her.
I never knew my papa. Mama sayed his name is Osner and worked her farm with her. She loved him and made him go away too Hayti. I will not ever see him. I'm nigh on 16 and a married woman. My husband is a goode good man Mr. Luke Greely. He is a kind man. He has a blacksmith shop in town and I am dressmaker like Mama saye for me to be. We are content essept for missing Mama. We buryed her in St. Ann Church cemetery in Charleston like she saye to doo. I suppose I will be the only child to

Shed a Tear on the Sod where my Mother lies. I have planted a little cedar at the head and food of her Grave. Also a Weaping Willow. I am not capable to write to you as I wish at this time. Let us look with hope to that day when we Shall meet in Heaven.

I remain your respectful friend,

Lilianna Fleur Abbott Greely

Dallas and Anna sat at the dining room table where Anna had been working on the letters. Anna reached for Dallas' hand. "Now we know the reason Amaelie disappeared from your family's history. It's a blessing your Great-grandmother saved this letter. And a shame she hid the knowledge."

"Yes, on the one hand, she must have really loved her sister. Yet on the other hand, the attitudes and morals of the times would have kept her from acknowledging or reaching out to a mulatto niece. Oh, that sounds so, so…I mean her biracial niece. By the 1870s, the Red Shirts, Wade Hampton's renaming of the KKK, was a terrorist organization. I would hope that Great-grandmother Lillie was not so easily intimidated. Maybe we'll never really know why no one ever spoke about Amaelie and Lilianna." Dallas shook his head sadly.

"You know what this must mean. The Greely name? Without the third 'e'? Where are the girls now? Still at the Abbott Museum? Shall we call them, Dallas?"

"Let me think on it. Go ahead and scan the letter." Dallas looked out the window at the blooming garden, considering. He turned to back to Anna. "Let's investigate a bit more if we can. Would you be a dear and

189

check the census records for 1870 to say, 1930? If the trail leads us where we think it will, we'll know for sure. Then we'll have solid data to tell. We'll call them later to find out what they've learned in the Carolinas. Then, we can tell them and email Lizbet Lilianna's letter. One thing we do know, Amaelie loved Lillie and honored their sisterly love. She named her daughter for herself and her sister: Lili for Lillie and Anna from Amaelie Ann - Lilianna."

Sandy and Lizbet drove through the Abbott Industrial Zone across from the museum when they finished their research. Lizbet wanted to see with her own eyes if there were any remnants of the old Greeley farm. Taylor Rice, the museum director said that the property line between the Abbott and Greeley farms was about 3 miles down Greeley Road. All they'd found were the construction site and a large house on a hill overlooking the Savannah River. They could only speculate it might be the original Greeley farmhouse. It had already been modernized and renovated into office space. "Sorry, Lizbet. I'm afraid we're not going to learn anything more."

They had just turned back toward Generostee Road when Sandy's cell rang. "Phara, where are you? Where? Delmas? In Haiti? Lizbet, she's in Haiti! Wait, Phara, slow down. What's happening? They? Who is after you? Phara? Phara? She's gone, Lizbet. All I heard was 'Come, help, I need...' and the call went dead."

18 Heating Up

THE SUN WAS BLINDING, as Sandy and Lizbet stepped out of the American Airlines terminal at Port-au-Prince's Toussaint L'Ouverture International Airport in search of a taxi. They were hit with a wall of intense tropical heat. "I love it!" Lizbet exclaimed. "After years of Boston blizzards and Nor'easters, I'd adore living in the tropics. The hotter, the better!" Sandy just rolled her eyes and kept fanning herself, while she scanned ahead for an empty taxi.

"We have a few hours to get our bearings and find out what we can about Phara's disappearance," Sandy said. "Then, we'll contact Bobbi. Lena Morris' call to invite me to fly down and join them to inspect the new Auguste SA Elite facility was certainly unexpected. Bobbi's text to go along with it but stay on alert means she's on to something."

"Sandy, do you think…."

"Welcome to Port-au-Prince, my friends." They turned to see a tall, strikingly handsome man in tan cargo pants, a white guayabera shirt and brown Teva sandals, smiling at them. "Dr. Troux, I presume? And Ms. Sheridan?" he said with a wide grin.

"How do you know us? Who did you say you were? We don't need a tour guide, you know," Sandy replied with a guarded look on her face.

"Ray Morgan texted your photo, and I must say it doesn't do you justice. I am JanJak Mathieu, head of the Caribbean branch of the Fugitive Task Force," he said, showing them his photo ID. "I am here to help you, and have you help me, find two people very important to me. Come. My car is parked ahead in the security section. One of the perks of my profession. I see you are wise to travel light. Are these your only bags?"

"Yes," Lizbet responded. "Sandy's carry-everything-you-need traveling style is starting to rub off on me. Just the bare necessities for this trip. We're staying at the Bishop Hood Foundation Guest House," Lizbet volunteered. "It's on…"

"I know where it is. My cousin, Father Gabriel Mathieu, is the director and pastor of the Foundation. You've made an excellent choice."

"Inspector Mathieu, before we check in, there's an urgent matter we have to address. I assume Ray told you about the disappearance of Haitian singer Phara Damour? Do you know if an investigation has been launched? If so, I'd like to stop by the National Police headquarters to see if there's been any progress," Sandy said.

"There won't be," he replied grimly. "And please address me as JanJak. Our police will wait the necessary 36 hours before even beginning the paperwork, and by that time, the trail will be cold. Just like it was with the disappearance of Dayanne Mathieu last week. Our Task

Force has taken over the investigation for both my sister Dayanne and our cousin Phara Damour."

"Sister? Cousin?" Lizbet asked. "You're related to both kidnapped victims *and* the director of the Bishop Holly Foundation?"

"Our family is large, and many of us are very involved in the fabric and culture of Haitian life. You'll find many Mathieu cousins as a well as many in the Damour and Holly branches of our family working on behalf of our people and our country."

"I'd love to hear more, but first tell us about Phara," Sandy said urgently. "She called me yesterday afternoon, clearly in trouble. She said something about knowing what Cassandra was tracking and that she was in Delmas. She was very frightened, talking very fast and breathing very hard, as if she were running. The last I heard was 'come, help...' before we were disconnected. No response when I tried to call her back.

"We tried to get help for her, but we were in South Carolina and couldn't reach anyone at the Port-au-Prince police headquarters who'd take us seriously. So, I called Ray and then we took the first flight we could to get here."

"That was wise. And knowing Phara was last in Delmas was essential," said JanJak. "I already had a team of agents in that area following up on a lead about Dayanne."

"So you think their disappearances are connected?" Sandy asked.

"Oh, yes. Phara and I spoke at length when she

193

arrived with our uncle, the author Stevenson Mathieu, the other day," he continued. "He lives in New Jersey now and was at Phara's concert. When he found out about the attack on her and where she'd been taken, he went to the hospital and wouldn't leave her side."

"Do you know why they flew here to Port-au-Prince?" Sandy asked.

"Once the International Fugitive Task Force had taken over the inquiry into Cassandra's murder and its connection to our sweatshop and trafficking investigation in the New York/New Jersey and Haiti/Dominican Republic areas, Phara was free to come home. We all felt she'd be safer here."

"But she wasn't. The thugs who attacked her in Montclair were still at large, weren't they? And when they discovered the DVD they stole from Phara only contained her music videos, they must have tracked her," Lizbet observed, astutely.

"You are correct," said JanJak. "But there was more. When she and our Uncle Stevenson arrived at Cynthia Stagoff's home in Montclair to collect her belongings, Cynthia gave her a small package that had been missed because her young children were playing with it. It contained a flash drive and a note from Cassandra to get it to Ray Morgan or me. We've had an IT security team at work in New York, extracting and deciphering the coded information on it."

"But how did Phara end up in Delmas?" Sandy asked. "That's an industrial area in Port-au-Prince, isn't it? Phara told me she lived south of the city in Carrefour."

"The note from Cassandra mentioned a location in Delmas to investigate, and I happened to mention the lead we had on Dayanne in that area," JanJak said. "I don't know why she would have gone there. She's not normally a risk taker. Something or someone must have lured her."

They turned down a side road flanked with old warehouses, some still in disrepair from the 2010 earthquake. "Here we are," the inspector announced, pulling his Suzuki sedan up next to an old industrial building. "We've set up a small command post in this area to facilitate our investigation." He turned to Sandy with a big smile. "One of my agents is coming toward us to speak with you."

Sandy turned to her right to find Ray Morgan standing there.

⤡

It was a busy day at Port-au-Prince's international airport. Another America Airlines flight, this one from New York, arrived two hours after Sandy and Lizbet. One of the passengers was a Manhattan fashion industry executive. He was met by a couple of rough looking Haitians in Army/Navy Store fatigues.

An hour later, a Delta Airlines jet touched down, carrying Bobbi and Lena Morris. Lena had arranged to have a limousine waiting for them to take them to the 4-star Marriot Port-au-Prince Hotel on Avenue Jean Paul II in the Turgeau section of the city.

As they were checking in, Bobbi said to Lena, "This

hotel is a little pricey, Lena. I usually stay in one of the smaller ones in the Petion-Ville district."

"Oh, Harvey pre-approved our expenses, and I think he'd want us to be safe and comfortable, don't you? Don't worry," Lena replied, a bit flippantly. "I'm sorry there was only one executive king room available, but I think your single guest room will be comfortable. The concierge said it has a good view of the pool."

She rattled on. "It's such a pity that your friend Sandy had some personal business in Carrefour and can't join us until tomorrow morning. I wonder what that business is – a tryst, of some kind?"

"I really wouldn't know, Lena. *Dr. Troux* doesn't confide her personal life to me," Bobbi said, feigning disinterest. "We're not such close friends these days."

"Oh, dear, well, ah, let's go freshen up and meet for a drink and then dinner at La Sirene. It's just off the lobby. I can't wait to savor their Pwason Gwo Sei – that's a lovely fish dish. And maybe I'll start with their carrot seafood salad," Lena said, attempting to lighten the mood of the moment. "I'll contact Sandy and tell her to meet us for breakfast in the hotel's Café Cho at 8 o'clock tomorrow morning. Might as well get off to an early start. Be a dear and call the concierge to confirm our car and driver for tomorrow."

Several minutes later, Bobbi was on her cell phone with Sandy and Lizbet. "She's a piece of work, that Lena. One minute, she's all respectful and sensitive to my feelings about the demotion, and I'm thinking I've misjudged her. The next, she's treating me like her assistant – no, her lackey. Oh, prepare yourself, she's gonna call you soon to invite you for breakfast."

Bobbi briefed her two comrades on her tour of Anderson County sites for the new Auguste International Innovation Center and the "training" of her replacement as head of *her* project. "I can't quite put my finger on it, but from time to time, she seems to be working from a different agenda."

"I don't doubt it," Sandy countered. "I know you'd like to feign a headache and skip dinner, but I think you should go and see what information you can wheedle out of her. We're beginning to get a bigger picture of bogus fashion labels, shady labor practices, and other criminal activity. Phara's been kidnapped, her cousin's still missing, and Ray's here working with a Caribbean task force headed by a relative of both missing women. Things are heating up.

"Oh-oh, there's that call from Lena," Sandy added. "Meet me in front of your hotel at 7:30 tomorrow morning. We can fill each other in on anything new. Hang in there, Bobbi."

The next day, when Sandy arrived at the Marriott, she was greeted by Bobbi and a steaming hot cup of coffee. "I asked for it black and extra, extra strong. You're gonna need it."

"You look like you could use it more than me, Bobbi. How was your evening with your new nemesis?"

"All I can say is brace yourself! That woman is going to unravel everything this program was meant to do. She doesn't believe in sustainability; she thinks Haiti is a great place because we can hire workers for peanuts; and she wants to cut some of Al's more expensive bells and whistles in the security program. He's gonna love that. I can't figure out why she was picked to head this project. She's an air-head! And totally opportunistic."

"Well, aside from all that Ms. Power, how was the dinner?"

"Tolerable, Sandy. Tolerable," Bobbi managed to say before they both burst out laughing. "OK, OK. Let's separate so we don't show up together. We're supposed not to like each other anymore, remember?"

Half an hour later, they were on Highway 8 headed toward the small city of Croix de Bouquets (Kwadèbouke in Creole), 12.9 km northeast of Port-au-Prince. This area was not badly damaged by the 2010 earthquake and hosted more than 10,000 displaced people in refugee camps. Auguste International had chosen this area as the setting for its new manufacturing facility in part to help boost local employment. The car turned left down a newly paved road, past a new school under construction with volunteer help from Seattle-based Architects Without Borders. They passed a young woman with a video camera who filming some children who'd gathered to watch the workers' progress on their school and mime a little for the camera.

The company's new facility had been designed to be totally sustainable. Solar panels were in place on the roof to provide a 100% power source. Manufacturing waste was collected and recycled. There were plans on the table to add a day care center for workers as well as subsidized meals and free healthcare. "At the moment, we have no problem getting both skilled and unskilled workers," Lena told Sandy. "This facility was designed to be state-of-the-art in technology, sustainability, and human resources management. One of our biggest objectives is to provide more training and opportunities for women."

Bobbi bit her lip to keep from saying what she was thinking. *Quite an about face from last night's dinner conversation.*

They entered the main office and were greeted by an attractive woman wearing a white cotton dress enhanced with exquisite hand embroidery. She offered a radiant smile of recognition. "Ms. Bobbi! Welcome back. We have missed your good spirit."

"Bonjour, Dominique. I'm so happy to see you again," Bobbi replied. "Let me introduce you to..."

Lena cut her off and introduced herself. "My name is Lena Morris, and I am the new director of the Auguste Innovation Program. Ms. Power is here to show me the ropes. This is Dr. Sandra Troux, an important new member of the Board. Please escort us to my office and then bring us a tray cold iced tea. Then, please tell Mr. Marcon we're here and ready to start our inspection."

Sandy and Bobbi were both embarrassed by her brusque, rude manner. Dominique looked like she was about ready to cry.

For the rest of the morning, as Ferdinand Marcon took them through the building, Lena barked orders and found fault with just about everything.

At one point, Bobbi started to intervene as Lena stood over one of the seamstresses, criticizing her work,

Sandy admonished Bobbi. "I'm sure Lena knows what she's doing. You mustn't interfere." Whenever there was a question to be asked, Sandy asked Lena. She chatted her up and snubbed Bobbi whenever she could find a plausible excuse. Bobbi, in turn, was careful to be distant and terse with Sandy.

When it came time to review the Innovation Lab, Lena had softened her manner a little. All the technicians and computer operators were male, and both Sandy and Bobbi became amused by her not so subtle flirtatious behavior. Most of the young men, fresh out of college, appeared totally embarrassed.

Bobbi was well aware that Lena was not using any of the standard protocol for a facility audit. She seemed uninterested in quality control, safety measures, employee programs, or efficiency measures. *What is the real purpose of today's tour? What kind of info do Klaus, Harvey and Al want her to bring back? She's asked for no feasibility reports, no G4 stats for sustainability, no metrics of any kind. What gives?*

The next stop was the Design Department. This time, Bobbi was asked to "sit this one out," and Lena took Sandy in, arm in arm. When they came out 30 minutes later, they seemed like the best of pals.

"Now, I'll be sure to get the proposal to you tomorrow so you can discuss it with your business manager. It's a good investment, I promise," Lena told Sandy, who was nodding and smiling. As they passed Bobbi, Sandy gave her a subtle eye roll that said: "You won't believe what I have to tell you."

On the way back to Port-au-Prince, Lena pressed

Sandy with questions about her world travels and her work as a cultural anthropologist. Sandy responded with enthusiasm, subtly turning each inquire to Lena's experience. As Lena chattered on, flattered by Sandy's interest, she described how she had initially come to Haiti.

"I was here on a vacation once. It was a cheap trip, and I needed to get away. I probably shouldn't have wasted my money. So anyway, I wanted to leave the hotel and see something of the country. So, I got on a tour. Well, you couldn't really go much of anywhere. There was so much poverty. Really, it was quite disgusting. Trash everywhere. Ragged children begging. Rivers filled with garbage. I mean, you'd think these people would have more pride," she sniffed in derision.

Sandy agreed with her to draw her out more. *There has to be a connection between her and Cassandra and the SA labels. My prickles do not lie.* Sandy's skin was prickling intensely. "So, what is your opinion of them as workers in the new factories?"

"I hope I can train some of them well enough to work in my, umm, our project. But you know these people…" Lena said disdainfully.

Bobbi, who sat between them, was not asked to participate in the conversation.

When they returned to the Marriott, Lena offered Sandy the use of the car for the night. Then, before she rushed off for her 4 o'clock spa appointment, she asked Bobbi to get a head start on their facility audit report. "Ciao, ladies. See you tomorrow!"

Sandy dismissed the driver, and she and Bobbi walked around the corner and jumped into a waiting black Suzuki. JanJak and Ray both turned around to ask how the day had been.

"Well," Bobbi began, "Miss I'm-such-an-important-board-member here just qualified for an Academy Award for Best Stab in the Back Friend. And pray tell me *Dr. Troux*, what was all that talk about a proposal and an investment?"

"Well, it seems our Ms. Lena Morris wants me to invest in *her* fashion company, under the Studio Augustus label. Or dare I say the pseudo *SA* label? And I am more and more certain that she was involved in Cassandra's murder. I'm just not sure how."

Lizbet had spent the day at the Bishop Holly Foundation, learning about the scope of work they were doing in rebuilding Haiti. Father Mathieu had first told her that Port-au-Prince had lost their beloved Holy Trinity Episcopal Cathedral in the 2010 earthquake. "It was such a central part of the spiritual life of the country, not just this city, that we have done all we can to raise funds for a new cathedral. Many people from all over the world have sent contributions. Even our school children have labored and given what little money they can. A new, stronger church structure has been designed and construction will soon begin. Of course, a building is not our spiritual center. That flows from our hearts and souls."

"That's what Phara Damour and her friends were doing in Montclair, New Jersey – raising money for Haiti, for the children of Haiti, for the hearts and souls of Haiti" Lizbet said.

"Oh yes, for six years, those good people in Montclair have contributed their time and money to help three non-profit organizations – NGOs who work for our people. The Edeyo Foundation from New York seeks to improve lives through education. Lamp for Haiti provides medical care and humanitarian aid for people in the slums of Cité Soleil. HELP, the Haitian Education Leadership Program, provides need-based and merit scholarships for our young people. Oh, it is very good work indeed. Just yesterday, I was talking with a young American filmmaker, I mean videographer, named Lisa Tan. She's creating a video about how young volunteers from America and other countries are working with young Haitians and various NGOs to make a difference here."

"I've been spending some time in your library here and speaking with some of the people who come to volunteer and support each other," Lizbet said. "You have a long history of community and service that's very impressive, Father Mathieu."

"Yes, community service was present from our very beginnings. But, please call me Father Gabriel. Everyone does," he said. "When my ancestor –my great-great-great-uncle – Bishop James Holly first came to Haiti in 1861, he struggled. But he also opened his doors to many people, especially those who were escaped slaves from America. Many of them came again and again to help him build his church. You know, one of my ancestors, my great-great- grandfather came many times. He helped build the first church building, rectory and school at Holy Trinity. He became so much a part of the church community that he even became a member of the Bishop's family. He married Bishop Holly's niece, Rebecca Holly."

Lizbet had been listening intently, and her mind was also racing with questions she dared not ask. *Could it be? Could it actually be?*

Father Gabriel continued. "This church was the chief conduit for communication with the families of American Freedom Seekers. Letters would come addressed just to Bishop Holly or Trinity Church, Port-au-Prince, Haiti. Sometimes there would be a name or return address, sometimes not. There was a wall where letters were posted for people to claim. Sometimes a priest or a parishioner would travel to villages to find the person who was sent a letter. Someone was always here to read or write a letter for someone in need."

"What happened if no one claimed a letter?"

"They were saved," he replied. "In fact, we stored our archive of letters here at the Foundation in the next room. It was lucky we did, for they would have been destroyed in the earthquake. Would you like to see them?"

"Oh, yes, I would indeed," she exclaimed.

That is how it came to pass that Lizbet Lee Sheridan, nee Lee Bong-Cha Alice Greely, found almost the last critical piece of her family puzzle. She had just finished reading the letter when Sandy and Bobbi walked into the room.

"I have something to tell you," Lizbet and Sandy said in unison.

"You first."

"No, you first."

"OK," Lizbet said. "Me first. Sandy, I have a letter in my hand, dated June 18, 1874 from Amaelie Fleurie Abbott to Osner Mathieu. Listen."

Mme. Amaelie Fleurie Abbott
St. Ann Episcopal Church
Charleston, SC

M. Osner Mathieu
Bishop James Holly
Holy Trinity Church
Port-au-Prince, Haiti

My dear Osner,
It is my great hope that you are well and safe in your new home. I am happy you are free. Times are very hard here. We struggle everyday to keep body and soul together. Fleetwood died without a will and the farm was taken from me. I worked in the general store in Storeville for a time but they drove me out when I started to show. It is a shocking thing for a widow to be with child so long after her husband's passing. I told people it was a rape by Yankee bummer – not untrue. I was shunned anyways and Fleetwood's brothers came and took my three sweet younguns away. I only see them once each sad Christmas. They do not know me now.

For a time, I knew not if the babe came from the times we lain together. Or that terrible night when that foul Yankee took me in the kitchen and I lost you forever. I lived in fear it were his. The birthin' was so hard I almos' died. Minette who saved me. I saw you in that sweet little angel face and cried with joy. You have a daughter named Lilianna after my Mama and sister.

Lilianna is 10 year old. She is a pretty child with light chocolate skin and curly chestnut hair. She is sweet, kind, hardworking and very smart. I teach her the 3 Rs, the Bible and how to sew so she has a skill and never has to do fieldwork again. But now we share crop together over at the Greeley farm. They were kind to take us in. Minette married a free Black from over at Lexington and is share croppin' and havin her own chil'ren.

Your letter of 2 year ago only jus reached me here. I rejoice that you are free in a free land. I tried to come to you with Lilianna. Almos all my sharecroppin money was sewed in my petticoat. We walk cross the 'tire state o South Carolina, eatin' off the land and sometimes beggin' It tok us a month to git to Charleston. I dressed in my ol' N'Orlins clothes and bonnet so the white stores would buy my old finery and the las of my jewelry Mama and Papa give me. 'For I left, I dug up the family silver and jewels I buried. Got enuf for 2 tickets to Haiti on a ship loaded with corn 'n'cotton.

But now it breaks my heart that only this letter will ever be held by you. Lilianna come down wit denghe fevero 'for we ever set sail. The capn throwed us off for fear he would get sick. He kept all my gold coins too.

Lilianna, our strong angel, is recovering. We will stay here in Charleston. I don have strength to walk back home. Osner, I know I will never see you again now. I love you. I love you.

With deep affection,
Amaelie Fleurie Abbott

When Lizbet finished reading, tears were rolling down her cheeks. "What do you think, Sandy?"

"I think you should read this letter that Dad and Anna found among Great Aunt Babby's treasure trove. It's from Lilianna Fleur Abbott Greely to her Aunt Lillie Fleurie Troux." She handed Lizbet Bobbi's tablet, which was open to the scanned copy of the letter.

"You know what this means, don't you?" Bobbi asked. "You two are cousins. Third or fourth cousins, thrice removed or something like that. Oh, heck, forget the details. *COUSINS!*"

Lizbet and Sandy were hugging, laughing and crying all at once.

"Thank you Amaelie Abbott, thank you Osner Mathieu!" Lizbet cried, looking up at the ceiling.

"Osner Mathieu? Amaelie Abbott?" Father Gabriel Mathieu exclaimed. "You're descended from my great-great grandfather and his first love Amaelie?" He walked over to the wall and took down an old daguerreotype photo of a group of church members from the 19th century. "Look! Here's Osner Mathieu standing to the right of Bishop Holly! He's your ancestor too! And let me tell you, you have cousins. There's lots of us here in Haiti! Uncle Stevenson, Phara, Dayanne, JanJak, and me for starters! You are a cousin-rich woman, Lizbet Sheridan!"

Bobbi stood watching this joyful moment and was immensely happy for her dear friends, especially Lizbet. Yet, she couldn't help feeling a tad left out. *Shake it off, Bobbi, shake it off.*

❦

Several miles away, in the industrial Delmas section of the city, the tide was starting to turn. Inspector JanJak Mathieu received a tip – a tip that might break his case wide open.

An informant reported two "high-class" women being held against their will, locked in a store room of an old abandoned button factory. A shipment of bogus fashions was nearing completion. A container ship with Liberian registry had just cleared the channel.

Things were indeed about to happen.

19   Stowaway!

THE MUSIC PULSED in a rhythmic konpas beat at a huge celebration that continued into the late night. When news of the discovery of a new Mathieu "kouzen" from America spread, upwards of 50 family members descended on the community center at the Bishop Holly Foundation. A spontaneous Byenveni Kouzen (Welcome Cousin) party for Lizbet ensued, warmly inviting in the new newest member of a large extended "fanmi" (family).

People brought food to share: Dire ak Pwa (rice & beans with coconut milk), vegetable stew, Lambi a la Creole (conch), banana pez (fried plantains), Pan Potate (sweet potato pudding), and a big Birthday sheet cake for Lizbet.

Father Gabriel ladled out a sweet fruit and coconut punch for everyone. "No alcohol allowed. This is Church property," he chided two strapping young cousins who tried to spike the punch with rum.

People sang and danced to the pulsating drum beats of konpas music, a mixture of African rhythms and old style ballroom. Then meringue, samba, jazz rock. Sometime during the party, someone brought in a boom box, and they listened to the sultry and much missed voice of their beloved cousin Phara. Her calypso song of Plus Près de Toi (Closer to You) that she sang at the Montclair concert, brought tears to all eyes. Everyone joined in with her jazzy rendition of God Bless the Child.

Father Gabriel leaned over to Lizbet, Sandy and Bobbi to say, "You all must come back in July for the Carnivale des Fleurs festival. There will be much music and dancing in the street, starting at the Champ de Mars plaza across from the Palais National (National Palace). Or, come next January for the big Calypso Festival."

To Sandy, he said: "C'est incredible that you and Lizbet are cousins. It is a miracle."

Uncle Stevenson approached and put his arms around Bobbi, Sandy and Lizbet, drawing them into a big bear hug. "It is good that Lizbet has found a new, big Haitian family. But do not forget that you three have been family for many years. You are more than cousins. You are sisters of the heart and soul."

"Yes," Father Gabriel agreed. "Rejoice, rejoice for you have been given a very rare gift. Now, let us all dance the night away!" And they did.

Sandy looked out at the crowded floor filled with people of all ages, right down to a 3-year-old dancing to the beat of meringue, samba, jazz, konpas, and krèyol rock. *As much as I hate to leave a good party, I need to make a discreet exit soon. Ray and JanJak are already at the stake out in Delmas.*

She caught Bobbi's eye and nodded toward the corner for a quick confab. "You and I need to do some work while Lizbet bonds with her new extended family, Bobbi.

I need to get to the task force stakeout of a possible sweatshop that may lead to recovering Phara and Dayanne, and…"

"Right, I need to go shake Lena's tree a little and see what falls out. She thinks she's got me primed for failure and you for her next promotion and meal ticket. Time to flip that around. Confuse her a little. Don't you think?" Bobbi

"Agreed. It's definitely time to 'blow this popcorn stand,' as we used to say as kids. You go ahead. I'll clue in Lizbet so she can cover for us."

"OK," Bobbi agreed. "I'll text you anything you need to know. Check in with you later."

A few minutes later, both women had discreetly left the party, and Lizbet & fanmi continued with the festivities. More hugs, kisses, dancing, and singing.

At the end of the evening, Father Gabriel called everyone together for a blessing.

"We thank you, Lord, for bringing our new dear cousin Lizbet to us. And her sister-friends Sandy and Bobbi. Bless the souls of our dear ancestors, great-great-grandpé Osner Mathieu and great-great-grandmé Rebecca. Bless his first wife Amaelie Abbott and their daughter Lilianna. Without each of them, none of us would be here.

"Please watch over our dear cousins Dayanne and Phara and bring them back to us safely.

"Finally, let us pause to remember and pray for our dear friend Cassandra Innocent. She was not yet a cousin, but she would have become one in July when she was to marry our cousin George Damour. She was my friend since we were children, and I miss her sweetness profoundly. As her favorite poet ee cummings wrote: 'I carry your heart, I carry it in my heart.' Now all of you – it is time to dance out this party and go home to sleep!"

The old rhythm & blues song "Good Night Sweetheart" played everyone, tired and happy, to their homes.

On her way back to the Marriot, Bobbi called Lena. "Hey, boss, just checking in to find out what's on the agenda next...Sandy?..Naw. I just got rid of her. I mean, *Dr. Sandy has left the building.* She went off with her new Haitian boyfriend for the night. Left me and our friend Lizbet flat, which is not a first. Can't really count on her, you know, if you really want her participation in the biz. She runs hot 'n' cold with people...Yeah, go ahead and call her if you want. If you make her feel important, she'll probably dump the boyfriend.

"Hey listen, I've been meaning to tell you I hold no grudges. I'm sure you think I'm bitter about our switch in roles at Auguste. Fact is, I'm kinda relieved. Those ol' misogynist so-and-so's at HQ were getting on my last nerve anyway. I'm ready for greener pastures, if you know what I mean, when your training period is over. Not that you really need training. Ah-huh, yeah, you're so right."

Bobbi listened to Lena, trying not to gag as she waxed on about how much she needed her to enhance the program for her and make her look good.

"Will do, Boss. So, what's on the agenda for tomorrow? Any more sites to explore? Any young designers to exploit?...Ah, yeah, Micheline Obin. I hear she's all the rage with the young professional crowd...She hangs out where?...A club over near Champs de Mer?...Yeah, Yeah. I could stop by now to maybe make a connection, maybe maneuver her into a contract. Wanna join me for a drink or two there?...Oh, sorry you're not feeling well...OK. I'll meet you at the Café Cho at 8 a.m. Ciao."

OMG! I can't believe I had to do that. The things I do to trap a felon. UGH! She leaned forward and told the driver, "Sorry, I forgot something back at the Bishop Holly Foundation. Could we go back?" *Time to get Lizbet and join Sandy et al at the stakeout.*

"Can we trust him? This Luc Savant, your informer?" Sandy asked JanJak. "How can you be sure the two women allegedly being held in that warehouse are Dayanne and Phara?"

Sandy had just arrived to join Ray and JanJak. The men had been sitting in an old beat up van across from a group of dilapidated metal-clad warehouses for several hours, with no activity on the street. The inside of the vehicle looked more like a TV van, with three big monitors and all sorts of media equipment that gave them the advantage of a 360 degree view of their surroundings.

"I've used Savant as a mole before," JanJak said. "He's always reliable, and he's risked his life for us many times. I am more concerned about the rookie detective I sent with him. Bertrand Holly has only been on our task force for 3 months. He was lately with the Haitian army, but he's green."

"Holly, you say?" Ray asked with a slight grimace. "Don't tell me he's another one of your legion of young cousins."

"They have to learn sometime," JanJak replied with a shrug. "He wants to make a difference in the world, thinks he can wipe out all the bad guys who prey on little children and women. He must understand that things are not that simple. And, I want to keep him alive long enough to accomplish that."

"So, you keep an eye out and essentially babysit him, right?"

"Something like that," JanJak said. "Right now, I have him rigged with a very small video camera hidden in a 'Vote for Hillary' button. He's supposed to turn it on when he gets close enough to see if they're holding any prisoners. He can get away with it since he still has that look of a teenager."

"What about Savant?" Sandy asked.

"He's rigged with an ear piece and mike so we can hear what's going on."

"Sir, we're getting a signal now," said one of the officers.

"Put it on the center monitor."

They all leaned forward. The picture was dark and the images faint and grainy, so it was hard to see.

"We're getting some audio now. I'll put it on

speaker."

"You see, Savant? How hard these little ones work?" a gruff male voice said. "And they're quick and obedient too. They'll fetch a good price in America."

"What? Do you see that? They're just children! Why, some of them can't be much more than six!" Sandy exclaimed.

Her cell buzzed to alert her to a text from Bobbi: *Lena's calling to set up a meet. We'll be there in a few.*

"What about the Auguste knock-offs? Are they all packed for the shipment?" Savant asked. "Our partner expects perfection, you know."

"Yeah, we added the last batch an hour ago."

"And the counterfeit labels? Can I see them?"

"They're in the back room with the Mathieu woman and that singer. I'll show you, but the kid stays here. The boss is very touchy about the labels."

"Well, we've got confirmation now," Ray said, with satisfaction. "They've got Dayanne and Phara."

Sandy had stepped away to take Lena's call. She'd heard the good news about Dayanne and Phara. "Listen, guys. I know you're ready to do your thing, but if your suspects get any hint of an impending raid, Phara and Dayanne will be at risk."

"We know...," JanJak began.

"I know you know what you're doing. I don't question that, but I can give you an edge from the inside. Lena wants me to meet an important 'colleague' from New York at this location. Like now, tonight. She's on her way here herself in about half an hour."

"Sandy, you're a very capable, courageous woman, that I know for sure," Ray began. "But you can't go in there by yourself."

"But she won't be alone," Lizbet and Bobbi chorused from behind them. "Don't worry. We were discreet. We parked the car we borrowed from one of my cousins down the block and persuaded one of your gendarmes that we were legit so he let us in."

"Lizbet, with all due respect, this is police business," JanJak objected.

"It's my business too, now that I know Phara and Dayanne are my kin."

"Look," Sandy began. "Lizbet and I will be fine, and we'll be great cover for your operation. Sorry, Bobbi, but you'll have to hang back so your cover's not blown with Lena. We might still need you as our secret weapon."

Ray thought for a moment, remembering all the times he'd seen Sandy in action. He turned to JanJak. "Actually, they do make a point. At the very least, it'll knock them off balance. And we have them under surveillance, so we can move in fast if we need to."

"OK, but you're both going to wear a wire so we can come in and save the day like Sir Galahad, if we have to," JanJak added, only half joking.

A few minutes later, Ray, JanJak and Bobbi focused on the center monitor as a small car carrying Sandy and Lizbet pulled up and parked on the other side of the building. Sandy and Lizbet got out.

"It looks kind of dicey, Sandy. I'm glad I'm here with you to provide a little extra protection," she nudged her friend playfully.

"Oh, there you are!" A young man in a business suit emerged from a door just behind them. "I'm Peter Johnson. I work for Bobbi, I mean, I used to. Now, of course, I work for Lena Morris. Lena asked me to meet you. She's running a tad late."

"And Bobbi? Is she coming with Lena, or is she already here?" Sandy asked, aware of this man's duplicitous behavior toward her friend.

"Oh, no. Lena sent Bobbi to check out this hot new designer at some club downtown. Right this way, ladies."

Fifteen minutes later, the task force in and around the van was preparing to move on the suspects. On the monitor, they had witnessed children chained to sewing machines and young women cowering at the machines threatened by large thugs wielding base ball bats. The audio made it loud and clear that this was one of those sweatshops fueled by the work of the youngest, most vulnerable migrant worker slaves. When Savant and Officer Holly moved on to an office down a dark hall, what they saw and heard made them mobilize their forces pronto.

"Stay here, Bobbi. If I signal we need reinforcements, call this number and tell Claude Rainier to get over here," JanJak said, as he gathered his gear.

Phara and Dayanne were seated in a corner of the office. They looked haggard, drugged and in shock. Lizbet had been pushed down onto the floor. Lena Moore had arrived and was screaming at Sandy. "Did you think you could fool me *Dr. Sandra Troux*? I knew you were patronizing me when I gave you my phony investment pitch. I knew you'd tell Bobbi everything. Now you'll suffer the same fate as these Haitian busybodies – suffocating to death in a hot ship container on a long, long voyage to Hell. And Bobbi? Once she sets me up to look good for the company, I'll make sure any incriminating evidence points directly to her."

Suddenly, pandemonium broke out. The odor of tear gas mixed with the stale stench of a hot metal building whose windows were bolted shut. Shouts of "Police! Lapolis! Drop Your Guns! Drop Zam Ou!" mingled with the sound of screaming, crying children, clearly traumatized by the noise, the smells and the encroaching violence.

Ray led the way with a squadron of men, charging into a phalanx of thugs who barely had time to reach their Glock rifles, much less use them. As the men battled to subdue the felons responsible for the kidnapping and deaths of juveniles too many to count, a second battle was in play in the upstairs office.

Lizbet had grabbed a heavy waste can and flung it hard into the groin of the thug who'd thrown her to the floor. Officer Holly threw him against the wall and handcuffed him, then helped Lizbet get up.

Sandy and Lena were struggling for control. As Sandy parried and kicked and chopped, using her best tai qi and karate moves, Lena answered in kind. "I figured you for a gutter fighter, Lena. You surprise me."

"Ha! I have a brown belt in karate, and I'm much younger than you. Prepare to lose!"

"Oh, I think not, Lena. I have a black belt." Sandy clearly had the upper hand, until Peter Johnson pushed her off balance.

Suddenly, Luc Savant, police informer, showed his true colors – traitorous sleaze bag. He knocked the young officer unconscious with the handle of a Glock pistol he had hidden in his boot. Then he grabbed Sandy. "We need to go, Lena. Now! Through your hidden door and up to the roof."

He threw an extra pistol at Peter Johnson. "You too, pretty boy! Shoot the old one and bring the other two. They're too drugged to fight you. Let's go!"

He held Sandy off balance and in a tight grip. *He's strong, but if I can just regain my footing and knock him off balance...there!* She managed to free herself, and almost had him when he succeeded in pushing her back down the stairs. She caught herself just as the door at the top of the stairs slammed shut. She heard the lock. Then, she heard the screams of children below and smelled smoke.

She did a quick about face, stopping in the office to discover that Peter Johnson had panicked and tried to run, but was now in police custody. JanJak had Phara and Dayanne in each arm. Lizbet grabbed her bag on top of the desk, stuffed in some papers that seemed important, and ran for the door.

Fire had broken out in the work room. Sandy, Ray and several of the task force were in there, freeing children, handing them to the older girls to carry out.

Just when they thought they had them all, Sandy heard a child cry out, "Mamé, Mamé!" She found her – a little girl barely about 5 years old – cowering near a corner, chained to a metal sewing table, just a few feet from the encroaching flames. She grabbed the closest heaviest thing she could find – a metal box containing scissors and various tools. With all her might, she smashed the chain's lock once, twice, three times until it clicked open. Sandy lifted the crying child in her arms just as the flames engulfed the corner.

She met Ray, running toward the stairs, carrying three small children in his arms. They both barreled down the hall and outside into the light and the fresh air. The building collapsed, just as the fire department arrived.

A quarter of a mile away, Lena, Luc, and two huge thugs dressed in Army/Navy Store fatigues, raced to the end of another flat-roofed metal warehouse, stepped through a trap door and into the building. In the ground floor garage, a black van was waiting for them. As they sped off, deeper into the Delmas district, Lena vowed with rage, "I'll get them, I'll get them."

"Lena, your cover is blown now and so is mine," Luc Savant cautioned. "It would be best to take your cache of money and jewels and disappear for a while. Perhaps in the Dominican Republic. I have friends there, and you still have your secret operation outside San Cristobal."

"I'm not defeated. They don't know how extensive my operation is. I'll get them sometime, somewhere," Lena said, her eyes now glazing with rage. "Find out where they are. And wherever…"

❧

The children and young women were all taken to the Holy Trinity Children's Hospital to be checked and cared for. Father Gabriel Mathieu was taking charge of finding them safe haven in the Holy Trinity Children's Home and among his parishioners.

Miraculously, Dayanne and Phara were in good condition, in spite of being drugged during their imprisonment. They hadn't been beaten or molested. Apparently, Lena had planned to ransom them until that morning when they saw her for the first time, and her cover was blown.

Ray suggested that they all go back to his hotel suite, which had acted as temporary HQ for the Fugitive Task Force. He wanted them to stay below the Haitian National Police radar, suspecting some ties with sweatshop criminals. Neither he nor JanJak thought it would be safe for them to return to their homes or stay with any relatives yet. After much appreciated showers and some food, they were resting.

JanJak took Lizbet and Bobbi back to the Holly Guest House to get some fresh clothes for Phara and Dayanne. Sandy went with them to the lobby, leaving Ray to watch over the exhausted women. She stopped in the store off the lobby for aspirin, toothpaste and brushes and combs for both women, and then spied herself in a mirror near the hotel's beauty salon. *Girl, you could use a haircut.* But it was way after hours, almost 3 a.m.: the shop was closed.

Fifteen minutes. That's all it took. For vanity to delay her. For two women who'd already faced and survived great danger to be endangered once again. For a man she was beginning to think the world of to be imperiled.

Lucky for all of them, Sandy had been just off the lobby near the rear service elevators – in time to see two non-uniformed hotel "staff" wheel a large laundry bin from an elevator and out the door toward a waiting a black minivan. She saw them dray Ray, Phara and Dayanne out and shove them into the vehicle. Ray was bloody. His arm was dangled at an odd angle. He had put up a fight. *No time to tell anyone at the hotel.* With no weapon on her, except her pocket knife, she ran to the hotel's nearby taxi stand, found a waiting driver, handed him a US$50 bill and said, "Follow that van and don't lose them!"

The driver, apparently a great fan of American cop shows, was thrilled. With a flashing grin, he said, "Don't worry, Missus. I'll stay on their tail! I will be like McGiver or those hot detectives Rizzoli & Isles!"

As they weaved through the city, Sandy called Bobbi on her cell. "Bobbi, Phara, Dayanne and Ray have been taken again. Yes. I'm racing after the van holding them. Put JanJak on."

"We've just turned down Rue Lysius Salomon. I think we're headed toward the port."

"Oh, yes, Missus, we are. Oh, hang on, they are making a turn. I will follow."

Sandy hung on for dear life, her cell phone dropping to the floor of the cab. She knew JanJak would marshal his forces to catch up. She also knew she couldn't wait for them. Before long, the taxi slowed as she and her "partner" in the chase spied the black van ahead, unloading their "cargo" into a huge orange shipping container. She was too late. She watched, as it was attached to a giant crane and raised high above. For a moment, her eyes couldn't believe it when she saw the name of the docked ship the container was heading toward: Starlight Argent.

Sandy picked up her cell phone and moved out of the taxi, first giving her "Rizzoli" driver a paper with JanJak's cell number and a scribbled note: *Phara, Dayanne, Ray in container on board Starlight Argent ship…Intercept…Am stowing aboard.*

She made her way stealthily toward the ship, undetected, just in time to see the container about to be lowered onto the docked ship. She took a quick photo with her phone and memorized what she could of the container's markings. Then two more containers looking identical to the first were also stowed onboard. *Which one was the right one?*

She spied some members of the crew carrying bags and boxes of food up the gangplank at the stern of the ship. She waited until the last one was halfway up, grabbed a box full of produce and hoisted it up on her right shoulder, hiding her face. She was wearing the old, baggy, worn-out guayabera shirt and brown trucker hat her "Rizzoli" driver had given her to disguise herself. She pulled the hat down more to cover her face. Once onboard, she dropped the box in a pile and disappeared, hiding herself away.

The ship had already reached the 12-mile limit and

was headed out into sea waters when Inspector JanJak Mathieu arrived at the port and at the right dock. Neither the National Police of Port-au-Prince nor the Port Authority was willing to reverse the course of the Starlight Argent.

20 Buried Alive

CONTAINERS ON THE STARLIGHT ARGENT were stacked six high, ten from port to starboard and ten from prow to stern, about 600 on an average ship. Stacked in a dense block, so that any container not on an end or with its doors exposed were impossible to access. Sandy ducked and hid, searching for the container that imprisoned Ray, Phara and Dayanne, and trafficked Haitian children destined for North American sweatshops, farm and domestic labor imprisoned in a container. After two days at sea, Sandy had made herself known to Captain Francois Langouste. *I have to chance it. There have to be records of the containers and their placement.*

The captain was initially suspicious of this silver-haired American, her fluency in French and her fanciful story of captives, UNODC officials, Haitian singers, trafficked children, but at last reversed his attitude. He offered Sandy a meal, her first in two days – curried coconut shrimp with sweet potato fries, while she told him in more detail about Phara, Dayanne and Ray. She told how anxious she was that they might be dying in a container stacked in the middle of all the others – inaccessible. Rescue impossible. She described what they

225

had found at horrible sweatshops in Haiti. How she, Ray and her friends were working with the Fugitive Taskforce in NYC/Newark and Haiti. She explained why she, Bobbi and Lizbet were in Haiti and how they were within moments of nabbing both a gang of traffickers and the ringleader, a possible murderer.

"That food was more than delicious; it was restorative, Captain Langouste. And now you understand why I stowed away. I escaped capture from the hotel only because I had gone down to get some items. I saw them being shoved into a black limo. I followed and by the time I found the right ship, several containers were being lowered. One of them in the middle of the block. I'm so worried my friends will die before we reach port and can release them – suffocate, die from heat stroke, bleed to death, something agonizing. Captain Langouste, this is a huge case and your help is critical. Isn't there any way to identify the right container, move it around and get them out?"

Sandy and the captain walked by the throbbing engines, various control rooms for water, sewage, crane, and electrical systems, and into the section of the ship with cabins and berths. "Here is yours, Dr. Troux, I hope you will be comfortable. Dinner is at 7:30 p.m.. Rest well. I will certainly send messages to all you've asked me to. But as I explained, we have to wait until the next port where we are off loading some containers before we can shift things around and find them. There are a number of containers marked with initial number that are due for Port Newark. But which one is the critical one?" He pursed his lips and raised his hands in a French gesture that said, who can tell? "We are another two days before we make Charleston, South Carolina in the United States, especially with the weather – maybe an early tropical storm. Perhaps we can make a stop earlier." At that the ship lurched. "You see what I mean? Believe me, Dr.Troux, I will do everything I can. I, too, am anxious."

"But you will send those messages. I have texted, but I'm not sure of a signal."

He ushered her to her cabin and reassured her he would send the messages. The cabin was simply furnished with a single bed and under bed drawer, a chair and a table. It had only a curtained space for hanging clothing. Sandy laughed to herself. *Lizbet might be appalled, but since I have only what I'm standing up in, looks great!* The whole cabin was a luxury suite when she thought of Ray and Dayanne and Phara, and those small terrified faces she had glimpsed. *A shower and a nap and then...I have to find them no matter what the captain says.* Three hours later, Sandy woke refreshed. She had washed out the clothes she'd been wearing and they were dry enough, clean and no longer stinking. She thought again and again of her friends and the children. She was sure she had seen children, sweating out their last body moisture. She heard a helicopter beating overhead. It circled and seemed as if it was going to splash down, but then it flew away. Not for the last time, did Sandra Troux wish for her friends Bobbi and Lizbet and for Ray.

She crossed to the cabin door, turning back to see if she had gotten all her belongings meager as they were while pressing down on the door latch. *Nothing. Locked in.* Moments passed as she got over her disbelief. *Sandy, you're losing it. How could you have been taken in by that old fox?* She looked out of her port hole to see the skies darkening and *yes, just as the Captain had predicted, the seas rising in a quickening storm.* Back to the cabin door. From her waist pack she took out her Swiss Army knife, the one she had been given by her mother, and set to work on the door lock. *I've got to find them and get them out of that death trap. If they haven't perished from thirst and heat, the rolling ship may batter them to death in the container.*

Sandy crept down the corridor, looking and listening for footsteps or voices. *So far, so good.* She remembered the layout of the ship's living and working quarters from Captain Langouste's tour and her stowaway time. She climbed on deck and ducked behind a container. From the bridge, the captain had showed her how the entire load of containers could be seen. In the bridge, there was no longer a helm, that old wheel, to steer the ship – only glowing banks of dials and computer screens. He explained that at night there were flood lights over the entire load of containers. *How am I going to find the right container without being found myself?*

Captain Langouste had also shown her three possible containers with the correct shipping information and their locations. Only one was possible for her to reach, if she could avoid discovery. It was the last container on the final row at the stern. *A one-in-three chance. Better than a sharp stick in the eye as Simone used to say. I'll take it. Now to make my way to the electrical controls, get back on deck, get to the* stern *without being seen, figure out how to open the container doors, pray they are not locked, stay on my feet with the deck rolling, and not throw up or get washed overboard. Piece of cake,* she thought grimly.

Luck and not a little running, ducking out of sight, finger crossing, and risk taking had also helped. She climbed up to the huge container doors that faced the stern and the churning heaving seas behind them. *Turn your head away, you'll throw up for sure.* In their haste to get the container on board and the ship underway, the padlocks threaded through the catches over the bars to which the rotating handles were attached *seemed, maybe, yes, not snapped completely shut.* With the heaving seas jolting her, and lashing rain and wind battering her, Sandy held on for dear life, for hers, for Ray's, for Dayanne's and Phara's, and for the children's. *Only let it be this container. It has to be.* She banged her fist against the catch to shove it upward in order to release the handle bars and swivel them outward. *This time has to work. Almost.* Her hand was bleeding. She banged upward again and the catch gave. Quickly she pulled out the handles, rotated them and lifted, the upright bars that held the door in place with sockets top and bottom released, and it swung open, almost swinging her out over the sea. She reached around the edge of the door and scooted onto the floor of the container. *Please, please let this one be the one.* She scrabbled up from her knees and stood facing the cavernous dark, outlined against the lighter sky and sea behind her. *Just like Amaelie. Only this time I'm going to get the buggers; they're not going to get me.* Her eyes adjusted. "Hey, Ray, wanna hug?"

Sandy heard the throbbing of helicopters and, better yet, a booming voice, announcing the U.S. Coast Guard coming aboard. "We'd better stay here. Safer, don't you think?" Ray was in terrible shape, dazed and feverish, arm definitely broken. Phara and Dayanne a little better, but battered by the rolling ship. *The children, yes,* she had seen correctly, *twenty-five children between 12-15 were in pretty bad shape. Really dehydrated, terrified, just skin and bones.* Sandy stripped off her shirt and held it out in the rain. "The children can suck some moisture from the cloth. Phara, Dayanne, can you tear part of skirts? As soon as I get them wet, pass them back to the children." She was quite a sight to the U.S. Miami Coast Guard cutters and helicopters alike, stripped to the waist in her bra, balancing in the open container door, doing what looked like the washing!

Ray's hospital room in UMDNJ in Newark, where the former captives had been airlifted was quiet and peaceful. He laid holding Sandy's hand. "Phara and Dayanne are down the hall, and the children are doing amazingly well. But there's no sight of Lena," she told him. "Somehow, she got away. Nobody knows where she is. Sandy had not given up on Lena. She was determined to get her. Bobbi and Lizbet walked into Ray's room.

"Here's your iced tea, Sandy," Lizbet said, handing her a tall cup. "Ray, you look pretty good for a guy with a broken arm and a fever, bopped over the head and locked up in a 110 degree stinky metal box with no water for two days."

"Glad to see you're back with us, Ray. You doing OK?" Bobbi walked over to his window. She turned back and then in that Star Trek mind meld thing she and Sandy did all too often, she and Sandy said, "Set a trap for Lena – how and what will get her? I'm sure she murdered Cassandra Innocent back in Newark to keep her real plans hidden. So she'll have to confess as well, since there's really no tangible evidence."

"Oh, I forgot," Lizbet said, rooted around in her bag and held up the plans she had scooped up from the desk in the Delmas building. "Will these help?"

A tactical huddle over, Sandy said, "Yes, I think it just might work. OK, Bobbi, you call the Boys at HQ and tell them you have some really incriminating evidence that puts you in the clear and points elsewhere. But, you have something important to do in Montclair before you come into the City. You're going to a quilt exhibit, honoring one of your best friend's aunt's artistry."

"Right, I'll say, I have the plans with me and will keep them with me safe until I turn them over to the President when I get into the office this evening. That'll give them time to contact Lena. I'm sure they are in contact. Maybe she's already back in NYC: one of those looking for something, someone in plain sight things."

"Lizbet and I will go to the exhibit, and if she doesn't show up there we'll take the walking tour to the Howe House. You stay out of sight, but nearby and we'll bemoan that you had to go to the office on important business, but that you gave me something to hold for you for safekeeping. We'll do a flanking two-pronged action. We'll be the bait."

~∾~

"Yeah, she's in Montclair at a quilt exhibit and has the plans. You'd better get them or we're all done for. A quilt exhibit, for God's sake! Unbelievable air head."

"Listen you assholes," Lena's suck-up-to-the-Boys manner gone, "you just take care of things at your end. I know what to do and how to handle everything. There'll be no loose ends here. You just make sure about your end."

~∾~

Jane Eliasof, executive director of the Montclair Historical Society welcomed New Jersey's own Faith Ringgold and other quilters to the Crane House's story quilt exhibit – *Story in Quilts: The Wellspring*. She introduced Lizbet, representing her aunt, Alice Greeley Mason, "who's lynching theme quilts are unique and so topical. Ms. Ringgold's and Mrs. Mason's quilts represent one way the organization is honoring the importance of African American women artists whose chosen medium and technique is quilting." Eliasof continued, "The highlight of this exhibit is a newly discovered Reconstruction Era quilter, Lilianna Abbott Greeley. And we are thrilled to be the premiere site for its first showing."

Lizbet concluded her remarks, "We are both so proud of Lilianna. Sandy and I have been friends since we were ten years old and now, through the Abbott family connection, we discovered we are cousins as well. This quilt is named *The Bridge of Love*. Lilianna certainly knew how love could bridge the greatest divides." Lizbet shot her friend a look that said love bridges.

After the exhibit, Sandy and Lizbet joined the walking tour that would take them to the Howe House a few blocks away. The docent explained that "the original owner of this house," gesturing to the newly repainted Crane House, "was Israel Crane, known as King Crane for his ownership and operation of the Newark-Pompton Turnpike in the mid-18th century. He was also a prominent merchant with ties to the cotton industry and an owner of slaves. His Federal-style mansion was built 20 years after the signing of the Declaration of Independence when Montclair was still known as Cranetown."

She waved the group along, "Less than a mile away, 369 Claremont Avenue is the address of one of Crane's former slaves. Come along, Ladies. In 1813, Crane purchased James Howe for $50. Crane left Howe his freedom, along with the house, $600 and some of his 'best land' in his 1831 will. Maybe he was being generous manumitting a slave, and maybe Howe was Crane's son! Their true relationship and Crane's motives are lost in time. However, the Montclair Township Council passed an ordinance in January 2008, designating both the house and the property as landmarks. It is dignified by its old age and significant past. Mr. Howe was finally given what he must have striven for all his life: liberty. His former home has great potential to educate us. It's a story that may not be easy to hear, but most certainly should be told. The failures of Reconstruction are evident in the segregations of our town and across the nation: African Americans struggled, and too many still struggle, to find their own way in society without much help. Africans arrived here against their will and were never given the start in a free life that they most assuredly deserved. Whatever were Israel Crane's motives, love, guilt, moral awakening, only in death did he do right by James Howe. Given the escalation of murders of African Americans by white men, the Historical Society hopes that honoring the strength and power of the amazing quilt artists and telling James Howe and Israel Crane's story will help bring about *a new day* in America. Thank you, Ladies and Gentlemen. I hope you enjoyed your tour."

"You want to solve mysteries, do you, Sandy Troux? Well, choke on them, an echoed voice drifted down on a flutter of little butterfly wings. Sandy staggered to her feet, steadying herself with a hand on a rough wall. Dazed, she looked up, shading her eyes, but couldn't see exactly what they were against the glare. One gently landed on her upturned cheek. She touched it as others floated down on her head and on a dark bundle lying nearby. Sandy turned around and around and then turned in the opposite direction. *Whew, I'm really dizzy or something. Drunk, maybe? Drugged? Where am I? Who's here?*

In the dimness at the bottom of the cistern, Sandy took one of the little butterfly wings and held it up to the light. Now that her head was clearing and her vision sharpening, she could see she was holding a little black shimmering rectangle. More rectangles floated down. Sandy squatted down and picked up a handful – all the same: the odd floating items she thought were butterfly wings were actually clothing labels. The raised glimmering letters read SA.

"Sandy, is that you?" Lizbet sat up, her hand to the back of her head. She, too was peering at the little black rectangles figured with a curving gold 'S' overlapped with a rounded capital 'A.'

"Labels," they both exclaimed. "They're fakes," Sandy added. The last little label fluttered down on the echoing voice.

"You stupid women, these are mine – my brand labels, the new Studio August clothing line. I've got all the new technology embedded in that shimmer – programmable micro-lens technology. This line will capture global share and make me a rich, rich woman. A 1% woman. A one percenter. I will be the top 1% of the 1%!" Lena Van Vleck Morris stood, leaning over the edge of the Howe House cistern, her hands on her upper thighs, laughing for all she was worth. "And you silly bitches thought you could stop me. But if you cooperate and hand over the plans, I will let you out."

Completely clear headed now, Sandy remembered how she and Lizbet strolled around the grounds of the Howe House, inviting an attack by Lena, while looking at the projected landscape plans for new plantings. They had come to an area still to be cleared of tangle where some workmen stood around a large round opening in the earth. Something about one of the men had resonated, tickled a faint memory. "Lizbet?" she remembered asking and then remembered nothing more. But now, she knew what had resonated. The shape of the biggest man was the shape of the man behind the tree in Military Park at Cassandra Innocent's murder and the shape of the man driving the sedan that rammed them at Port Newark and bolted away into the storm and probably the same man – men – who stalked Anna and Dad. And Haiti as well? Lena's men.

"Come on, come on," Sandy muttered under her breath. "Lizbet, say something to her. Get her going. I'm going to edge around. I think I see some loose stones over there. Just the right size. I want you to distract her. See how she's leaning over? I'll see if I can strike her with a shot to the head.

Lena Van Vleck Morris leaned over further, attempting a view of the bottom of the cistern. "You can't get out you know. And everybody's gone. We're the only one's here. How is that, you wonder? These are my men, MY men, who are working this job. They have orders to make this cistern safe, so they are ready to put the cover back on and then cement it in place. You'll be buried alive, if you don't drown first. It is a cistern after all. Unless of course, you give me the plans." Lena teased and leaned over even further, "Oops! a little too much there. Almost went in myself and joined you in your final resting place." She chuckled again as she knelt on the cistern lip, peering over unmindful of its crumbling edge. "There is something so satisfying, so symmetrical, so balanced even, that the two of you, descendents of the same family of slave holders and slaves, yes, I know your little secrets, AND cousins at the same time, will spend your last days – if it would take days for you to drown or suffocate – and an eternity together here at the Freed Slave House – freed by one of my ancestors. You do see the irony, don't you?"

Lizbet called up to her captor, "One of your ancestors?"

"Oh, you two are really stupid. "I'm descended from Natty Crane, get it? Nathaniel Israel Crane, descendent of Israel Crane. Surely you know this history? I am a Crane on one side and descended from Clyde Van Vleck on the other. You know THE Clyde van Vleck. Maybe you are related to me, too, Mzzz Lizbet. Surely you figured that out. Especially you, Know Everything Lizbet Sheridan. Or you, Ms. Mystery Solver Troux. What's the matter, cat got your tongues? Oh, oh, that was soooo childish." A gold locket swung out over the cistern opening as Lena pushed her head further and further forward.

"NO, I don't know," Lizbet called up. Sandy nodded as if to say keep her talking and distracted. She edged further around until she was opposite Lena. *Pray I have the strength and enough width to get a good trajectory.*

"Some of the land Howe inherited is where he had this cistern dug. You see the irony now, don't you?" She slapped her thighs with glee. "A freed slave, making the prison for me to use. I've enslaved The Great Sandra Troux and the Walking Encyclopedia Lizbet Sheridan," she chanted again. "No one will ever, ever know what happened to you two."

Sandy sidled around a bit more and cut her eyes at Lizbet who began to whimper and beg, "Please, Lena, Ms. Morris, please, we won't tell anything. I promise. Sandy promises, don't you, Sandy?" They shot glances at each other in agreement.

"Oh the Great Sandra Troux is going to beg. I want to hear that!"

"I am begging, Lena, I mean Miss Morris. I'm begging, too. Please, Lena. I'll call off the Fugitive Task Force. I'll say I was mistaken. I'll say I tripped and fell when we were exploring and hit my head and I don't remember anything. You'll have time to get away. I've got the plans right here. I'll destroy them. 'Plans, what plans,' I'll say. I won't remember about plans, or how we met, or about Cassandra's death, or labels, or anything. After all, I'm an old lady. We don't have such good memories. Please Lena, think about my daughter, my grandchildren."

"Oh, yes, Cassandra, Cassandra Innocent," Lena sneered. "She thought she was so smart, too. I fixed her. She thought she was going to wreck my operation. Nobody gets in my way. And she didn't."

Sandy held her breath. Now to get her to confess. "No, Lena, you're the smart one," she began carefully. We're down here, and you're up there. You fixed Cassandra. How was that possible? How could you? You were with us."

"You really must be slipping. Not only did I fix her myself, I grabbed the diaries right from under your noses. You were so wrapped up in talking to that dolt Oliver, you didn't even see me snag the leather case with MY ancestors' diaries. I walked right out with all that stuff in my tote bag."

"OK, I see. But how could you fix Cassandra? You were with us all the time," Sandy said tentatively and paused, as if she were at last working out how the murder had happened. "So, you lied about breaking your heel. Is that it?

"You really are slow witted. Don't know why everyone thinks you're so smart. It was simple. She didn't suspect a thing. I just walked up to her and slid the knife in her back, walked away, handed it to one of my men, and came to the luncheon with that lame excuse, which all of you believed.

"You think you're so wonderful, so amazing, so all that! You and your so-called friends, friends for life, so smug, so…" she sputtered. Her bile was so acidic she couldn't think of worse things to say. She took a deep breath and sneered, "Do you know where your *friend* Bobbi, Ms. Almighty Too Good Bobbi Power is right now?" She leaned further over.

"No, you haven't hurt her? We were expecting her here. We've been so worried that she hasn't come." Sandy called up, sounding distraught while gauging the angle of her shot and how much room she had for her pitch. Lizbet began to sob loudly her face in her hands. She peeked through her fingers at Sandy. "Where is she?

You've been tormenting her? Why? What did she ever do to you but mentor you, help you navigate that anti-woman world. Teach you all the strategies to stay afloat and succeed. Do you know? What have you done with her?" Sandy put steely anger in her tone.

"Oh, you'll never guess where she is right this second."

"I think I just might guess, Lena. In fact, I think I know where she is right this second," Sandy said suddenly, speaking calmly.

Lizbet scooped up a double handful of labels, floating on the pools of water, puddling the floor of the cistern, threw them in the air and laughed, "Me, too. I know where she is right this second."

Lena scowled at this unexpected turn and scrabbled at the edge as she leaned over even further enraged that her insults and Sandy and Lizbet's perilous situation now seemed to amuse instead of frighten them.

"Yes, indeedy," Sandy grinned even wider, "I do know. Because you, YOU stupid woman have never, ever gotten her. But you should have. She is a truly good woman. She would always have helped you. That's what REAL women do for each other. We support each other. We do everything to make the world right. We stick together. That's real power. That's Bobbi's power!

"So, Missss murdering, thieving, double-crossing, job-snatching, larcenous corporate spy, I have a long overdue message for you."

Sandy reared back, wound up and shouted while she snapped her arm and fired off the sharp rock she had been weighing, "YOU, Lena Van Vleck Morris, ARE FIRED!"

Lizbet burst into gales of laughter and danced around tossing the labels in the air.

Lena, a furious Lena, an enraged Lena, leaned just a fraction too far forward, the mortar of the compromised cistern edge stone blocks crumbled a bit more, Sandy's rock hit its target square on her nose causing her to jerk her hand up in self-protection, Lizbet's gleeful dance distracted her, and Bobbi who had been standing behind her just in Sandy's sight, placed a daintily Prada-shod foot in the middle of Lena's back and tipped her over the edge. "Yep," Bobbi echoed, "you are so fired."

21 All Threads Meet

"YEP, THEY GOT THEM ALL: Lena and the Black Sedan Guys in Montclair; the shipping guys at Port Newark. Tony and Lou snagged them. The Boys at HQ; the thugs in Haiti, the Captain in Miami. A clean, coordinated sweep, thanks to local PD in Montclair and Newark and Miami; and that fabulous Fugitive Task Force." Sandy sat on the edge of Ray's bed. "You should have seen Lena, fighting, mud splattered, foul mouthed. It was a great sight." She pushed him down when he tried to get out of his bed to say goodbye to Lizbet and Bobbi.

"So, Lena was behind everything," Sandy said. "She found out about the meeting that Cassandra had in Military Park. Cassandra was just getting too close to the truth. She was a loose end that had to be tied up. Cassandra thought she was meeting Phara, and Phara thought she was meeting Cassandra. But, Lena intercepted the texts and changed the times just enough so that they missed meeting, giving her enough time to go to the park and kill her, just as she said. Then, she handed off the knife to one of her black sedan guys. And then came to lunch with us. Cold. Very cold."

"Bobbi took up the account. "The HQ boys," as she

called them," my supervisors, can you believe it? They thought they were playing her, but she was playing them all the time. She got them to embezzle money to pay for her criminal operation. But, they thought she was going to be the scapegoat for their illegal corporate operation. Check and checkmate. It'll take months to sort everything out. But that's OK, because I'll be doing that."

"Bobbi, you going now?"

"Into the City to be reinstated, get that corner office, a raise, a promotion, and take back my project. I'm also going to reinstate Pierre St. Claire as CMO so he can retire at the end of the year with no loss in benefits, as he originally planned.

"Oh, and Colin is flying over next week. We're going down to South Carolina to look at how we can use his new fiber source, stinging nettles, to make the most gorgeous, gleaming fabric you ever saw – beyond sustainable." She gave Sandy and Lizbet hugs. "We good?"

"Always," they replied.

"Wait a minute. Don't leave yet. I have news, too. First, I want to show you something." Lizbet took out a gold locket. "This is the locket *That Woman* was wearing. Amaelie's locket, which Natty Crane stole. So, look. I pried up the frame around the picture of Amaelie and see…"

"Oh, my," Sandy said, tearing up. Ray squeezed her hand tightly.

"Amazing," Bobbi said eyes wide.

"Yes, it's them, a pencil sketch of Amaelie and Osner.

And under Fleetwood's photo is one of Lilianna." She put her thumbnail under that frame to show Lilianna's photo at about twenty-one. "They were always together even if they were miles and even centuries apart." Lizbet said, passing tissues out to Sandy, Bobbi, and Ray and taking one for herself. "Now my other news is good, too. Amanda and her wife have invited me back to Greensboro. They have someone they want me to meet. Tra La!"

When the friends had gone, Sandy and Ray were quiet for a while. Again, he started to get up. "Not so fast." Sandy walked quickly to the door, peeked out and then locked it. She pulled the sheet back from Ray, gave an appreciative look, stripped off and slipped in beside him. "This time, you're my captive."

The End

SNEAK PEEK

Peril at the Pilato

1   Missing in Euskadi Herria

SANDY WAS SHAKEN. The frantic call from her goddaughter Sophie Rose Power in California had jolted her awake. It was 1:30 a.m. But, already, she was primed for action.

"Calm down, Sophie. Take a breath. What do you mean your Mom's missing?"

"She's visiting our cousins in the Basque Country of Spain and having a great time. They're wonderful, warm people, welcomed her with open arms, even had a birthday celebration for her the day she arrived."

"Yes, that I know," Sandy said, more patiently than she felt, but she knew Sophie needed to unwind a little so she could question her. She waited.

"Well, the Santiagos Festival in their town of Ermua just ended on Thursday, and some of the younger cousins thought it would be great fun to drive to Donastia-San Sebastian in Gipuzkoa Province and spend the weekend.

It didn't take much pleading to convince Mom to go as chaperone.

"She sent me a text message that she'd be back Monday around noon my time, so we could Skype then."

"It's only Saturday, Sophie. What happened between yesterday and now? Do you know?"

"I got an emergency telephone call from our cousins Ismael and Inma an hour ago. A telephone call! They never do that. They always email and set up a Skype call.

"They haven't heard from them at all since they left. No calls, no texts, no emails. Nada. All their cell phones go to message. It's 8:30 a.m. Sunday in Ermua, and there's been no word for more than 36 hours!"

"I assume they've already checked for accidents?" Sandy asked, knowing the answer would be yes.

"No reported accidents along the route they were taking. In fact, none at all in the two provinces they were driving through. The police even insist that the ETA separatists in the entire north autonomous region have been quiet for months. So they don't suspect terrorist activity."

Sophie paused. "Wow. That gives me chills all the same."

"OK, Sophie," Sandy said, her take charge adrenalin pumping. "Give me your cousins' phone numbers – home, cell, work, and their email address. Ray's in Dublin at a conference, but I'll call him and get a referral to local police in Bilbao or Donastia-San Sebastian or both. I'll also contact your cousins for an update. As soon as I can talk to someone on the ground there, I'll text you."

"I want to go over, Aunt Sandy, if she isn't found by the end of tomorrow, I want to go over. My passport's up-to-date."

"OK, just in case, check for flights that go through O'Hare to Bilbao or Madrid," Sandy said. "I don't want you embarking on a search and rescue alone. Got it?"

"Got it. Thanks Aunt Sandy. Love you."

"Love you, too, sweetie. And don't worry. They probably just had car trouble, and they're in an area with no cell reception. Think positively."

You too, Sandy. Think positively and positively don't worry!

FOUR DAYS EARLIER

Bobbi sat in the first row facing the Pilato court. It was just off the town square in the small Basque town of Ermua in Bizkaia Province. Her cousin Inma was explaining the nuances of the ancient hand ball game of pilato. "I've seen a version of this game in Bridgeport, Connecticut back home. They call it Jai Alai, and the court has four full walls, not two. And the players had these huge baskets attached to one arm," Bobbi told Inma in her basic Spanish. Inma spoke little to no English and Bobbi's facility with Spanish was middlin' at best. Yet, the two had bonded instantly and somehow they always managed to understand each other.

"Every town and village in Euskadi Herria (the word for Basque Country in the Basque language) has a Pilato court in their center square. It is where the young boys learn the game and old men and women cheered and booed and taught them. It is a sport that fills us with great pride."

Bobbi knew that the game was very historic, traditional, and a source of our national identity for every Basque or descendent of a Basque in the world. It was played in many countries where the Basque had emigrated to, even the United States, with some variations here and there. It had been part of the Olympic Games at one time.

As she watched the game, she also scanned the crowd of Inma's friends, relatives and neighbors. It was time for the yearly Santiagos festival (known as Santixauak in Basque). Many people scheduled their vacations around this 4-day event. So there were also visitors to the small town from other parts of the province as well as other areas of Spain and surrounding countries. Most of the people gathered for today's afternoon game were "townees" as they'd be called back home. And most were passionately engrossed in the game.

"Do Jon and Luken play Pilato, Inma?"

She tilted her head back and laughed. "Oh, no, not my two tech-loving sons. They'd both rather be at their computers. When they're not, Jon is with his girlfriend, and Luken is playing music with his marching band. My husband, your cousin Ismael, and his brothers played the sport as boys and young men, but not so much now."

Their pleasant afternoon was interrupted by a disgruntled old man sitting behind them. He suddenly stood up, shaking both of his fists at a man who was backing away from the court into the main square. He yelled in Eustadi, the old Basque language, which was having a resurgence in the country. Inma didn't understand many words, but there were several people in the crowd who looked shocked and turned a hateful gaze toward the old man across the square. A man who suddenly made an angry hand gesture and stormed away.

There were shouts of "Traidor!" "Traidorearen!" and other phrases, not in Spanish, that Bobbi couldn't decipher.

"Traidor? Traitor? What is he a traitor for, Inma? Did they say?"

"To the Euskaldunak, to the Basque people. He and his father and his grandfather fought with Franco against their own people. Some say his father sent maps of the mountains of Bizkaia to help the Germans who bombed Guernika and Durango. He was later stoned to death. That man and his brothers vowed revenge."

Bobbi shook her head in disbelief as she watched the old man hobble away.

To be continued...

BOOK EXTRAS

Cast of Characters

This list of names is provided to help interested readers keep track of the many characters that populate *Secrets at Abbott House*. Nearly all spring from the imaginations of the authors and are not based on any real persons, living or deceased. Exceptions, such as historic figures, are identified.

Recurring Characters:

Dr. Sandra (Sandy) Troux: Series *shero* who is an amateur detective, retired university professor of Cultural Anthropology, widow of Peruvian artist **Joaquin Quinn**; daughter **June Troux Quinn**, son-in-law **Tim Booker**, and two granddaughters **Kat** (Katelyn) and **Charlie** (Charlotte).

Bobbi (Barbara Ann) Power: Sister sleuth and lifelong friend; divorced, single adoptive Mom of college-age China-born daughter **Sophie Rose**, high-tech expert and EVP of Global Marketing & New Business Development at an international fashion company

Lizbet (Elizabeth Lee) Sheridan: Sister sleuth and lifelong friend; lesbian, widow of wife **Joan Davis**; two grown sons, **Liam** and **Robert**; retired restaurateur and food specialist; a 1950s Korean/African-American adoptee, birth name Lee Bong Cha; adoptive parents were **Delores Lee Sheridan** and **Robert William Sheridan**; birth parents were **Lee Ae-Sook** and **Ben**

Greely, an American GI killed in Korean War

Dallas Walter Troux: Sandy's father and noted international journalist, retired; author of several historic investigative books on prominent political and military figures from the post-WWII era

Anna Green Troux: Dallas' second wife; originally au pair for the Troux family; became executive/research assistant after completing her business degree

Simone Cecile DuBois Troux: Dallas' first wife; Sandy's deceased photojournalist mother; born in France

Ray Morgan: Agent at United Nations Department of Crime (UNDOC) and Sandy's love interest.

U.S. Segment – Current Time Period

Lena Van Vleck Morris: Director of Marketing at Auguste Fashion Marketing International;

Phara Damour: Internationally renowned Haitian Stagoff; headline act in Montclair Concert for Haiti

****Cynthia Stagoff:** Organizer and manager of the Annual Montclair Concert for Haiti

Cassandra Innocent: Phara's childhood friend works for "Sweat Free Communities" and UNDOC

Oliver Tichenor: Director of New Jersey Historical

Society and **Sarah Pennington**, speaker at NJHS

Detective Breshelle Allison and **Sergeant Iris Pedilla:** Newark police officers with the major crimes unit

Appollo DuBane and **Samuel LaFitte:** False UPS delivery men

Helen Pawlawski: Bobbi's 85 year-old neighbor

Sally Soames: Bobbi's tenant.

Lou Lombardi and **Tony Marrara:** Port Newark longshoremen working undercover

Emmet Brown: Head of Security at NYC office of Bobbi's company, Auguste Fashion Marketing International, and Bobbi's friend

Executives at Bobbi's Company: **Etienne D'Arsenault**, Chief Executive Officer (CEO); **Lucio Veigas,** President of US Operations; **Klaus Vandervoort**, Chief Operations Officer (COO); **Harvey Steinbert**, Chief Financial Officer (CFO); and **Pierre St. Claire**, Chief Marketing Officer (CMO) and Bobbi's mentor and manager.

Bobbi's colleagues: **Hector Alberiz**, Executive Vice President of Manufacturing (EVP); **Stuart Ames**, Executive Vice President of Finance (EVP); and **Al Mackenzie**, Executive Vice President of Research & Development (EVP).

Betty Wilson: Senior Vice President of Human Resource Management (SVP).

Other Auguste Co-Workers: **Peter Johnson**, Bobbi's NYC administrative assistant; **Julianne Lopez**, Bobbi's Newark administrative assistant; **Harvey Simmons,** HR manager at Newark Center; **Carol Atkins**, president's executive assistant.

Detective Sam Roberts and **Officer Kevin McNally:** Montclair police officers

Aunt Babby (Babette Troux Scott): Dallas' aunt

Alice Greeley Mason: Story quilter, specializing in Lynching Stories from Black History

Amanda Mason: Alice's daughter

****William R. Trotter**: Civil War historian and neighbor of Alice Greeley Mason

Lucy Benedict: College intern and tour guide at Abbott Farm & Museum in Iva, South Carolina

Taylor Rice: Director of the Abbott House Farm & Museum in Iva South Carolina.

June (Junie) McIntire: Anderson County, South Carolina

****Jane Eliasof:** Director of Montclair Historical Society

U.S. Segment – 19th Century

Lillie Elise Fleurie Troux: Amaelie Abbott's younger sister; married to **Jacques (Jack) Pierre Troux**; Dallas Troux's grandparents.

Amaelie Ann Fleurie Abbott: Lillie's older sister; widow of Henry Fleetwood Abbott

Henry Fleetwood Abbott: Amaelie's husband, mortally wounded in the first major battle of Civil War

Amaelie and Henry Fleetwood Abbott's Children: **Henry Fleetwood II** (b. 1854), **Hezikiah Jackson** (b. 1856), and **Georgiana Belle** (b. 1860).

Osner Mathieu: Slave owned by Henry Fleetwood Abbott

Lilianna Fleur Abbott Greely (b. 1864): Bi-racial daughter of Amaelie Abbott

Minette: Amaelie's slave personal maid

Clyde Van Vleck: Union soldier from New Jersey

Nathaniel (Natty) Dey Crane: Scalawag and Union soldier from New Jersey.

** Actual Person

Haitian Segment

**Bishop James Theodore Holly: First Africa-American Bishop in the Protestant Episcopal Church; missionary Bishop of Haiti and pastor of the Holy Trinity Church in Port-au-Prince; historic figure who aided U.S. fugitive slaves and immigrants

Dayanne Mathieu: Missing Haitian fashion designer and boutique owner

JanJak Mathieu: Member of Caribbean arm of Fugitive Task Force

Father Gabriel Mathieu: Episcopal priest and director of the Bishop Holly Foundation

**Stevenson Mathieu: Haitian author who lives in Brooklyn, NY

**Lisa Tan: American freelance videographer and video editor

Captain Francois Langouste: Captain of the Liberian-registered container ship Starlight Argent

** Actual Person

Glossary

Bushwhacker: An irregular Confederate soldier or guerilla soldier during the Civil War.

Bummer: One of a horde of deserters, stragglers, runaway slaves and marauders who wreaked havoc on locals during the U.S. Civil War and also as part of General Sherman's army. The term was shortened to "bum" after 1870.

Capisce: Italian slang for "Do you understand?" Pronounced Capeesh.

Cormorants: Any of several voracious seabirds (Phalacrocoracidae) native to the Americas, Europe and Asia. They are noted for a long neck and distensible pouch located under the bill used for holding captured fish. Cormorants are used in China for catching fish. A second definition: a greedy person.

Creole: A person born in the West Indies or Spanish America of European ancestry (usually Spanish). Creole also describes a person born in Louisiana of French or Spanish ancestry mixed with African American. They speak a "creolized" form of French or Spanish.

Daguerreotype: An early photograph produced on a silver or silver-covered copper plate. There were also sometimes made on solid silver sheets. Images in daguerreotype portraits were typically unsmiling since the process of taking them was too long for people to hold a smile.

DNA Taggants: Plant-based genetic markers used on cartons and labels to authenticate products and detect counterfeiting.

Elbertas: Elberta peaches are slightly tart freestone hybrid peaches, named after the wife of the 19th century Georgia farmer who first cultivated it. Once highly popular, it has been replaced by sweeter peach varieties, though less luscious, in the American palette.

Glock: A handgun commonly used as a sidearm by law enforcement agencies and military organizations around the world; a popular choice for civilian home defense.

Guayabera: A loose fitting men's shirt (sometimes called a Wedding shirt) with two vertical rows of closely sewn pleats running the length of the front and back; often worn untucked.

Haitian Creole/Krèyol: "Creolized" French spoken as the native language of most Haitians.

Juneteenth: Also known as Freedom Day, Juneteenth is the oldest nationally celebrated commemoration of the ending of slavery in the United States. Originating in Galveston, Texas in 1865, the observance of June 19th as the African American Emancipation Day has spread across the United States and beyond.

Kroner : A cupronickel coin and monetary unit of Norway and Denmark, equal to 100 Euro. (Abbreviation: Kr., kr.)

Micro Lens: A small lens, generally with a diameter less than a millimeter (mm) and often as small as 10 micrometers (μm). The small size of the lenses means that a simple design can give good optical quality.

Micro printing: One of many anti-counterfeiting techniques used on currency and bank checks, as well as various other items of value. Very small text, usually too small to read with the naked eye, is printed onto the note or item.

Phragmites: Any of several tall grasses of the genus Phragmites, having plumed heads. They generally grow in marshy areas.

RECs: Renewable Energy Certificates (RECs) are tradable, non-tangible energy commodities in the U.S. that represent proof that 1 megawatt-hour (MWh) of electricity was generated from an eligible, renewable energy resource (e.g., electricity).

Scalawag: A native white Southerner who collaborated with the occupying forces during the Reconstruction era of the American South. A scalawag is considered a scamp or rascal, motivated by a desire for personal gain.

Story Quilt: A quilt that features an image(s) appliquéd in the center panel and surrounded by two fabric frames. The inner frame contains the text of the "story," written or embroidered; the outer frame serves as a border of solid fabric or patchwork.

UGRR, Depots & Stations: A network of secret routes and safe houses used by 19th century escaping slaves or freedom seekers in the U.S. in a flight to free Northern states and Canada. Safe houses and business were known as depots or stations; a conductor was someone who moved people from one place to another.

Family Trees

If you study these family trees, you'll find that Sandy and Lizbet are third cousins! Amaelie Abbot is Lizbet's great-great grandmother and Sandy's great-great-great aunt.

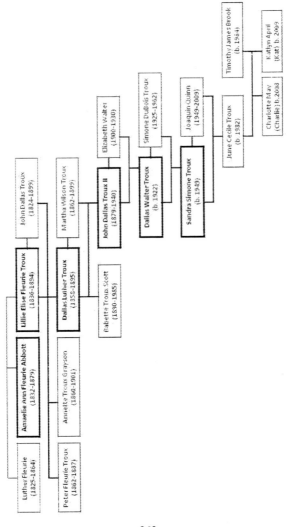

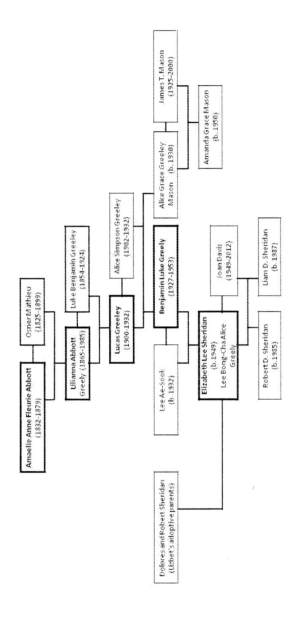

A Ride on the Underground Railroad

There are so many books and articles and websites rich with human stories and historic facts about the Underground Railroad that we could not do justice to this important topic. The ingenuity and bravery of the people who organized, operated and rode the UGRR throughout the U.S. from roughly 1830 through the end of the American Civil War in 1865 cannot be underestimated. People we now consider the sheroes and heroes of the time, both black and white, deserve our respect, admiration and gratitude. It's not just the luminaries of history – like Harriet Tubman and Frederick Douglass – who should be remembered. It's all the unnamed conductors, stationmasters, and Freedom Seekers who risked their lives every day for their fellow human beings. Let freedom ring. Let it always ring.

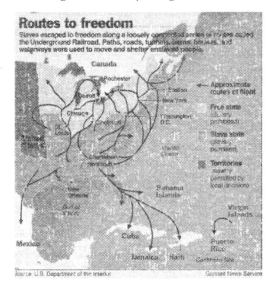

Freedom Seekers escaped west to Mexico, as far north as Canada and as far south as Jamaica, Haiti and Puerto Rico. The factual and fictional aspects of the UGRR highlighted in this book are only a tiny portion of the extensive networks that actually existed.

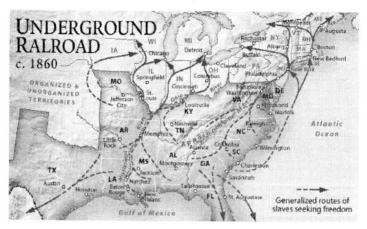

A more detailed map of the routes to freedom

The Role of Story Quilts

Story quilts offered hope and an important means of communication for African American women as well as escaping slaves traveling on the UGRR. The main feature of a story quilt was the center pictorial panel of appliquéd shapes that told a story, be it everyday life on the plantation or Bible stories full of messages of deliverance and freedom.

African American women were sometimes allowed to meet socially in quilting bees, where they would talk more freely and convey coded messages that could be passed along. For example, "bugs in de wheat" meant "look out for patrollers." A quilt hanging in a window or doorway that had black patches signified to UGRR freedom seekers that "this is a safe house." Triangular patches represented prayers for a safe journey.

For the History Buffs Among Our Readers

Here is a sampling of some of the many books written about the Underground Railroad and this period in American history. We invite you to visit your local library and as well as the many sources available via the Internet to find out more.

Blockson, Charles L. *The Underground Railroad.* New York, NY: Berkley Books, 1987

Bradford, Sarah H. *Harriet Tubman: The Moses of Her People.* Auburn, NY: W.J. Moses Printers 1869; Reprint, Secaucus, NJ: Citadel Press, 1961

Farrow, Anne , Joel Long and Jennifer Frank. *Complicity: How the North Promoted, Prolonged and Profited from Slavery.* New York, NY: Ballantine Books, 2006

Franklin, John Hope and Loren Schweninger. *Runaway Slaves: Rebels on the Plantation.* New York NY: Oxford University Press, 1999

Gara, Larr. *The Liberty Line: The Legend of the Underground Railroad.* Lexington, KY: University of Kentucky Press, 1961

National Park Service. *Underground Railroad: Official National Park Handbook.* Washington, DC: U.S. Printing Office, 1998

Siebert, Wilbur H. *The Underground Railroad: From Slavery to Freedom.* New York: Macmillan Company, 1898; Reprint, New York, NY: Arno Press & the *New York Times,* 1967

Switala, William J. *Underground Railroad in New York and New Jersey.* Mechanicsburg PA: Stackpole Books, 2006

Wright, Giles R. *Afro-Americans in New Jersey: A Short History.* Trenton: New Jersey Historical Commission, 1988.

Wright, Giles R. and Edward Lama Woneryor. *New Jersey's Underground Railroad Heritage: "Steal Away, Steal Away," A Guide to the Underground Railroad in New Jersey.* Trenton: New Jersey Historical Commission. (pdf) http://www.newjerseyhistory.com

Some Online Sources:

http://baristanet.com/2013/07/montclair-historical-society-directors-hope-for-the-james-howe-house/

http://christineadamsbeckett.com/2013/02/22/the-james-howe-house-a-local-manifestation-of-the-failure-that-was-reconstruction/

http://churchillhistory.wikispaces.com/file/view/Underg round_Railroad_Map/323881468/Underground_Railroa d_Map

http://www.nytimes.com/2007/10/14/opinion/nyregio
nopinions/14NJpatton.html

http://untappedcities.com/2012/01/17/the-
underground-railroad-in-new-york/

Books About Story Quilts

Story quilts are not just about the craft of quilting.
They offer a unique perspective on the everyday lives of
enslaved African Americans from the point of view of the
population with the least amount of power: women. Here
is a small list of books to begin exploring this topic.

Fry. Gladys-Marie. *Stitches from the Soul: Slave Quilts from the
Ante-Bellum South*. New York, NY: Dutton, 1990

Hopkins, Deborah. *Sweet Clara and the Freedom Quilt*. New
York, NY: Knopf, 1993.

Houck, Carter. *The Quilt Encyclopedia Illustrated*. New York,
NY: Abrams, 1991.

Lyons, Mary E. *Stitching Stars: The Story Quilts of Harriet
Powers*. New York, NY: Scribners, 1993

Meeske, Susan. *Quilt Me a Story*. comminfo.rutgers.ed/
professional-development/child lit/books/Meeske
.pdf

The Shadow of the KKK during Reconstruction

The 19th century characters in *Secrets at Abbott House* lived through very perilous times in the post-Civil War Reconstruction period of our country. One can imagine the fears Amaelie Abbott lived with as she raised her biracial daughter in a world that had been turned upside down by war, starvation, poverty, confusion, fear, and the disruption of the areas' infrastructures. The emergence of the Red Shirts, the KKK and other agents of racist hatred and violence aimed to restore white male power. This domestic terrorism would have impacted the daily lives of these characters.

The Ku Klux Klan (KKK) is a white supremacist group originally formed in 1865 in Pulaski, Tennessee, when Confederate Army veterans formed what they called a social club. The first leader (called the "Grand Wizard") was Nathan Bedford Forrest (1821–1877), a former general in the Confederate Army. On April 12, 1864, in the final days of the Civil War (1861–65), he led a massacre of three hundred black soldiers in service of the Union Army at Fort Pillow, Tennessee.

The Ku Klux Klan waged a campaign of terror against blacks in the South during Reconstruction (1865–77), the twelve-year period of rebuilding that followed the war. Klan members, cloaked in robes and hoods to disguise their identity, threatened, beat, and killed many blacks. While the group deprived its victims of their rights as citizens, their intent was also to intimidate the entire black population and keep them out of politics. White people who supported the federal government's measures to extend rights to all black citizens also became the victims of the Klan. Membership in the group grew quickly and the Ku Klux Klan soon had a presence throughout the South.

In 1871, the U.S. Congress (the country's law-making body) passed the Force Bill, giving President Ulysses S. Grant (1822–1885) the authority to direct federal troops against the Klan. The action was successful, causing the group to disappear—but only for a time. In 1915 the society was newly organized at Stone Mountain, Georgia, as "The Invisible Empire, Knights of the Ku Klux Klan, Inc." This time the group widened its focus to include Roman Catholics (people who believe in the Roman Catholic religion headed by a Pope based in Rome, Italy), immigrants (people from one country who permanently settle in another), and Jews, as well as blacks. Members of all of these groups became targets of KKK harassment, which now included torture and whippings. Proclaiming its mission of "racial purity," the KKK became a national organization and managed to get its members elected to public office in many states in the North as well as the South. By the 1940s, with America's attention focused on World War II (1939-1945), the Klan died out or went completely underground. The group had another resurgence during the 1950s and into the early 1970s, as the nation struggled through the Civil Rights Movement (a campaign for equal rights for African Americans that began in the South during the 1960s). The Klan still exists today, promoting the extremist views of its membership and staging marches.

For the History Buffs Among Our Readers

Here is a sampling of some of the books written about the Klu Klux Klan. We invite you to visit your local library and as well as the many sources available via the Internet to find out more.

Bartoletti, Susan Campbell. *They Called Themselves the KKK: The Birth of an American Terrorist Group.* Boston, MA: HMH Books for Young Readers. Reprint Ed., 2014

Chalmers, David J. *Hooded Americans: The History of the Klu Klux Klan.* Durham, NC: Duke University Press Books. Third Edition, 1987

Powell, William S., Editor. *Encyclopedia of North Carolina.* "Red Shirts." (doctoral dissertation, James L Jones) : Chapel Hill, NC: University of NC Press. 2006

Prather, H. Leon. "The Red Shirts Movement in North Carolina, 1898-1900." *Journal of Negro History.* 62:2, 1977

Hard Times in Haiti

Ayaiti, Ayiti, Hayti or Haiti has fought, faced and survived hard times periodically since Christopher Columbus' flagship, the Santa Maria, ran around on the northern shore of this Caribbean Island in 1492. Claiming it for Spain, and planning a slave state, Columbus named the island Hispaniola. It was populated by the Taino Arawak people whom Columbus planned to enslave as agricultural workers. Within decades, the island was cleared of the Taino, and African slaves began being imported into the most brutal slavery anywhere in the world. In 1698, the island was split under the claims of the French and Spanish, the former's colony being named the Pearl of the Antilles or Santa Domingue and the latter Santo Domingo. Rum, coffee, cotton, sugar, and the slaves to work the fields and produce these goods made France and Spain rich for more than 100 years. Never docile, slave revolts marked the French colonial years until revolutionary leaders Toussaint Louveture and then General Jean Dessalines won victory for the western portion of Hispaniola and renamed Santa Domingue Ayaiti or mountainous country, the first colony to win its freedom from slavery and become a free nation: January 1, 1804.

The political history of Haiti has periodically been turbulent up to the present time. Haiti's relationship with the United States has been equally fraught and difficult. Despite frequent petitions for the U.S. legislature to recognize Haiti as an independent nation, from the early

1800s to 1865, Southern politicians blocked this status. They were anxious that the example of a former slave state would incite rebellion in their own states. Legislators passed laws to keep Haitian merchants away from U.S. soil because slaveholders there did not want their slaves getting ideas about revolt. However, the two countries continued trade, albeit at disadvantageous prices to Haiti. The U.S. embargo of Haiti lasted 60 years, but Lincoln declared it unnecessary to deny the country's independence once slavery in the U.S. began ending. He encouraged newly freed slaves to emigrate there to attain a freedom he did not deem possible in the U.S. Thus, Reverend Bishop James Theodore Holly, the son of freed slaves, immigrated to Haiti, with his family and free African Americans to minister to Haitians' educational and spiritual needs.

Despite the efforts of people like Holly, slavery is still widespread in Haiti. According to the 2014 Global Slavery Index, Haiti has an estimated 237,700 enslaved persons, making it the country with the second-highest prevalence of slavery in the world, behind only Mauritania. Haiti has more human trafficking than any other Central or South American country. According to the United States Department of State 2013 *Trafficking in Persons Report*, "Haiti is a major source, passage, and destination country for men, women, and children subjected to forced labor and sex slavery." Haitians are trafficked out of Haiti and into the neighboring Dominican Republic, as well as to other countries, such as Ecuador, Bolivia, Argentina, Brazil, and North

American countries as well. Haiti is also a transit country for victims of trafficking en route to the United States. After the devastating 2010 Haiti earthquake, human trafficking a.k.a. slavery 'by force, fraud, or coercion to exploit a person for profit,' has drastically increased"

Irrespective of this difficult history, the people of Haiti are resilient, vibrant and amazingly energetic. Their art, music and spiritual life has international appeal and reach, not the least, the annual Haitian Concert organized by Cindy Stagoff in Montclair, NJ on behalf of the Edeyo Foundation, the Haitian Education and Leadership Program (HELP) and Lamp for Haiti.

For the History Buffs Among Our Readers

There are tons of historic and travel books, as well as online sources, full of information on the history and culture of Haiti. Here are a few that we consulted.

Dubois, Laurent. *Haiti: The Aftershocks of History*. London, UK: Picador, div.Pan Macmillan. 2013

Goldstein, Margaret J. *Haiti in Pictures*. Minneapolis MN: Lerner Publications Company. 2006

Hintz, Martin. *Haiti: Enchantment of the World*. New York, NY: Children's Press, div. Grolier Publishing. 1998

Lefebvre, Claire. *Creole Genesis and the Acquisition of Grammar: The Case of Haitian Creole*. Cambridge, UK: Cambridge University Press 1998

Preszler, June. *Haiti: A Question and Answer Book*. Mankato, MN: Capstone Press. 2007

Torres, John A. *Threat to Haiti.* Hockessin, DE: Mitchell
    Lane Publishers 2009

Online Sources:

https://en.wikipedia.org/wiki/Slavery_in_Haiti

http://edeyo.org/

http://uhelp.net/

http://lampforhaiti.org/

.

Interview with an Ancestor
By Lizbet Sheridan

Lizbet Sheridan: Great-great Grandmother Lilanna, it's wonderful to meet you.

Lilianna Greely: Come here, Sugar, let me love your neck. Yes, I can see some of my Mama in you and some of your Papa. You sure are a pretty little thing.

Lizbet: Thank you. So Grandma, what can you tell me about those early days in South Carolina?

Lilianna: You've got to remember, Sweetpea, that I was born in 1864, so I was a babe at the end of The War, that's what we call the Civil War, ha! And since my Mama was free, so was I. Your slave status came from your Mama. Not your Papa. So Amaelie was a free white woman (well, I always wondered just how "white" she was, but that's another story), and so I was free even though I was a little darkish.

Lizbet: When did you start to remember?

Lilianna: Well, now let's see, got to think back, was a powerful long time ago. I have one memory of being strapped to my Mama's back while she hoed. Was not too much to eat after the war, and of course, Papa was gone and the others had gone off with Sherman.

Lizbet: Anything else?

Lilianna: Well, of course, the Red Shirts were real bad.

Lizbet: Red Shirts?

Lilianna: Yes, those Red Shirts were terrible. After Old President Grant outlawed the KKKers, Mr. Wade Hampton, here in South Carolina, wanted to run for governor, twice. He organized the Red Shirts to scare the Blacks. Scare them, kill them. Why, I remember when I was just a little girl before we walked all the way to Charleston. I was coming home doing Mama some errand, and I heard some horses and I hid in a ditch. Well, don't you know those Red Shirts had a poor young man, dragging him by the neck and all tied up with ropes and pulling him behind their horses and laughing to beat the band. Mama was angry at me for coming back so late, but when I told her what had happened, she just hugged me and hugged me. Didn't say anything, but just hugged me. I think she cried, too.

Lizbet: Oh, my God!

Lilianna: Well, well, no God seemed to help that poor boy or lots of others. Does make you wonder sometimes. When I got older, I heard about a poor boy who was caught by them and they treated him even worse. They put him in a wooden barrel, rolled him down to the river, pushed him in and then shot holes in the barrel. Let's talk about something not so sad.

Lizbet: OK, how did you meet Mr. Greeley?

Lilianna: Well, now that meeting did indeed seem Heaven sent. I was taking a parcel of dressmaking to this white lady's house down in the Battery section. Oh my, a grand house, pink with two big porches one top the other, white columns and all. Anyway, it was just so simple. I tripped on a stone. Mr. Greeley had been there doing some work. He helped me up, waited for me and that was it. We were married just a month later. I was only 15, but you grew up fast back then. I found out from Mama just a little time before she died that she knew this great strapping man when he was a little boy. The Greeley's would send him over rent free to help her after her white husband died. That was my Little Luke. Now what do you think of that, Grandchild? Want some lemonade? Think that's enough for today.

No, wait a minute. I have one more thing to say. All these killings of these young people, these women and these men, by the police and by that crazy white boy who shot up the church right here in Charleston. Doesn't it seem like the Red Shirts or the KKK are still riding? Now let's see about that lemonade and some sweet potato pone. It's really good. Help me up, child.

Lizbet felt a hand shaking her shoulder. "Wake up, Lizbet, here's your cold lemonade and some Charleston style sweet potato pone. It's sorta like corn bread, sorta like a cake. Real good," Amanda said. "Now hurry and get ready, we're going to meet Elise O'Connor. I think she's just right for you.

A Sampling of Recipes

The Carolinas

The cuisine of the Carolinas reflects a compendium of flavors and cooking styles brought to the area by the Irish, Scots, Scotch-Irish, French, and Germans who settled this region as well as Native American, Caribbean and African influences. Southern cooking is known for its pan-fried chicken dishes, deep pit barbecues, oyster roasts, gumbo, catfish stew, cornbread, grits, biscuits with red-eye gravy, black-eyed peas, and a variety of greens, beans, and other vegetables. The coastal area of North and South Carolina is marked by a variety of seafood choices, most notably shrimp and oysters dishes. The recipes here, some shared by the characters of this book, will provide just a taste.

Grits

1 cup quick cooking (not instant) packaged grits
2 cups water
1-1/4 cup milk
1 teaspoon salt
1 teaspoon butter or non-dairy margarine

Combine grits, water, milk, salt and butter in a sauce pan. Bring to a boil. Reduce heat, cover and cook on low heat, stirring from time to time until grits are stiff. Top with butter or red eye gravy.

Grits 'N' Shrimp

1 cup grits
1 cup cheddar cheese, grated
4 slices bacon, cut into ½-inch pieces
1 pound medium shrimp, peeled and deveined
2 plum tomatoes, coarsely chopped
2 scallions, finely sliced

Cook the grits following package directions (or use the recipe above). Stir in the cheddar cheese. At the same time, cook the bacon in a large skillet over medium heat until crisp, about 6 to 8 minutes. Transfer to a paper towel to drain and set aside; drain the skillet of excess bacon grease. Add the shrimp and tomatoes to the skillet and cook, tossing occasionally, until the shrimp are opaque throughout, about 3 to 5 minutes. Stir in the scallions and the bacon and serve over the grits.

Vegetarian Chili

2 tablespoons olive oil
1 clove garlic, finely minced
1 large yellow onion, finely chopped
1 cup vegetable stock
1 medium red bell pepper, chopped
1 medium green bell pepper, chopped
2 medium carrots, cut into small slices
1 cup mushrooms, finely chopped.
1 medium zucchini, cut into small chunks
1 can (15.5 oz.), garbanzo beans, drained
1 can (15.5 oz.) pinto or black beans, drained

1 can (15.5 oz.) stewed tomatoes or crushed tomatoes
1 teaspoon cumin
1 tablespoon chili powder
Salt and black pepper to taste
Water, if needed

Brown garlic and onions in olive oil in a large skillet or sauce pan. Add vegetable stock, peppers and carrots; simmer for 10 minutes until peppers and carrots begin to soften. Add remaining ingredients one by one and simmer 15 to 20 minutes. If the chili cooks down too much, add water. Garnish with non-dairy sour cream or soft tofu and finely chopped scallions. Serve with Grandma's Gluten-free, Non-dairy Cornbread (see recipe on the next page).

Grandma's Cornbread
(Traditional Version)

1 cup all-purpose flour
1 cup yellow corn meal
4 teaspoons baking powder
½ teaspoon salt
1/4 cup sugar
1 cup milk or dairy free equivalent
1 egg
1/3 cup butter or non-dairy margarine

Preheat oven to 425 degrees and heat 9" cast iron skillet on top of stove. Coat the skillet with a little melted butter or margarine or cooking oil.

Sift dry ingredients and set aside. Beat the egg and

mix in the milk. Add to dry ingredients gradually, mixing until the batter is blended and slightly stiff. Add more milk, if needed. Do not over mix.

Melt the butter or margarine in the skillet and pour into the cornbread batter and stir to combine; it should sizzle. Quickly pour the batter into hot skillet and place in pre-heated oven. Bake for 20 minutes or slightly longer until golden brown. Test for doneness with straw or thin knife blade. It should come out clean when inserted into the cornbread.

Cool cornbread in skillet for 5 minutes or so. Place a dinner plate on top of the skillet and corn bread. Invert and turn cornbread out on a plate. Cut into pie shaped slices. Best served piping hot and topped with butter or margarine, jam, honey or molasses.

For delicious midnight snack: Crumble stale corn bread into a glass of cold milk and eat with a spoon.

Grandma's Gluten-free, Non-dairy Version

1 cup brown rice flour
1 cup organic yellow corn meal
4 teaspoons salt-free baking powder
1 teaspoon salt
1 cup+ non-dairy milk, such as coconut, soy, almond, or rice milk
1/3 cup organic honey
1/4 cup olive oil
1 whole organic egg

See above for Grandma's Traditional Cornbread.

Red Eye Gravy

1 slice, country ham
1 tablespoon unsalted butter
1 to 2 cups, cool black coffee
½ cup cold water
Pinch of salt, if desired

Soak ham in cold water for 20-30 minutes to remove some of the salt. Pat dry, cut through fat border to prevent curling; then cut ham slice into 2 pieces. Heat skillet and add butter.
Fry country ham in hot skillet until slightly brown; remove ham and set aside on a plate.

To deglaze the pan, pour coffee into the hot skillet and scrape pan drippings from bottom.
Add cool water and bring to a slow boil; reduce heat and add salt if desired. Fat will rise to the top leaving a "red eye" of coffee and drippings

Pour over hot baking powder biscuits or grits. To make biscuits, use cobbler topping recipe below, arranging biscuit rounds on a baking sheet. Place the uncooked biscuits on sheet with shoulders lightly touching for nice high biscuits.

Blackberry Cobbler*

Go out to a field on a hot summer day and pick several quarts of blackberries! OK, if you don't want to do that, buy them from your grocery store or favorite fruit stand.
   * *You can substitute blackberries with peaches, apples, raspberries, or blueberries.*

Filling

2 quarts blackberries, rinsed and cleaned using a vegetable soap
1 cup granulated sugar
½ teaspoon salt
2 teaspoons lemon juice
2 tablespoons butter or non-dairy margarine

Biscuit topping

2 cups all purpose flour
3 teaspoons baking powder
1 teaspoon salt
½ cup butter or non-dairy margarine
3/4 cup milk
2 tablespoons granulated sugar, to sprinkle on topping (optional)

Sift dry ingredients together. Cut cold butter or margarine into the flour mixture until it is the texture of coarse meal. Make a well in flour mixture, add milk and stir quickly using a fork. (Mixture will be loose.) Turn onto a lightly floured board, sprinkle lightly with flour and gently pat dough into a rectangle or circle 1/2 inch thick. (You can also use a rolling pin.) Cut biscuit dough into rounds using a biscuit cutter, small glass or clean, empty can.

Assembly

Preheat oven to 450 degrees and coat baking dish with butter or margarine. Toss blackberries with mixture of sugar and salt. Pour into baking dish and dot with butter, if desired. Arrange biscuit rounds so they are gently touching. Bake cobbler for 45 minutes to 1 hour or until filling is bubbling and biscuits are golden brown

Dish out and pour heavy cream over cobbler or top with vanilla ice cream or whipped cream, if desired. * You can also substitute the blackberries with other fruit, such as peaches, apples, raspberries, or blueberries.

Cookbook Starters

There are many, many cookbooks that focus on Carolina cuisine as well as many other approaches to Southern cooking. You have only to search your public library or the Internet to find a selection of books to inspire your appetite. The list below will get you started.

Algood, Tammy. *The Complete Southern Cookbook: More Than 800 of the Most Delicious, Down Home Recipes.* Running Press: Philadelphia. 2010

Algood Tammy. *Sunday Dinner in the South: Recipes to Keep Them Coming Back for More.* Thomas Nelson Christian Publishing: New York. 2015

Deen, Paul and Melissa Clark. *Paula Deen's Southern Cooking Bible.* Simon & Schuster: New York. 2011

Dupree, Nathalie and Cynthia Graubart and Rich McKee. *Mastering the Art of Southern Vegetables.* Gibbs Smith: Layton, Utah. 2015

LaBelle, Patti. *LaBelle Cuisine: Recipes to Sing About.* Clarkson Potter, The Crown Publishing Group: New York. 1999

South Carolina Family and Community Leaders. *The New Carolina Cookbook*. University of South Carolina Press: Columbia. 2007

Wiegand, Elizabeth. *Outer Banks Cookbook: Recipes & Traditions from North Carolina's Barrier Islands*. Globe Pequot Press: Guilford, CT. 2013

Woods, Sylvia. *Sylvia's Family Soul Food Cookbook: From Hemingway, South Carolina to Harlem*. William Morris Cookbooks: New York. 1999

Zumstein, Debra and Will Kazary. *Carolina Cooking Cookbook: Recipes from the Region's Best Chefs*. Gibbs-Smith: Layton, Utah. 2007

Haiti

Haitian (*Kréyol*) cuisine has evolved over the years, blending the unique flavors, dishes and cooking methods of the cultures that formed this Caribbean island nation. Strong elements of French, Spanish, African, and native cooking are enhanced by savory spices and very hot sauces (known as *pikles*) that give Haitian food its distinct tropical zing.

Rice and beans dishes (*dire ak pwa*) with either red or black beans are popular staples as are various vegetable, fish and meat stews. Most meals include plantains (similar to bananas, but not as sweet) that are often parboiled, sliced and deep fried. The Haitian palate offers a variety of fish and shell fish dishes as well as fried or barbecued (*grio*) pork, goat and beef.

There is a wealth of vegetables and fruits available that populate a variety of dishes: combinations of potatoes, corn, squash, okra, cabbage, eggplant, and cabbage; mangoes, bananas, avocados and other tropical fruits.

Kawòt ak Seafood Salad
(Carrot and Seafood Salad)

4 cups carrots, grated
2 cups cooked seafood mix (shrimp, crab meat, etc.)
½ cup Passion Fruit Vinaigrette
½ red onion, julienned
Salt and pepper to taste

Vinaigrette

1/3 cup passion fruit juice
2 tablespoon sugar
1 cup extra virgin olive oil
2 shallots, diced
½ teaspoon garlic powder
½ teaspoon onion powder
1 clove fresh minced garlic
Salt and pepper

Using a food processor, mix together all ingredients except the shallots; pulse. Add shallots after pulsing. Combine carrot, seafood, onions, and Passion Fruit Vinaigrette in a large salad bowl; mix. Salt and pepper to taste. Let stand for 20 minutes at room temperature before serving.

Riz et Pois Rouge ak Coconut Lèt
(Rice & Red Beans with Coconut Milk)

1 tablespoons olive oil

1 onion, chopped

3 cloves garlic, finely chopped

1 medium green pepper, chopped

1 cup brown rice, uncooked

2 cans (15 oz.), red kidney beans, drained

½ teaspoon ground cumin

¼ teaspoon dried oregano

¼ teaspoon crushed red pepper

1- ½ cups coconut milk

1 cup water

Preheat oven to 350 degrees. In a large saucepan, heat the olive oil, garlic, onion and green pepper. Sautee until the onion and pepper soften, about 3 minutes. Add the remaining ingredients and mix thoroughly until blended. Transfer to a 2-quart casserole dish; cover. Bake about 55 minutes or until all the liquid is absorbed and the rice is cooked.

Pwason Gwo Sèl
(Fish in Spiced Clear Broth)

2 whole snappers, scaled, cleaned and gutted

3 limes

Coarse sea salt

1 lemon, diced

6 cloves of garlic

3 shallots, julienned
3 tablespoons, olive oil
4 cups water
1 stalk scallions, chopped
½ green pepper, julienned
½ red pepper, julienned
2 tablespoons butter or non-dairy margarine
1 sprig of parsley
1 sprig of thyme
6 cloves
Pepper

Place snappers in a medium bowl and cut 2 slits on both sides of each fish about 1 inch apart. Wash fish with cold water and the juice and rind of 2 limes. Rinse. Sprinkle sea salt liberally along with the juice of 1 lime. Stuff cavities with diced lemon, 2 cloves of garlic and shallots. Sprinkle with pepper and brush with olive oil. Marinade for at least 2 hours or preferably overnight. Reserve liquid that collects in the bowl.

In a deep skillet pan, add 4 cups of water, scallions, green and red pepper, parsley, thyme, and cloves. Bring to a boil. Reduce heat and add snappers, reserved fish liquid and margarine. Simmer for 10 to 15 minutes.

Bannann Peze
(Twice Fried Green Plantains)

2 to 4 green plantains
1 cup vegetable or corn oil
1 tablespoon vinegar

1 tablespoon salt
½ teaspoon garlic powder
1 cup hot water

Peel plantains and cut each one at an angle into 5 pieces. Add oil to a deep frying pan on medium heat. In a small bowl, add remaining ingredients and set aside. Place plantain pieces in hot oil and cook 5 to 7 minutes on each side. Remove and flatten each piece. Soak in hot water mixture, then return to frying pan. Continue cooking over medium heat, turning each piece until they are crispy and golden brown. Serve hot.

Pain Patate
(Sweet Potato Pudding)

4 lbs. sweet potatoes
4 well ripened bananas, peeled and mashed
½ cup butter or non-dairy margarine
1 can (8 oz.) cream of coconut
1 can (8 oz.) coconut milk
4 tablespoons butter or non-dairy margarine
¾ cup brown sugar
1 tablespoon finely ground ginger
2-½ tablespoons vanilla extract
1 tablespoon each, cinnamon and nutmeg
½ teaspoon salt
1 cup raisins

Preheat oven to 350 degrees. Wash and peel sweet potatoes and cut in small pieces. Using a food processor, finely grind sweet potatoes with the coconut milk. Set aside in an 8 to 10-quart sauce pan. Peel and finely blend bananas; add to sweet potatoes and mix well. Add all remaining ingredients except the raisins and mix well. Cook on medium heat, stirring constantly with wooden spoon until brown (about 35 to 40 minutes). Simmer for about 5 minutes more on low heat. Remove from heat and mix in raisins. Pour the mixture into a 15-inch oven safe dish and bake for 35 minutes or until golden brown. Sprinkle with sugar and let sit for ½ hour before serving.

Cookbook Starters

Haitian recipes are found on the Internet in increasing numbers in blogs as well as in cookbooks. Here are a few of the cookbooks on this cuisine that we found listed.

Menager, Mona Cassion. *Fine Haitian Cuisine.* Second Edition. Pompano Beach: Educa Vision, Inc. 2012

Pambrun, Rachel. *Haitian Cookbook: A Beginner's Guide.* Create Space Independent Publishing Platform. 2012

Valme, Samuel. *Dinner Ideas for the Haiian Cook.* Smashwords. 2014

Various Authors, Meghan Bourke (creator) and Deby Santulli (creator). *Heather's Home Orphanage Haitian Cookbook.* Create Space Independent Publishing. 2014

Yurnet-Thomas, Mirta and Thomas Family. *A Taste of Haiti.* Expanded Edition. Hippocrene Cookbook Library. New York:Hippocrene Books 2003.

What's Real? What's Not?

As in previous books of Sandra Troux Mysteries, *Secrets at Abbott House* draws liberally from history and current events. Sometimes 'author' Crystal Sharpe even seems to anticipate the news! How scary is that?

What's Real?

- Micro-lenses are definitely real and are used in Norwegian paper currency as an anti-counterfeiting technique. As far as the authors know there are no programmable micro-lenses.

- Sexual relations between southern white women and enslaved or free black men during the colonial, antebellum or Civil War eras was much less frequent than the more commonly known instances of white men begetting more slaves on black slave women. However, sexual relations between white women and black men did occur, however infrequently they show up in the historical records.

- Trafficking of people and children for forced labor, whether for the bedroom or the factory floor, is all too real. Some trafficked people are indeed transported in shipping containers.

- The New Jersey Historical Society and Military Park, both in Newark, are real places. The authors have taken some poetic license with their appointments.

- The Newark Police Department is located where the novel states, as is Hobby's Deli. The menu described in the novel was abridged. Go! Nosh! Enjoy!

- Faith Ringgold is one of the most famous story quilters and children's authors in contemporary America. She is a New Jersey resident.

- Nancy Drew is also real, as real as a fictional character can be. She is a product of New Jersey – the original "Jersey Girl" and was "born" in Newark. Her creator, Edward Stratemeyer lived on 7th Street in Newark. The house still stands. Stratemeyer is buried in Evergreen Cemetery, Hillside, NJ. Nancy Drew, in her 85th year of being 18, continues to entertain and inspire girls the world over.

What's Not?

- Abbott House Museum and Farm are complete creations of the authors as is the Abbott Redevelopment Zone.

What's a Little of Both?

- Applegate Farm is a real ice cream place on Grove Street in Montclair, NJ. Although not confirmed by historians, Applegate is commonly acknowledged to have been a minor stop on the Underground Railroad. However, the tunnel and the history museum in the barn are concoctions of the authors.

- The Howe House on Claremont Avenue is definitely a real place and was indeed willed to James Howe, a freed slave of Israel Crane. Crane was one of the founders of Cranetown, which was initially part of Newark and later became Montclair. Some sources suggest that there were a series of escape tunnels under Montclair, some connecting to the Howe House as well as to safe houses and caves. However, the cistern behind the Howe House is a creation of the authors.

- The Montclair Historical Society is indeed a real organization. It owns the Crane House and several other historical buildings in Montclair. As far as could be determined, there is no walking tour from the Crane House to the Howe house, which remains privately owned while designated an historic property by the Town of Montclair in 2008.

Suggested Book Club Questions

1. Racial Identity has been a topic of heated, sometimes deadly discussion, in the past and certainly in the present and is certainly a main theme in this book. Cultural anthropologists have shown that genetic differences between people with different skin color or eye shape are almost indiscernible. So "RACE" is not a real thing, but something that people have made to serve political and economic purposes.

   a. How did racial categories serve to prop up the Slave system described in this book?
   b. What do you think is behind the racial killings of the present?
   c. How do you identify yourself?

2. Sandy and Lizbet have a complicated and sometimes divisive relationship in this book all around the issues of race, power, privilege and slavery. How do you think they resolve those issues, or do they? Bobbi and Sandy have strains in their friendship. What are these?

3. Haitians and Dominicans who share the island of Hispaniola have had a bloody relationship for several centuries. Recently, the Dominican Republic organized mass deportations of "dark skinned" Dominicans with "Haitian features" born of Haitian parents living, working, and even

owning property in the Dominican Republic. How does the government justify their politics of color?

4. Women's friendship is another key topic in the book. What are the strains that nearly divide these lifelong friends? How do you feel about your women friends?

5. The main villain in Secrets is a woman. What motivates her to be so bad? What kind of person is she?

6. What makes Sandy, Bobbi and Lizbet sheroes? Why do you think the authors do not call them heroines? Do you know any sheroes? What about yourself? Why do you think sheroes are important role models for today's young people?

7. Age is another important theme in the entire Sandra Troux Mystery series, no more so than in this book. How do you feel about women and age? About your own age?

8. Another key theme is sustainability and corporate responsibility. How do you think Bobbi will transform her company since she will have a more powerful position? How can companies change to equate the economy with the environment and the environment with the economy? How can you

implement sustainability in your life and work environment?

9. The artistry of women who all too typically are limited in time and materials by poverty and over work, has all too often been edited out of what is considered Art. What forms of Art do you see women making? And do you see there being institutional changes in conceptions of Art as it relates to women? What art do you create?

10. Relationships of all kinds are at the heart of this book: friendships, genealogies, sexual, racial, and environmental. Typically, a thriller is only about action upon action. How is action redefined here to create a new kind of thriller?

The Authors

About Crystal Sharpe

Crystal Sharpe is the pen name created by Baby Boomer co-authors Virginia Cornue and Linda Lombri. Ms. Sharpe was inspired by the famed Carolyn Keene – the pseudonym created by juvenile book publisher Edward Stratemeyer for the writer(s) of his fictional Nancy Drew detective series. Most of the books in that series from 1930 to 1979 were written by Mildred Wirt Benson, the first woman to earn a Master's Degree from the University of Iowa's journalism program in 1927. As the series' first ghost writer, she provided text for twenty-three of the first thirty ND books. Harriet Adams wrote most of the remaining 175 original ND classics until 1979 when she updated many of the early books.

Following in this great tradition of mystery writer pseudonyms, the intent of creating "Crystal Sharpe" as the author of the *Sandra Troux Mysteries* is to pay homage to the original series' "author." This series has inspired generations of girls and women around the world since its introduction more than eighty-five years ago.

In 2006, Virginia and Linda met in Shanghai when they accompanied their daughters on a return visit to China – the country of the girls' birth. To their amazement, they discovered they both lived in Montclair, NJ. A casual dinner in the fall of 2010 sparked the creation of this new book series. Why not write a new mystery series centered around three 60-ish women who were childhood fans of Nancy Drew, Agatha Christie and characters like *Prime Suspect's* Jane Tennison, and who now wanted to reinvent themselves as international sleuths? Why not, indeed?

As a girl, Virginia wanted to *be* Nancy, girl sleuth, and grew up to be the next best thing – a cultural anthropologist. At first, Linda, too, wanted to *be* Nancy – but ultimately decided she would rather *be* 'Carolyn Keene' and write books with a girl detective as the heroine. Linda grew up to be a marketing communications director.

Now decades later, manifesting their childhood ambitions, Virginia and Linda have collaborated on the *Sandra Troux Mysteries*. *Secrets at Abbott House* (Book 3) joins their other novels, *The Mystery of the Ming Connection* and *Masquerade on the Net*. They are at work on Book 4, *Peril at the Pilato*, with more to come.

About Virginia Cornue

Virginia Cornue is an author, award winning women's rights activist, cultural anthropologist, and part time professor at Bloomfield College. She is the author of *The Dragon's Daughters Return (2007)*, which chronicled the experiences of middle-school age daughters and their adoptive families returning to visit China; and *Draw on Culture: China (2009)*, an educational activity book. She is the co-editor of *So Much Blood: The Civil War Letters of CSA Private William W. Beard, 1861-1865*, and is researching another Civil War era non-fiction book, *A Secret Upcountry*.

Virginia earned her Ph.D. in cultural anthropology from Rutgers University (2001). Her manuscript, based on her dissertation, was *Sex, Tenderness and Discrimination: Chinese Women in the Great Global Market Revolution*. She holds a B.F.A in Dramatic Arts from the University of North Carolina (Chapel Hill) and did masters work at the New School for Social Research. Virginia co-founded and/or directed a number of non-profit organizations: The National Organization for Women (NYC chapter); The Service Fund of NOW; the Women's Funding Coalition-NYC; and Newark Emergency Services for Families. She was the recipient of the 1998 Susan B. Anthony Award for Service and Advocacy for Women and the 1989 Newark (NJ) Humanitarian Service Award.

She lives in Montclair, New Jersey with her daughter Mei-Ming who is a junior at Brandeis University.

About Linda Lombri

Linda Lombri is an author, marketing communications consultant, freelance writer/editor, interior book designer, and home economist. She heads her own communications firm, *Lombri Writes!* Her clients have included businesses in a variety of market sectors, as well as entrepreneurs and fellow authors.

In addition to the Sandra Troux Mysteries series, Linda is working on *Tapestry & Patchwork: A Family History Sampler*, a book of essays based on family immigrant stories, to be published in 2016. Another project, a trilogy of how-to booklets on navigating the "third act" years, will be out by the end of 2015.

Linda has an a M.S. degree in Design from Drexel University's College of Media Arts & Design, and a B.A. degree in Home Economics in Business from Queens College (CUNY). In her varied career, she was a home economist for Standard Brands, Coats & Clark and Butterick Fashion Marketing, and then a marketing services director in the consumer packaging industry. During her tenure at International Paper's Shorewood Packaging division, she branded and developed its *greenchoice*™ *Environmental Solutions for Packaging & Displays program,* which was awarded a 2008 Sales & Marketing Excellence Team Award.

She lives in Montclair, New Jersey with her daughter Anita, a senior at Colorado College.

Acknowledgements

We are very grateful to our enthusiastic editors, consultants, beta readers, photographers, and graphic artists. With their "crystal sharpe" eyes, they helped us edit, revise and refine our manuscript.

John Blythe, historian and genealogist for first suggesting a time shifting plot, plus information about South Carolina

Stuart Chase, Montclair resident and provider of information about undocumented UGRR sites in Montclair, NJ

Andrew Cohen, photographer extraordinaire, door photo, front cover

Deputy Chief Todd Conforti and Lt. Dave O'Dowd . and their colleagues in the Montclair Police Dept for their assistance in providing some police color for our story

Ryan Durka, front cover template design for the series

Jane Eliasof, Executive Director of the Montclair Historical Society for the generous use of the Crane House meeting room

Frank Gerard Godlewski, provider of maps of 19th century Montclair and information relating to the UGRR in Montclair

Patricia Lander, editor, who also shared her real life story of a Civil War ancestress burying the family silver to protect it from General Sherman's hard-war tactics in South Carolina

Linda Long, photographer, author photo, back cover

Stevenson Mathieu, NYC writer and native Haitian for providing key information and great guidance during a 2009 trip to Haiti

Jane Pendergast, editor extraordinaire

Judith Rew, designer, front and back cover, spine

Gigi Schwartz, avid mystery buff and beta reader

Corinne West, designer, STM logo

COMING NEXT

The Haunted Spa Down Under

Called to a walkabout by green activist Dr. Alira Yarra, Sandy & Co. take a wild ride through the Aussie Outback and the Great Barrier Reef. They unravel a labyrinth of corporate greed, purloined relics and stolen lives, amidst a backdrop of an endangered ecosystem and ancient Shamanic wisdom.

Intrigue in Istanbul

Sandra Troux meets (the shade of) Agatha Christie in this tale of danger and intrigue. When Agatha Christie ran away from her first husband in 1926, she disappeared. Did she flee to Istanbul? Sandy, Bobbi, and Lizbet check into room 411, Christie's preferred room in the Istanbul Pera Palas Hotel. What do they find behind a secret wall panel that Christie hid on one of her frequent in the 1920s and 1930s? How does following in her travel footsteps lead Sandy, Bobbi and Lizbet to their most thrilling adventure yet? The trio of sheroes encounters a heart stopping mystery of cultural tension, terrorism, murder, and love (re)claimed.